Richard Collins

Missionary Enterprise in the East

with especial reference to the Syrian Christians of Malabar and the results of

modern missions

Richard Collins

Missionary Enterprise in the East
with especial reference to the Syrian Christians of Malabar and the results of modern missions

ISBN/EAN: 9783337239084

Printed in Europe, USA, Canada, Australia, Japan

Cover: Foto ©Andreas Hilbeck / pixelio.de

More available books at **www.hansebooks.com**

MISSIONARY ENTERPRISE

IN THE EAST

WITH ESPECIAL REFERENCE TO THE SYRIAN CHRISTIANS

OF MALABAR AND THE RESULTS OF MODERN MISSIONS

BY THE

REV. RICHARD COLLINS, M.A.

LATE PRINCIPAL OF THE CHURCH MISSIONARY SOCIETY'S SYRIAN COLLEGE,
COTTAYAM, TRAVANCORE, SOUTH INDIA

HENRY S. KING & CO.

65 CORNHILL & 12 PATERNOSTER ROW, LONDON

1873

CHAPTER VII.

CHAPTER VIII.

APPENDIX.

ILLUSTRATIONS.

MISSIONARY ENTERPRISE

IN

THE EAST

CHAPTER I.

A tropical evening—The journey westwards—The Palghaut Pass—
The elephant and palanquin—A traveller's mishap—Trichoor—
The Roman Catholic pop-guns—The Bible at Trichoor—A digres-
sion to Ootacamund—The missionary conference—Climate of the
Hills—The Coonoor Ghaut—Ootacamund—Katy—Badaghars
and Todas—Hill congregations.

I AM SITTING ALONE in my room where I have breakfasted,
tiffined, dined, and often burned the midnight oil for—
with some few exceptions—nearly the last twelve years.
My residence is at Cottayam, in Travancore. It is ten
o'clock P.M., and the 1st of December, 18—. Nothing
can surpass the perfection of climate that we have at this
time of the year. The monsoon is over, and has left the
earth rich ' in all manner of store ;' and, as the sun is now
near the tropic of Capricorn, we have no excessive heat

indoors. The thermometer in the middle of the day (in the 'shade' of course, and not under an apple tree in the garden, like some people's 'shaded' thermometers in England, but in the middle of this room, which is forty feet long, far away from all radiation) seldom stands higher than 88°, and in the morning and evening is generally about 76° or 77°: it is just between the two now as I sit here. Every one else has gone to bed.

The 'bearer' is snoring in the verandah (he has extra pay for sleeping there as a watchman, and, I suspect, has a touch of opium in his nightcap, for I have several times found it very difficult to rouse him, and scarcely know whether real thieves—of whom, however, we are not much afraid—would succeed any better); the hum of voices from the College is hushed; everything human has conspired to 'leave the world to silence and to me,' at this delicious hour. And yet not 'darkness,' for the moon, which is near the full, and was risen when the sun set, has kept alive the twilight.

Nor does all the air so 'solemn a stillness hold' as at night in extra-tropical lands. The 'beetle' here, too, 'wheels his droning flight,'—but not the beetle alone. One has just come in to invade my solitude—a monster,—and having knocked his head against the punkah, now lies sprawling on the table. After him in pop a couple of bats, which, cheated of their prey, as

I suppose, are chasing each other round and round the room within an inch of the ceiling; for I have my doors and windows wide open both east and west. Innumerable crickets are hailing one another from every conceivable corner; the frogs in the valley are croaking their night-long chorus; two owls are conversing in the mango trees; the night-jar and chaunting hawk are turning night into day; and there are even flowers, as my reader will know, in this climate, which wait till the sun has gone before they unfold their beauties and unlock their treasuries of perfume. At this moment a magnificent brugmansia, not far off, with flowers of purest white fully six inches in length; a moon-flower, which is creeping over the trellis-work at my door; and a night-flowering cereus, are all in their beauty and are filling the air with delicious fragrance. Two mandarin-orange trees, too, are just in full bloom, and are adding their quota.

I have just been to look at them, and found them centres of most busy life: the moths are holding a perfect revel about them; scores of ' sphingidæ ' on the wing are attacking the flowers with their long probosces. And so amid all this revel of nature, though alone, I cannot feel lonely. It is just the hour for a retrospect,—for gathering up the threads of thought and weaving them afresh.

No subject better deserves the attention and study of

Englishmen, both in its religious and political bearings, than our great Eastern Empire. No country presents a history more pregnant with interest. India,—the land of the Vedas; the land of the Great Moguls; the land of Clive's conquests; the land over which Dutch and Portuguese, and French and English, have had many a fierce struggle; once the apple of discord among the nations; and ever the world's cornucopia, from whose scattered riches Tyre built her walls and clothed herself in purple, and Solomon enriched his capital with gold and ivory and peacocks, and Alexandria filled her libraries, and Venice reared her palaces. You have read something already of her ancient literature and her modern idolatry; of her religious schisms and strange mythologies; of the proud supremacy of her brahmans and of her exiled Buddhism; and when you have made the far East your home, you try to go everywhere—or ought to do—with your eyes and your ears open.

I landed at Madras on the 28th of December, 1854; but, as my chief experiences of India belong to the south-western coast, I shall confine my narrative to that. The greater part of my journey from Madras westwards was too much, no doubt, like other recorded journeys for me to linger over it. The excitement of the first starting just at sunset (I had a companion, and we travelled by palanquin), the hum of the bearers, the flare of the torches, the midnight halt and the fire, and bearers' supper, under some 'wide-spreading' banyan, the rest during the scorching day in the 'public bunga- low,' and the start afresh in the cool of the evening, would form but a tale thrice told. Our route was by Tanjore, Trichinopoly, and Coimbatore. At the next stage, Palghaut, we were fairly in the Malabar country.

During the night we had passed from the eastern to the western side of the Western Ghauts; and a most wonderful transformation in scenery, climate, produc- tions, people, and indeed almost everything, is due, as it would appear, entirely to this mountain range. While to the east of the Ghauts lies the almost treeless plain of the Carnatic, broken only at intervals by solitary conical hills, such as the hill at Trichinopoly, to the west is a beautifully undulating country, richly wooded to the sea.

While to the east from May to September the Car- natic is parched up with hot land-winds, on the west the black clouds of the south-west monsoon are gathering over the Ghauts, and pouring their floods of water on the jungles of Malabar; and while from September to January the north-west monsoon is de- luging the Carnatic, the west is beginning to glow under cloudless skies. While on the east, if there are any forests, they consist chiefly of the dreary and monotonous Palmyra,[1] the hills on the west are clothed with forests of teak,[2] and angely,[3] and blackwood,[4] and cedar,[5] and cotton-trees,[6] and bamboos;[7] and the valleys are luxuriant with the cocoa-nut [8] and the areca-nut,[9] the pepper-vine [10] and the betel-vine,[11] and a profusion of beautiful creepers, which festoon the river-banks and charm the eye at every turn. The very people, too, of the west, though of the same race, are different from those of the Carnatic in colour, language, and physique, as well as in many of their habits : not the least conspicuous difference, at first sight, is the wearing of the *kudumi*, or *tuft of hair*, on the top instead of the back of the head; the latter being the fashion through the rest of India.

The road from Coimbatore to Palghaut lies through what is called the Palghaut Pass. This is, in fact, a continuation of the plain of the Carnatic, stretching through the Ghauts, and is of considerable width. Through this pass the Ponnany river flows westwards; and, following its course, on the northern bank, is laid the railway, that now runs from coast to coast. To the north of the pass the Coondas, a branch of the Neil-

[1] Borassus flabelliformis.
[2] Tectona grandis.
[3] Artocarpus anjeli.
[4] Dalbergia latifolia.
[5] Cedrela toona.
[6] Bombax Malabaricum.
[7] Bambusa arundinacea.
[8] Cocos nucifera.
[9] Areca catechu.
[10] Piper nigrum.
[11] Chavica betel.

gherries, terminate in rugged peaks; and on the south
the Anamallies rise about 5,000 feet above the level of
the sea, forming the northern extremity of the range
of mountains that runs down to Cape Comorin. A few
years ago this pass was filled with a dense jungle, or
rather forest, of bamboos and other trees. It was greatly
infested by both elephants and tigers, and, nearly up to
the time of my passing through it, it was considered
so dangerous for travellers, that an escort of sepoys was
allowed to every European journeying between Coimbatore and Palghaut. The jungle was subsequently cleared
for some distance on each side of the road, and ryots
were encouraged to settle and cultivate the soil.

The shikâree's gun also was often heard among the elephants, for the destruction of which, I believe, Government
offered rewards. I remember seeing in the collector's
bungalow at Coimbatore a great number of elephants'
tusks, trophies of jungle sport, the largest of which I
could with the greatest difficulty lift from the ground.
These were all due, I was told, to the enterprise of
a single English gentleman, who had recently shot a
goodly number of these giants of the forest with his
own rifle. Thus the ryot and the shikâree together
rendered the pass less dangerous.

It was, however, but a very short time before I was
there myself, and after the sepoy escort had been dis-

continued, that an English gentleman and his wife narrowly escaped destruction. They were travelling in palanquins on a beautiful moonlight night, and were half-way through the pass, when the bearers shouted 'Âna! Âna!' that is, 'Elephant! Elephant!' Upon which the panic-stricken men put down the palanquins and decamped with the utmost precipitation. The gentleman had the presence of mind to rush to his wife's palanquin, drag her out and hurry her off to a large forest tree, which was not far distant, and up which some of the cowardly bearers had already scrambled. They were fortunately able to climb up to a large bough, out of harm's way. Meantime, a solitary elephant, of gigantic dimensions, walked leisurely up to the lady's palanquin, examined it, turned it over with his tusks, tossed it up in the air, seemed exhilarated with the crash when it fell, played with it as one might imagine a Brobdignagian cat with a ball, lifting it about with his trunk, first by one pole and then the other, and finally stamping on it with his foot, and in apparent fury crushing it to atoms. The second palanquin had its turn, and shared the same fate. I need scarcely say that this game was witnessed by the travellers in breathless excitement from their perch in the tree. The elephant at length disappeared in the jungle, apparently unconscious of the near proximity of so many human beings; but our friends had to remain in their uncomfortable berth till morning dawned, and a caravan of country carts that passed afforded them the means of continuing their journey.

At Palghaut we dispensed with our palanquins and continued our journey to Trichoor in country carts. These carts, well known to old Indians, are of very rude construction, mounted on two large, clumsy wheels, and covered with a coarse kind of bamboo matting. When used as a conveyance, as they often are in the 'Mofussil,' a good quantity of rice-straw is spread on the bottom, on which the traveller places his mattress. The pace is usually very slow, but the bullocks are sure-footed and very enduring. It is, however, not an uncommon thing, especially on the very bad roads we often meet with in India, for these 'bandies,' as they are called, to upset. We were fortunate enough to reach the end of our journey without an accident of this kind; but, at one of the public bungalows at which we stayed, a gentle- man arrived shortly after us, whose bandy-man had been less expert than ours; he had upset his load; and the gentleman, who was asleep at the time, narrowly escaped a severe injury from a box which had fallen on him. As it was, the only inconvenience which he suf- fered, beside the delay occasioned in mounting the cart again on its wheels, was that a bottle of cocoa-nut oil,

which he had to replenish his lantern, and which had
been hung up in the roof of his bandy uncorked, had
discharged its contents over his head ; so that, when he
appeared among us, he presented a peculiarly unctuous
and uncomfortable appearance.

The country through which we passed was one expanse
of wooded mountains, grassy hills, winding rivers, and
fruitful valleys. On reaching Trichoor, we were reminded
how much these hills and valleys, though lying in native
territory, owe for the development of their resources to the
British rule. Trichoor still has a witness to the rapacity
of that Mysorean tiger Tippoo in the almost perfect
remains of an earthwork that was thrown up by the
country Nairs, or Malabar soldiers, on his approach. His
soldiers spread devastation far and wide ; and there is
no doubt he would have been victorious to Cape Comorin,
had not European energy aided in resisting him.

Trichoor is a large and populous town, and contains
a bazaar of some size. In most of the houses in this
bazaar was something or other displayed for sale —
rice, cocoa-nuts, copra (which is the fruit of the cocoa-
nut dried ready for the oil to be expressed), cotton
cloths, grass and bamboo mats, earthen pots, usually called
chatties, lanterns, areca nuts, betel leaves, plantains, chillies, pumpkins, and vegetables and spices of various kinds
common to the country. The majority, however, of the

houses in the towns of south-west India are detached, each standing in its own compound, which is generally well stocked with cocoa-núts, Palmyras, mangoes, pepper, yams, and many esculent roots, so that such towns often cover a large tract of country. They are generally divided into a number of separate hamlets—a hamlet of brahmans, a hamlet of Sudras or Nairs, a hamlet of Christians, a hamlet of carpenters, a hamlet of black-smiths, and so forth, according to the chief divisions of caste.

Trichoor is the largest town in the Cochin territory, and contains a large pagoda, dedicated to the worship of Shiva, which claims to be the oldest in that part of India. No doubt the Brahmins established themselves there early; for the place derives its name from the temple-god, its proper name being Trishivaparoor. Near to the temple is a celebrated Hindu college. The rajah of Cochin also has a palace there, and the British resident, a residency.

Among other objects, a Roman Catholic church, of some pretensions, arrests the eye on going through the bazaar. As we passed we observed a number of people collected about it; flags and banners of all kinds were fluttering in the breeze; and from the sound of shooting that was going on, you might have supposed that a detachment of riflemen were practising in the churchyard.

On asking the meaning of this, we were informed that a number of iron tubes were stuck in the ground all round the inclosure, which were charged with gunpowder, and we saw men running about and firing them one after another by means of lighted fuses at the end of sticks. We were further informed that when anyone confessed to the priest, if he paid a coin called a *putthen*, that is nearly an English penny, his sins might be blown away by having one of these things discharged! Sometimes a train of gunpowder is laid from one to the other round the whole circle, so that they may be fired off in a volley. The noise is terrific. Once, subsequently, I had to pass a night near to one of these churches during some festival, when these explosions, the beating of tom-toms, the clashing of cymbals, and the shrill tones of innumerable hautboys were reverberating through and lacerating the air, and torturing my nerves till nearly daybreak. Thus, I grieve to say, the Roman Catholics too often, living among the heathen, learn their ways. The musical instruments on such occasions are invariably hired from the neighbouring pagoda, and the use of the pop-guns is to be traced to the same source.

It is gratifying to know that this religious mummery is not the only representative of Christianity among the hundreds of Hindus in Trichoor. The Church Missionary Society has had a missionary there for some years. There is a substantial mission house, and a commodious mission church where several hundreds every Sunday join in worshipping God, according to the Protestant formularies of the Church of England. The leaven of Christianity here, as in many other parts of India, is also at last reaching even the very penetralia of Hinduism. One of the native clergymen of the Church Missionary Society, the Rev. Ooman Mamen, when residing at Trichoor, had frequent intercourse with the pundits of the Hindu College. He ventured to show them a translation that has been made by another native minister, the Rev. George Matthan, of Dr. Mullen's ' Dialogues on Hinduism.' This led to many interesting discussions on the relative merits of Vedaism and the revelations of the Christian Scriptures; and ultimately one of the pundits expressed a wish to possess an entire copy of the Bible in the Malayalim language.

At the suggestion of the Rev. Ooman Mamen, this was presented to him by the Bible Society, and I had myself the pleasure of selecting the sheets from the Bible Society's depôt at Cottayam, and having them bound in two volumes in the best style which the binders at the Cottayam Printing Establishment could command. Thus in one of the most ancient Hindu places of learning on the western coast the word of the Living God has at last found a home. Those only, perhaps, who are conversant with Hinduism in the Mofussil will be really able to appreciate at their full value such evidences as this, that 'old things are passing away.' A few years ago the bravest pundit in the College would not have dared to have a Bible in his possession. I have heard quite recently that the pundit in question is still a thoughtful student of the Holy Scriptures.

It was subsequently my lot to travel the same road again both on my way to Ootacamund and Madras. I visited the former place on the first occasion to attend a missionary conference. The conference was composed of missionaries of several denominations, and from various parts of the Madras Presidency. There were English Independents, English Baptists, English Wesleyans, and English Church- men, Scotch Presbyterians, German Lutherans, and Ame- ricans of various persuasions. All were much at one, I think, on the leading doctrines of the gospel; and, stand- ing on the basis of a common Christianity, the members of the conference worshipped God at the commencement and close of every sitting with evident ' unity of spirit.' To my mind there was something very edifying, and indeed typical in this. I could not help thinking, as I stood among them, of John Wesley's dream. There are no denominations in heaven; all are Christians there. But though this meeting was an undoubted benefit and refreshment to the individuals who composed it, tending to enlarge the spirit of Christian love, and to draw out any puny minds from the corner of selfishness and exclusiveness, in which some minds do love to seclude themselves, I cannot remember that I was much struck with the real missionary results of the discussions. Many things were, of course, said which claimed general approval; but the one question of real importance that was discussed was that of education, especially among those natives employed in our missions; one party, among whom our Tinnevelley brethren figured conspicuously, maintaining that a slight education, and that without English, was best; the other, that no education of which a man is capable could go too far, but that the better taught the man, the more efficient the instrument.

Around this point there was great fighting; but, strange to say, no one was beaten, each combatant remained 'of the same opinion still.' Thus it seemed to me that the conference worked out no result. The missionaries went back to their homes, one to educate his young men more vigorously than ever; another to look upon the knowledge of English, and even a smattering of Western lore, as still more decidedly, in his mind, prejudicial to the spread of true godliness. The latter class won the day for a time, with the Church Missionary Society; for soon in Tinnevelley the learning of anything English was discountenanced in the schools, a mistake which affected other missions also. A reaction, however, has already commenced, and men are beginning after all to be convinced that, though 'a little knowledge' may be 'a dangerous thing,' absolute knowledge, however little, gives absolute power.

The scenery and climate of the Neilgherry Hills are thoroughly charming to the parboiled visitor from the plains. The refreshing breezes, and many reminders of old England, conspire together to delight the senses. At Ootacamund the thermometer never stood higher in my bedroom for days together than 60°. In Coonoor, which is 1,500 or 2,000 feet lower down, it would be between 60° and 70°. And then the wild roses, and many ground flowers, the song of the blackbird, which is the exact counterpart of its English cousin—something at every turn is like a voice from 'Home.' I shall not soon forget my delight at finding Dodabet, the highest mountain on the Neilgherries, nearly 9,000 feet above the sea, covered with most delicate anemones. The last anemones I had seen were growing in a wood near my father's house, in which I had spent many an hour in my youth.

The Coonoor Ghaut, by which the Neilgherries are ascended from the Coimbatore side, is rich in glorious peeps, here up to the towering heights above, then down to the glaring plains below. At every step the air becomes cooler and more exhilarating. The first time I ascended it, I was doomed to walk. I had engaged a man at Metapollium to let me have a pony early in the morning. The bungalow at Metapollium is fifteen miles from Coonoor, five miles being a level walk, or perhaps a little downhill. I was to meet the animal and its attendant in the early morning at the foot of the Ghaut itself, five miles from Metapollium and ten from Coonoor. I reached the point in good time, but found no pony there; and after waiting for some time in vain, was compelled at last to use the only means of locomotion with which kind nature had provided me. Breakfast I had had none, for not a biscuit was left in the Metapollium bungalow. I was in consequence excessively fatigued with the ten miles walk uphill: but the charm of the scenery kept me up.

One of the prettiest peeps that I had was from a broad rivulet a little below the bridge at Burliar. I stopped to sketch it, and refreshed my parched throat with some of the sweet running water. In the small valley above the bridge I purchased a few plantains, but they were of too coarse a kind to be very enjoyable. When I gained the bridge at Coonoor, though I had thoroughly enjoyed my walk amid the wild roses, and honeysuckles, and rhododendrons, I nevertheless felt thankful to see the Public Bungalow on a hill at no great distance; and then I ate a hearty breakfast, as indeed I was fully entitled to do after a fifteen miles' walk ; and, after first admiring the charming prospect around dotted here and there with snug little bungalows, beautiful gardens, and a church tower capping a hill in the distance, I slept from sheer fatigue till four o'clock in the afternoon.

Higher still we rose, next morning, towards Ootacamund, familiarly known as Ooty. Not so picturesque as Coonoor, Ooty is still the more favourite resort for pleasure and health-seekers. The breezes are cooler than at the latter place, and the prospects more extensive. It is situated in a wide valley, in the midst of which is a lake of no very great beauty. Round the lake is the fashionable drive. The grander scenery in the neighbourhood of Ootacamund is only to be found by quitting the valley, and visiting the outlying country. From Dodabet the scene all round is simply grand ; but yet Coonoor is to my taste by far the more pleasant residence, and is far richer in picturesque peeps. How Turner, Creswick, Richardson, Collingwood Smith, would have revelled here in communion with nature, sketch-book in hand !

On the old road, between Ootacamund and Coonoor, lies Katy, the residence of the German missionaries. I breakfasted there with Messrs. Merike and Metz, the resident missionaries. These missionaries have worked for some years among the hill tribes, but with no very marked success at present. Their few converts are chiefly from the Badaghars, a low tribe of most decidedly filthy habits. The stench of a Badaghar house, to say nothing of a village, is unique. Pigs, buffaloes, men and women, and dogs, herd together in a delightful proximity. I saw several of the chief converts, and a small school of Badaghar children. It was pleasant to see that they were redeemed, at least during schoolhours, from their native dirt ; and let us hope that they will grow up to be men and women who shall appreciate the ineffable boon of heaven—redemption from the filth of sin. But, at present, the Badaghars seem 'slow of heart to believe.' Still more backward in appreciating the message of the Cross are the more wealthy, proud, and exclusive Todas. These people belong to the old Dravidian race, like all the other ancient hill tribes of whom I have any knowledge. They are the lords of the hills, and Europeans pay them a quit rent for the lands they occupy. They live in small villages, called Toda Munds, and in peculiar stone-built, compact, but small huts. They are few in number, and are said to practise the degrading custom of polyandria. The German missionaries have preached the gospel here ; but hitherto I believe they have received but few, if any, converts.

The Gospel Propagation Society has a native ordained

missionary at Ootacamund, who presides over a small
Tamil congregation, the members of which are chiefly
drawn from among the Christian servants of the visitors
and residents. At Coonoor the American Dutch Reformed Church maintains a missionary. For some time
the Scudders resided there, and had a neat chapel, in
which a small Tamil congregation assembled. This
mission was commenced by the late Paul Pacifique
Schaffter, one of the Church Missionary Society's missionaries in Tinnevelley, when at Coonoor for his
health.

CHAPTER II.

Meteorological notes—The bullock bandy—A thunderstorm—The
Backwater—Legend of Parasu-Râma—Cranganore—Solomon's
gold, ivory, and peacocks—St. Thomas, the first Indian Missionary
—The Jews—The decline of Cranganore—Rise of Cochin and
Calicut—The early European adventurers—Cochin harbour.

On our return from the conference at Ootacamund (I
was accompanied by a friend), our journey from Trichoor
to Cochin was nothing less than an adventure. It was
in the month of May, when the south-west monsoon is
ushered in by terrific thunderstorms, which usually
occur about sunset. From November to May we have
on the western coast a steady sea-breeze during the day,
in which the thermometer seldom rises above 84° or
85° in the shade; and at night we have a gentler land-
breeze, which lasts till a few hours after sunrise.
During the sea-breeze I have repeatedly noticed an
upper current of air from east to west; that is, exactly
opposite in direction to the sea-breeze. This upper
current I believe to be permanent at that time of the
year.

When the south-west wind which brings the monsoon first sets in, probably about March, it has, I sus-

pect, in the first place, to wage war with this contrary upper stratum of hot air from the Carnatic. In confirmation of this I may say that I have frequently seen overhead whirling clouds suddenly generated, as though by the conflux of opposite currents of air of different temperature. As the south-west current increases in power, the great barrier of the Western Ghauts begins to oppose the onward march of the contending elements, and the result is the formation of rapidly developing rain-clouds between the mountains and the sea, which discharge themselves with more or less of electrical excitement. These periodic showers increase in frequency and intensity from about the beginning of April till June, when the monsoon itself sets in with strong gales from the south-west, and generally a week's, probably a fortnight's, downpour without much intermission, but now unaccompanied by any electric phenomena. The monsoon lasts till September.[1]

The morning was brilliant; not a cloud. Our next halting place was to be Karupadnam, about fifteen miles from Trichoor, which place we had hoped to have reached in the course of the afternoon, so as to be well-housed in the Public Bungalow there before an evening storm—should one come on—could overtake us. But from various causes of delay, not uncommon

[1] See Appendix.

in India, and an unusual difficulty in procuring bullocks, it happened that, instead of starting at ten o'clock, we did not start till two. Our bullocks, moreover, were none of the brightest, and seemed much disinclined to leave home. It was excruciating to see how the driver worked himself to the utmost pitch of excitement, shouting himself hoarse, prodding the unfortunate beasts with a savage-looking stick, and twisting, and not unfrequently biting, their tails with a frantic desperation. The animals soon resented this ill-usage; for we had not gone a mile before they became utterly unmanageable, and started off from the road, rushing with us across a common, in defiance of every effort of the handy-man. We expected a speedy upset; but, with the assistance of our two servants, who were fortunately with us, they were at last stopped, and coaxed back into the road.

More careful driving kept us now on the highway, but our progress was not very satisfactory. When should we reach Karupadnam? In the meantime ominous clouds began to gather in the east. Distant thunder muttered, and evening drew on. Before sunset the heavens became rapidly overcast; and as the light declined in the west, the east became more and more brilliant with the lightning, that never ceased to fly from cloud to cloud, revealing the dense masses of

watery vapour that were rolling towards us. Presently
we were in the blackness of darkness, the lightning
seemed exhausted for a time; an oppressive hush per-
vaded everything; the very frogs in the distant paddy-
fields seemed more deliberate in their intermittent
croaking; the sound of the bandy-wheels became painful
to the ear; there was not a breath in the air; a faint
streak of dim light grew in the east horizon, giving a
more solid appearance to the intense blackness overhead;
and then a sharp flash of lightning, which gave a bluish
tinge to everything, followed almost immediately by a
prolonged roar of thunder, revealed to us that we were
now in the very heart of the storm. Flash after flash
succeeded; the whole heaven roared with thunder; the
sound of distant wind broke on our ears, and soon over-
took us: it seemed as though it would have lifted the
bandy from its wheels. The rain poured in torrents, the
lightning was incessant. 'Look there,' cried out my companion; 'did you see——?' His sentence was broken
by a most terrific crash; not a roll, like the sound of
more distant thunder, but a sound as of splitting, like a
sudden rending of everything around and above us, and
which had instantly followed the most imposing spectacle
I ever saw: a stream of lightning seemed to join earth
and heaven; and, at the same instant, a large forest-
tree, apparently about thirty or forty yards from us,

leaped out from the darkness, and stood for a moment in the midst of that strangely-lighted landscape a tree of fire; the stem, the branches, every twig, every leaf, being for one second drawn in flame. That tree had been struck by the lightning.

Our position now was by no means agreeable. The rain continued to pour in torrents. The poor bandy-man was exposed to the full fury of the storm, for the roof of the bandy did not extend more than eight or ten inches over where he sat. He declared he could go no farther; that he did not know the way; that he would die of the cold. Our servants, however, volunteered to walk before the bullocks, so as to keep the road; and, by the help of the occasional flashes of lightning, which were now becoming less frequent, and for which we were sometimes at last obliged to wait, we managed to crawl along. Still, however, the rain was pouring in torrents; we had no means of obtaining a light, and we did not know where we were, all being strangers to the road. Our intense longing was to reach a house of some kind, and we determined to stop at the first we should find, and to put up for the night at any price. But no house appeared, and the way seemed interminable—every five minutes, no doubt, seeming an hour. At last we saw a light in the distance and found a house, as we had hoped.

Here, however, we were still doomed to disappointment:

the house belonged to a Brahmin, and no bribe could induce him to let polluted individuals like ourselves and our pariah bullock-driver enter his compound. At last, though inhospitable, the Brahmin was polite enough to furnish our servants with two torches, made of the leaves of the palm, and condescended, after a long palaver, to tell us that there was a village a few hundred yards farther on, where no doubt some of the 'lower caste' people would allow us to put up. The torches helped us on our way for a time, but the drenching rain ultimately put them out, and we were in the dark as before. We went a good many hundred yards, and began to fear the village was a myth. At last, however, after groping along for nearly another hour, we did reach a village, and there we stayed all night. But our night was not a very blissful one. The villagers, to a man apparently, had gone to bed; not a soul would answer our summons as we tried house after house. At last we stopped opposite to a good-looking house with a moderately wide verandah in front, its width being about four feet, and the roof projecting about another foot over that. Our servants knocked at the door; no answer. They offered fabulous sums of rupees for a night's lodging for two sahibs; still no answer. They thundered at the door and threatened, but with no better success; no doubt the inmates were thoroughly frightened. At last we took French leave, left our bandy, and took possession of the verandah.

Our servants managed to procure a light from a passer-by who was carrying a torch, the only man awake, as it seemed, in the village, but whom we succeeded in making a friend of. We got up a fire, boiled some water in our travelling-kettle, and soon enjoyed some tea. Our servants and the unfortunate bandy-man managed to dry their clothes, and even to make themselves merry over the fire : and ultimately we wrapped ourselves, as well as we could, in our rugs, and stretched our limbs for sleep. I remember waking about daybreak, rather cramped from the hardness of my bed, but none of us was any the worse for his out-door sleep. In the morning we found that we were not far from the Karupadnam bungalow. Thither we betook ourselves, before the inmates of the house, in the verandah of which we had so unceremoniously stayed, were stirring, and, after a hearty breakfast, set out for Cochin in a boat that was already waiting for us, and in which we were to have a six hours' row on the Backwater.

A more glorious morning never dawned than that after the thunderstorm. There was a charming freshness in the air after the rain ; a faint mist hanging still about the eastern mountains caused them to assume a most intense purple at sunrise ; and when the sun was at last fairly above them in all his glory, the stretching Back-water sparkled, where the land-breeze just brushed it, like a thousand diamonds. Our boat lay in a creek beautiful with Nymphæas, principally *Nymphœa rubra*, towering above which rose the lotus (*Nelumbium speciosum*), called by the natives *thâmara poo*. The bank was thickly grown with the screw-pine (*Pandanus odoratissimus*), and on the hill behind the pretty orange blossoms and pale leaves of the *Mussœnda frondosa* (one of the *Rubiaceæ*) were conspicuous.

We embarked about eight o'clock, and our oars were soon laid aside for the sail to be hoisted, as the sea-breeze sprang up; and the fourteen rowers, who had pulled in most excellent style, rested awhile and tucked up their legs under them, chewing their betel [which consists of a fresh leaf of the *chavica betel* (one of the pepper family), rubbed over with a small portion of quicklime, and chewed together with a portion of a nut of the *Areca catechu*, and some tobacco], while we scudded along at the rate of four or five miles an hour; then they resumed their oars and gave us one of their country songs. Many a white sail besides our own was glittering in the morning sun; many a big baggage-boat, too, we passed, laden with merchandise and pushed along by bamboo poles; and here and there we passed the fisherman in his tiny craft, a small paddle in one hand and his fishing-rod in the other. In fact the Backwater was alive, and showed good evidence that it was the great highway of that part of the country.

This Backwater, which runs parallel with the sea coast

from Quilon to near Calicut in varying widths, is a particular feature in the scenery of south-western India. It is separated from the sea by a narrow strip of sand, which is one long dense garden of cocoanuts. It has but one or two outlets into the sea, the principal of which is at Cochin. The rivers of the interior discharge themselves into it, so that in the monsoon season it is full of fresh water, while in the dry season it becomes salt, and rises and falls with every tide. There can be no doubt that the flat tract of country in which the Backwater lies has been mainly formed, like the deltas of great rivers, by the deposits of the several small rivers which drain the neighbouring hills. But it is not improbable that there has been also a rising of the coast through volcanic agency. There is, I think, a probable reference to this fact in a legend in the end of the 'Brahmânda Purâna,' where the god Parasu-Râma is described as standing on the shore at Gokurnum, and commanding Varuna (the Hindu Neptune) to retire with his waters from the coast. If such be the case, we have but a parallel to the rise of that immense tract of country near the mouth of the Indus, which took place in 1819, when an extensive plateau, computed to have an area of upwards of seven hundred square miles, was raised about ten feet above its former level; while at the same time another adjoining tract of six hundred square miles was submerged and converted into a lake—

the lake of Sindree. Moreover, the whole appearance of the south-western coast of India is calculated to produce the impression that it may have been thus raised.

Even now that mysterious power is not altogether quiescent. Considerable changes have been witnessed even by the present generation. In some parts the sea encroaches—in others recedes. Allepie, for instance, is nearly a mile further from the sea than it was twenty-five years ago. In 1856, as I well remember, repeated shocks of earthquake were experienced along the coast; previously also, in 1823, 1841, and 1845, severe shocks were recorded at Trevandrum, the capital of Travancore. In several cases the shocks seem to have been propagated from the north-west. On September 1, 1856, a ball of a pendulum in the Trevandrum Observatory, seventeen feet long, is recorded to have been moved about four inches in the direction N.W. by N., and S.E. by S., which is about the direction of the coast-line. The legend to which I refer is, I think, of sufficient interest for me to give it, furnishing, as it no doubt does, a clue to the early history of Brahminical influence in the district now comprising Malabar, Cochin, and Travancore, and anciently called Kêrala; and giving also a fair specimen of Hindu poetical imagery.

According to Hindu mythology, Parasu-Râma was the sixth avatâr, or incarnation of Vishnu. He is repre sented to have been born—the son of Jamadagni, of the race of Bhrigu—at the commencement of the second, or *Treta Yuga*, for the purpose of punishing the tyrannical kings of the Kshatriya, or military race of Hindus. According to this mythology there have been four *yugas*, or ages of the world—the *Krita*, the *Treta*, the *Doâpara*, and the *Kali*. The *Treta*—the silver age of the Hindus, at the commencement of which Parasu-Râma was born—contained 1,296,000 years; the *Doâpara* 864,000; and the *Kali Yuga*, the iron age of vice, dates from 3000 B.C. He was therefore born no less than 2,164,860 years ago. The most advanced of our chronologists will hardly wish to carry us much further back in the history of the human race than this. But setting aside the enigmatical chronology of the Hindus, we may no doubt allow that a real Parasu-Râma did live *some* years before the Christian Era; though how many it would be at present, I think, difficult to say, notwithstanding the increasing light that is being thrown on Indian chronology by the researches of Max Müller and other Oriental scholars. At the same time we may bear in mind that since he is represented to have been an incarnation of Vishnu, who was a post-Vedic god—that is, a god who was introduced into the Hindu mythology subsequent to the age in which the Vedic hymns were written—we must not assign to him too high an antiquity.

Let us say, then, that *some* centuries before the Christian Era there lived a powerful and influential Brahmin, named Râma, who belonged to one of the most aristocratic families — the clan of the Bhrigus. In his time it would appear that there were certain jealousies existing between the priest caste, or Brahmins, and the royal and military caste, or Kshatriyas, which led to most sanguinary results. Parasu-Râma, whose name means Râma-with-the-axe (*parasu* meaning an axe), was the great hero of the Brahmin cause in some or all of these engagements. Thus we are told in the 'Vishnu-Purâna' that 'Parasu-Râma cleared the earth thrice seven times of the Kshatriya caste, and filled with their blood five large lakes;' that he 'presented the earth to the ministering priests;' that, having 'given the earth to Kasyapa, this divine hero retired to the Mahendra mountains, where he still resides;' and that in this manner 'there was enmity between him and the race of the Kshatriyas, and the whole earth was conquered by him.'

The legend is as follows, and I give it as I find it in a copy obtained for me by my Pundit: After a description of how the sons of Sagara (who was King of Oude) dug a hole, and descended into the infernal regions in quest of a certain horse that had been stolen by Indra and deposited there; and how, since they had been consumed by the fire of Kavila's anger, one of their descendants implored Gunga (the goddess of the Ganges) to descend into Pâtâlum (Hades) and moisten their ashes; and how at last Gunga yielded to their entreaties, and, having flooded the abodes of Kavila, welled up through the hole dug by the sons of Sagara, and covered with destruction a city on the Malabar coast, named Gokurnum—we are told that 'the inhabitants ran about in great distress, and when they saw that Gokurnum, the holy temple, was so speedily immersed in the ocean, they were deeply grieved, and consulted what they should do.'

The result of their consultation was, that they went up in a body to the summit of the Sahya mountains, that is, the Western Ghauts, anciently called *Sahya* or *Delectable*, in search of Parasu-Râma, to whom their complaint was as follows :—' Hear the cause of our now coming, O thou that possessest mercy. We, who once lived at Gokurnum, are now afflicted by the sons of Sagara, who dug a hole and descended to the infernal regions, and were burned with the fire of Kavila's anger; and now all the country where the sons of Sagara dug has become ocean : and because Gokurnum, the great temple, has sunk beneath the waves with its sacred waters, we are greatly distressed.' In this strain they supplicate Râma, who at last vouchsafes to accompany them to the sea-shore.

The legend then goes on to describe the proud god marching down from the mountains to the shore, where he stands and surveys the scene. And then, 'with a voice in thunder rolling,' he summons Varuna, the Hindu Neptune, to appear before him. Varuna, however, though he hears the words of Parasu-Râma, neither returns answer, nor does he make his appearance. The exhibition of this rebellious spirit on the part of the sea-king is very distasteful to Râma, who causes the air to thunder with his reiterated commands that Varuna should leave his ocean throne and obey the summons. Varuna, however, still maintains an obstinate silence. Bhârgava, as Parasu-Râma is also called, then has recourse to a threat :

> 'Soon with my arrow will I dry this sea,
> Till not a drop of ocean shall remain ;'

and the legend goes on to tell us that immediately there fell from the skies a bow and arrow. But in the description that follows I will endeavour to give as nearly as possible a literal translation, and to keep up in some measure the poetical element :—

> 'And then the feet of Shiva worshipping
> Bhârgava took the heaven-sent bow, and strung
> With wildest rage ; and clutching in his grasp
> The arrow forged by Bhrigu, both his eyes
> Starting their veins blood-red, he clanged the string.
> Then trembled the three worlds, and all the earth,
> With oceans, islands, mountains, deserts, quailed.

And then upon the string that arrow dread,
That, winged with flame, burns awful, like the fire
Of the great day of doom, Bhârgava fixed,
And muttering *maistras* stood. Then hid the sun
His disc behind the cloud of dust that rose
From off the trembling earth ; a comet streamed
Across the sky, the lightning flashed, and blood
Rained thick. Then terror seized the tribes of heaven ;
Siddha,[1] and Muni,[2] Chârana,[3] and all
The singers of the gods, the cause unknown,
Ran here and there, and mad with fear lay hid.
And the inhabitants of ocean all,
Huge alligators, fishes, serpents, whales,
And crocodiles, and tortoises, were scorched.
The waves rolled up, and deluged all the shore,
And all the waters of the ocean boiled.'

At last, influenced by the entreaties of the various denizens of the deep, who are beginning to suffer wofully on account of Varuna's obstinacy, the proud sea-king is glad to humble himself before Parasu-Râma, and offers to obey him in anything he commands. Upon this Parasu-Râma indulges in a laugh—' Ah, you dog, why did you not obey my summons sooner !' Thus, it is worth while to observe in passing, is a deified Brahmin made by a Brahmin poet to treat one of the old Vedic gods as a slave ! And so, through all the later Brahminical systems, the gods of the earth (*bhu-deva*, as the Brahmins call themselves) make themselves the gods

---

[1] A species of demi-god supposed to inhabit the region between the earth and the sun, or Indra's heaven.

[2] The spirits of saints are called *Muni*, or *Rishi*.

[3] The dancers of the gods.

of heaven too, that the 'profane vulgar' may know and fear.

But to resume our story. Parasu-Râma removes the dread arrow from the bow, and commands Varuna to bring up the holy temple, and remove his waters to a respectful distance. Varuna complies, and promises to remove the bounds of his kingdom as far from the shore as Râma shall bid. Upon this Râma relinquishes his bow and arrow; and, having taken in his hand a golden spoon, such as is used for sacrificial purposes, he flung it over the waters towards the south. It fell at Cape Comorin, where the waters removed from the shore for two hundred *yojanas*, which expresses in round numbers the distance between Gokurnum and the Cape. The legend concludes by telling us that 'Gokurnum, the great temple, then became level with the earth; the city, the village, and the plain came in sight little by little, and all the sages blessed Parasu-Râma. And thus Parasu-Râma gave Kêrala to the Brahmins.

Such is the legend; and the phenomena with which the author of the 'Brahmânda Purâna' is dealing are the phenomena of earthquakes. And I cannot doubt that this description is built upon a tradition known to the poet, that Gokurnum and the coast to the south were once raised out of the waves by subterranean force. It should, however, be remembered that the object of

the author of the 'Brahmânda Purâna' really is to
establish the fact that the Brahmins have a divine right
in Kêrala. 'Thus,' he says, 'Parasu-Râma gave Kêrala
to the Brahmins.' It is not improbable that in that
misty period of Indian history, when the only figures
that can be dimly seen are Parasu-Râma and the Kshatriyas, the former fighting against and almost annihi-
lating the latter—'that dark chapter,' as Professor Max
Müller calls it, 'marking,' as he thinks, 'the beginning
of the hierarchical supremacy of the Brahmins'—the
Brahmins then first established themselves in the hilly
country between the Western Ghauts and the sea, called
Malayâla or Malabar, that is, 'hill country.' And it
was no doubt subsequently necessary for the Brahmins,
who were in the first instance immigrants, probably from
Madura, to keep up their prestige by a renewal from
time to time of their claim to the patronage of Parasu-
Râma, the great Brahmin hero. This would be especially
necessary in Malabar; for, from the important and
wealthy Kshatriya families still there as rajahs and lords
of the manors, the rajah of the Cochin territory being
among the number, we may conclude that they were
formerly there in great force. Hence, no doubt, the
legend that the low lands by the sea, probably reclaimed
in these comparatively recent times from the domain
of ocean, had been miraculously wrested from Varuna's

hands by Parasu-Râma, for the special behoof of the Brahmins. And hence Parasu-Râma became the *patron-saint* of Kêrala. Scarcely is there a temple of note to be found which has not its own legend of its having been founded by him. Every Brahmin *grâma,* or village, claimed the immediate protection of this demi-god. Every youth to this day, in Kêrala, knows the legend of the 'Brahmânda Purâna;' and yearly, from the 27th of August to the 3rd of September, the great feast of the *Onum,* there is a universal holiday with great rejoicings, when it is supposed that Parasu-Râma descends from the Mahendra mountains, or Indra's heaven, and visits his people.

But our boat has been progressing under sail and oar, and we are now opposite to a place of great interest from its historical associations. To our right is Cranganore, now only a small village, but once the most prominent seaport on this part of the coast. That old time-battered watch-tower, which crowns that corner of land jutting out into the Backwater, is all that remains of its ancient forti-fications. To the south, where you see that narrow strip of sand between the Backwater and the sea, and on the other side of which you see the white lines of the breakers, as the swell of the Indian Ocean there expends its momentum, there was some centuries ago an opening into the Backwater ; through this opening the largest ships could enter, and found in the waters on which we are now scudding along one of the finest harbours in the world.

Probably on the very spot over which now our little boat is sailing, ships of Hiram's and Solomon's navy had anchored in safety nearly 3,000 years ago, while the monsoon has swept over the coast; for this, I have little doubt in my own mind, was one of the ports where Hiram's 'shipmen that had knowledge of the sea,' and 'the servants of Solomon,' collected their cargoes of gold, ivory, apes, and peacocks. India was one of the first, if not the first, of gold-yielding countries. It was the El Dorado of Phenicians, Egyptians, Arabians, and Persians. Though it is probably many centuries since the ancient gold-fields of India were exhausted, as the diamond-fields of Golconda may be ere long, yet some memories of the past still live unmistakably in the names of places. The Ponnany, a river that drains the Coondas, and part of the Neilgherries, and still yields a small quantity of gold, carries in its first syllable a memory of the past; *Pon* in the oldest dialect of the country signifies *gold.* On the Coromandel coast too we have a Pennar river, which is properly *Ponnar,* or *gold-river.* Ivory has always been, and still is, one of the exports of this part of India: and with regard to Solomon's peacocks, it is unquestionable that they came from the Western Ghauts; for as Dr. Caldwell has pointed out in the introduction to his 'Comparative Grammar' of the Drâvidian tongues, the Hebrew word for peacock, which occurs in the Book of Kings, is identical with the name of this bird in the ancient vernacular of the country, and is to this day current in the Tamil language to express the peacock's tail.

Could the stones that lie about on this now almost desolate spot become vocal with human speech they would have many a tale to tell of the 'days that are no more.' Many a romance, that no magician's art can now extract from the past, has been enacted in the heart of this Indian Tyre, where the fiery sons of Ishmael, and the demurer Armenian, and the turbaned Persian, and the bearded, hard-bargaining Jew, have met for commerce. Here, according to local tradition, was the gospel of the Lord Jesus preached first in India. While St. Paul was engaged in the busy centres of the west, Athens, and Corinth, and Rome, another apostle had found his way to Cranganore.

With the strong faith that no doubt characterised St. Thomas's life from the day when was wrung from him the exclamation 'My Lord and my God,' and a zeal heightened by a never-dying remembrance of his first unworthy doubt, and of his Lord's condescension in affording him every evidence of His resurrection, he sought the most glorious country of the old world, and its then probably most prominent city. And in Cranganore he preached the gospel of the Lord Jesus to the swarthy sons of India.

Nor, as I believe, was it only to Hindus that he brought the message, for there was probably already a settlement of Jews here. Certain it is that a large colony of Jews settled at Cranganore soon after the destruction of the Temple by Titus. According to their own account, 10,000 Jews came there from Palestine in the year A.D. 70. This is a large figure. But if even we allow that a tithe of that number came, we must conclude not only that Cranganore was a place of considerable importance and celebrity, but that Jews had most likely already settled there. Here it was that, coming probably with some Jewish refugees, the first Christian missionary in India preached of 'the world to come,' and 'the resurrection of the dead;' and that missionary an apostle. The Christians of St. Thomas, or Nazarene Christians, as they often style themselves, still exist in considerable numbers on the coast, having originally spread north and south from Cranganore.

As not a few writers of note have expressed doubts as to the truth of the tradition concerning the Apostle Thomas's mission to India, I shall take occasion in a future chapter, when I am to speak more particularly of that ancient Christian Church which claims him as its founder, to enter at length into my reasons for accepting that tradition as most probably founded on fact.

In the meantime we must leave Cranganore, and speed on our way to Cochin. Years ago, by one of those strange vicissitudes which so often mark the progress of time, Cranganore was shorn of her glory. It was no Nebuchadnezzar, no Alexander, no Titus, that blotted out her name from history, and 'laid her stones, and her timbers, and her dust in the midst of the waters;' and made her 'a place to spread nets upon'—a mere village, as she is now, of a few fishermen's huts: she fell a prey to the geological instability of the coast, before referred to. Like so many things of earth, the very foundation on which she was built was insecure: the entrance to her harbour became choked up; the remorseless monsoon washed away her bulwarks; and, losing her trade, she lost also her inhabitants.

It was in the year A.D. 1341, about a century and a half before that great European pioneer, Vasco da Gama, first sighted the Malabar coast, that the Backwater ceased to discharge its monsoon flood of waters into the sea by the Cranganore outlet, and forced another passage some miles further south, thereby forming the present beautiful harbour of Cochin. Cranganore, deprived of her harbour, gradually dwindled down to its present state of insignificance, the Jewish colonists being among the last to leave it.

Its trade fled northwards to Calicut, and southwards to the new harbour of Cochin; and these two were, in their turn, the scenes of the earliest adventures of those European navigators who, late in the world's history, found in

India, what centuries before Phenicians, and Persians, and Arabians, and Egyptians had found, a mine of wealth and luxury. A wonderful chapter is that in the history of western Europe, when, fired originally by the Crusaders' rhapsodies on the 'glowing Orient,' brave men first sought through the waters of the Atlantic a new route to the spices, and the silks, and the pearls, and the diamonds of the East Indies. Who shall ever sift for us out of the world's history the whole truth as to how much we ourselves as a nation owe for our knowledge of navigation, of geography, of astronomy, of ethnology, of history, of language—and, by these as stepping stones, for a growth in knowledge in a thousand other matters—how much we owe for our wealth as well as our luxuries, our intelligence as well as our commerce; nay, for our very position among the nations of the earth, directly and indirectly, to India!

And now we are nearing the Cochin harbour. A small forest of masts is visible. Some scores of *patamers*—for so the native vessels are called—are lying at anchor. Not a few ships of European build are there also. Some have French, some Dutch, some English colours flying. Several noble-looking vessels, of apparently from 600 to 1,000 tons burden, are by the wharves busily receiving cargo; others are at anchor out in the roads. Signals are flying from the flagstaff that stands on the top of that old substantial tower, once part of a Portuguese cathedral. They are evidently signalling to that steamer out at sea, which, leaving a long line of smoke behind it, is making its way northwards. And here, close by us, getting up steam to follow ere long probably in the same direction, is another iron-built steamship, which is just receiving a boat-load of passengers, perhaps the last for the season; for the monsoon is at hand. We are already experiencing something of the swell of the Indian Ocean as it rolls in, subdued, but not quite broken, at the mouth of the harbour; and in another minute we shall be at Cochin.

CHAPTER III.

The Jewish Synagogue—Feast of Tabernacles—The Shâsana on copper plates—Anthropological theories—Emigration of the Jews from Cranganore to Cochin—Portuguese and Dutch—The Jewish watchman—The fort of Cochin—Missionary lesson from the history of St. Paul—Protestant Church of Cochin—Cathedral ruins—Vasco da Gama—Roman Catholics banished by the Dutch —The Hortus Malabaricus—Evening rendezvous—Journey to Cottayam—Phosphorescence on the Backwater—Cottayam and Travancore.

Cochin, as I have already said, is a place of considerable interest in connection with the history of the western coast of India. My own sympathies were especially drawn out towards the old Jewish colony. And I had not been in Cochin long, on my first visit, before I made my way to the Jewish synagogue—a visit I have since not unfrequently repeated. It was Friday, and I wished to be present at their evening service. Their settlement is about a mile up the harbour, the synagogue being but a stone's throw from the water; so, accompanied by a few friends, I went by boat.

The synagogue is a more imposing place than I had expected to find. A good number of lamps hung from the ceiling, all in brightest glass shades, and many brilliant with lustres. The reading-pew and other benches were scrupulously neat and clean, and in fact in every respect just such as are to be seen in a synagogue in Europe; and the floor was laid with those inimitable old Dutch tiles with which our great-grandfathers were wont to decorate their fireplaces, and which recalled to my memory the fireplaces of an old rectory that I used to visit as a child—such tiles as those from which Dr. Watts is said to have received his first lessons in Bible history at the lips of his mother. And then the handsome robes, nearly all of silk, and the noble bearing, for the most part, of the Jews, both young and old, completed what was really a grand picture.[1]

After the service the rolls of the Law were taken from their silver cases and shown to us. They were all written at Amsterdam, and were no doubt brought to Cochin in the time of the Dutch, who were good friends to the Jews. I have since then been in the synagogue during the Feast of Tabernacles, when there is more than ordinary fervour of worship and a very full synagogue. On that occasion the men all reverently march, one after another, up to the

[1] I have since seen Holman Hunt's celebrated picture of the Finding of Jesus in the Temple, and was instantly struck with the extreme fidelity, both in physiognomy and dress, with which each figure is drawn. It carried me back at once to the synagogue at Cochin; and I could scarcely persuade myself that I had not seen the exact original of each character there.

Law, and devoutly kiss it. The women, too, then come into the body of the synagogue, and likewise kiss the sacred volume; after which the children are held up by their fathers to perform the same act of devotion.

We also went to the house of the Chief Rabbi, a fine old man. He there showed us the copper plates of which, if I remember rightly, you read in Buchanan's 'Christian Researches,' on which is engraven, in an obsolete Tamil character, a *Shâsana*, or royal grant of privileges, made to them by the Gentile authorities of the country probably not less than 1,000 years ago. The grant is made by Erasy Virma, a prince whose capital was Cranganore, and who is supposed to be identical with one of the Perumals, a race of princes who ruled in Malabar in the early centuries of the Christian Era. The witnesses to the grant are seven petty rajahs, or nobles, of the surrounding States.

Many of the privileges sound strange to European ears; but it must be remembered that they were granted in a country where to this day a low-caste man must wear a cloth of a certain cut, and must not carry an umbrella, or ride in a palanquin; where a low-caste woman must not cover the upper portion of her person, or wear, in short, anything but the prescribed cloth round her loins. To Joseph Rabban, the Chief Rabbi of the Jewish colony at that time, and to his heirs, it was permitted, amongst other things, to wear clothes of five colours, to ride horses and elephants, to be preceded by a servant, to have a certain kind of lamp carried before them (this is a custom still only belonging to the higher classes), to use the palanquin, and to carry an umbrella of state. In addition to such privileges, it was enacted that seventy-two families should be free of rent and taxes.

The reader is aware, no doubt, that there are both black and white Jews in this Cochin colony. On their unconscious heads have been built the most contradictory anthropological theories. Do the black Jews prove that in the course of many centuries a white race will become absolutely black under a tropical sun? Do the white Jews prove that climatic influence has no effect in bronzing the skin? Answer: the black Jews are not Jews at all in their origin. Their physiognomy at once shows that they are Malabars. I questioned the rabbi we visited about them, and he said simply, ' They are our *servants.*' There can be no question that they were originally the *slaves* of the white Jews, obtained in most cases, probably many centuries ago, from the lower castes of the country. In the same way there are many Portuguese, so called, now in India, who are as dark as the lowest-caste natives. They profess to be, and have often been supposed by Europeans to be, the descendants of the Portuguese. That some of them carry Portuguese

blood in their veins I could not say; but there is very good evidence that they are, in almost every case, descended from the domestic slaves of the Portuguese, who were bought, and baptised with Portuguese names.

The white Jews are the Jews proper. Some of them, however, have a decidedly olive tint, and are by no means so fair as a European Jew. And though some are undoubtedly very fair, comparatively, it would be difficult to prove that European and Asiatic Jews have not joined the colony even so late as the time of the Dutch; and hence difficult to prove through them that the influence of climate is *nil* in this respect. They are still in communication with the north. I have seen both a German Jew and also a Jerusalem Jew at the same time in the synagogue. And in their palmier days there was no doubt occasionally, if not frequently (and local reports favour this view), an accession of new blood. I doubt, therefore, whether the white Jews of Cochin are an answer in the affirmative to M. Pouchet's question 'What nation has been transformed?' The white Jews of Cochin he cites as an instance of a race ' remaining pure.' No doubt they are purely Jews by descent, but is their colour pure? I think not. There has been a change, and a change as great as I should have expected, especially as I cannot doubt an occasional infusion of new blood from the north.

It should be remembered that even the Hindus are not all black. We have in fact almost every grade of colour. A man's colour tells you at once of his *occupation*. The black man is the ground slave, who, like his ancestors for how many centuries, has worked day and night exposed to sun and rain, and wind and storm; his house a few cocoa-nut leaves, supported by half-a-dozen sticks, which he seldom troubles. His master, the landowner, the well-to-do Nair, who carries his umbrella in the sun, and lives and sleeps in a good substantial house, is brown, but by no means black. The Malabar Brahmin, who has never earned his living by the sweat of his brow, is probably wealthy, perhaps a lord of the manor, never appears in the sun but well-clothed and under his umbrella, is seldom ever brown; he is oftener a dingy white. I have seen a high-caste woman all but as fair as a white Jewess.

As a rule a man's colour belongs to his caste; indeed the Âryans have always used the word 'colour' to denote 'caste;' they found the aborigines, as we should suspect, darker than themselves, and therefore called them men of 'colour.' These Turanian aborigines (if they were aborigines) had been already bronzed in tending their flocks, or subduing the Indian forests and plains to the plough. What colour were the Âryans when they invaded India from Central Asia? Were they not as fair— or, put it in this way, could they have been much less fair, than the Jews when they colonized Cranganore from Palestine? And what colour are the Âryans of India now? They are all shades, from a nearly European fairness to a deep chestnut colour. Has this been the result of the mixture of an originally white race and a dark Turanian race? I think not. It has been the result of climate. The lady who lives in seclusion in her capacious house, under the shade of her tope of mangoes and palms, is fair. The slave who lives and works in the paddy-fields is black. The Âryan woman, who has 'kept at home,' as her ancestors have done for centuries, has preserved her complexion in the same degree as the Jewess, whose ancestors did the same.

For the same reason the Brahmanee woman from the woody valleys of Malabar is generally fairer than her sister of the naked Carnatic, who is exposed to a fiercer sun and heat. The Jew of Cochin has not lived in the field, but in the merchant's office; he has not handled the plough, but the ledger. I should not therefore expect that his colour would be much modified; at least not in a greater proportion than that of the high-caste Hindu, who has been in India perhaps three times as long. There is nothing whatever in the mere skin colour of different Indian castes to throw a doubt on the unity of the human race. There is everything to indicate that the colour is induced.

But to return to the Jews. They are now a small and comparatively poor people. They delight to dwell upon their days of former glory in Cranganore. They date their decline from the time of Portuguese ascendency at that port. It is probable that at that time the principal trade of Cranganore was in the hands of Jewish merchants; and though it had lost its harbour, it was still, no doubt, a trade centre of some importance. Accustomed to see the Jews oppressed in Europe, the Portuguese were not likely to treat them with any great consideration in India. At all events, local accounts tell us that in 1565 the Jews sought the protection of the Rajah of Cochin, and obtained from him a grant of land, on which stands the present Jew town. The Dutch, on the contrary, seem to have befriended them during the whole time of their supremacy on the coast.

An amusing tale, as I learn from the chaplain of Cochin, the Rev. T. Whitehouse, is still current among the Jews, illustrative of their hatred of the Portuguese, and attachment to the Dutch cause, even before the Dutch were established in Cochin. The first attempt of the Dutch upon the Portuguese fort of Cochin was unsuccessful, and on the approach of the monsoon they suspended hostilities for a time. The Jews aided them in their retreat, which was accomplished in the night with such tact that the Portuguese were all unsuspicious of what was going on. After the last Dutchman, one Boerdorp, it is said, who had been running to and fro the greater part of the night shouting the word of command in the deserted trenches, and challenging imaginary intruders with 'Who´ goes there?' had embarked, a Jew still sounded the hours on the abandoned ground till after daybreak, till in fact the Portuguese at last discovered that their enemies had fled. The account, however, no longer amuses us when we find that the poor Jews suffered severely for this act. Before the Dutch returned to the siege at the commencement of the dry season, the Portuguese had wreaked their vengeance on the Jews by burning both houses and synagogues, and slaughtering all the Jews they could lay hands on.

The fort of Cochin was built by the Portuguese in 1503. It was a mile and a half long, and a mile broad. It was the first European fort in the East, and was built only five years after the renowned Vasco da Gama first rounded the Cape of Storms. Goa was a later conquest, and for a time Cochin was the residence of the Portuguese Viceroy of India. It is therefore a place of great historic interest, and was, in fact, the first stepping-stone to that European supremacy in the East which is now, in the providence of God, centred in our own nation. The Dutch took it from the Portuguese in

1663, and the English from the Dutch in 1795. The Dutch reconstructed the fort on a smaller area than that occupied by the former one. The traces, however, of their industry in this respect are fast disappearing. The stones of the few remains of the Dutch ramparts are being daily carted away to mend the roads; and what was once the fort is now the town of Cochin, a grotesque medley of Portuguese, Dutch, and English houses and offices.

Efforts have not been wanting to instruct the Jews of Cochin in the truths of the Christian faith. For some years a European missionary resided there, the Jews having a great share of his attention. I am not aware, however, that any individual amongst them has acknowledged the Messiahship of Jesus. Amidst what—in a human sense at least, and we can only judge of things from a human standpoint—we must regard as brilliant successes in the mission field, there are very many instances of failure. If we want to arrive at anything like a system of evangelistic work, we should take particular note of every such case. In every progressive work more is learnt from failures than by successes. What has been the defect in the instrumentality, when evangelistic labours in India have not been followed by an adequate result? I am possessed by a growing conviction that the defect lies chiefly, and in a much greater degree

than is popularly believed, in the *foreign element* of
our agency, and in the absence of the 'gift of tongues.'
This is a matter to be tested by observation, and I
dare say I shall have more hereafter to say about it.
There is an all-important missionary lesson to be found
in St. Paul's attitude in Jerusalem: 'When they heard
that he spake in the *Hebrew tongue* to them, *they kept
the more silence:*' and afterwards, when before the
council, he cried out, 'Men and brethren, I am a
Pharisee, the son of a Pharisee,' the result was 'We
find no evil in this man; but if a spirit or an angel
hath spoken to him, let us not fight against God.' The
accents of the national Hebrew, from the lips of a
son of Israel, appeased, as though by magic, one of the
angriest mobs ever congregated; and the mere declaration of national brotherhood at once split the most
bigoted council of the old world, and claimed an over-
whelming majority for the acquittal of the prisoner.
This was but in accordance with the laws that govern
human nature. And who disregards law, does it not
with impunity. The Pharisee must speak to the Pharisee, the Jew to the Jew, the Hindu to the Hindu. A
national agency should be the watchword of every
missionary society.

It was quite dark when we got back to the parsonage,
where we were staying; and as night comes on early

within ten degrees of the equator, we were early to bed
The next morning, after *Chota Haziree,* or early breakfast, which generally consists of a cup of tea or coffee
and a slice of toast, we walked through some of the quaint
streets, and traced the outlines of the old Portuguese and
Dutch fortifications. Afterwards we went into the large
Protestant church. It belonged originally to the Fran-
ciscan monastery, which stood near, and is, I suppose, the
oldest Portuguese church now standing in the East. The
Dominicans and Augustinians also had splendid churches
here, but they have long since been demolished. The
cathedral, of which the massive tower alone remains, the
English Government having destroyed the rest of it to
make room for the oil casks and cotton bales of the merchants (truly we *are* a nation of ' shopkeepers!"), must
have been a costly and noble edifice. I judge from the
granite bases, some of which are exposed, and capitals of
pillars still lying about. The cathedral tower is now
surmounted with the flagstaff.

It is interesting to know that the renowned Vasco da
Gama was originally interred in the present Protestant
church. He had been sent out a second time to this
coast as Viceroy of India. Scarcely, however, had he
reached Cochin than he died ; in 1524, it is said, on
Christmas Day. Though his bones rested in the Cochin
church for some years, they were eventually removed to

Portugal by one of his sons. The epitaph is said still to exist, I believe, in Lisbon: 'Here lies the great Argonaut, D. Vasco da Gama, first Count of Vidigueira, Admiral of the East Indies, and its first discoverer.'

With the influence of Portugal on this coast came also the influence of Rome. Not only were there the grand churches and monastic establishments in the fort of Cochin itself, with the cathedral and its bishop and staff of clergy, but throughout the country there were scattered Romish missionaries, and especially along the Coromandel coast, and among the fishermen. Among these was the famous Francis Xavier, whose first scene of labour was near Cape Comorin.

But the Dutch were as stern Protestants as the Portuguese had been zealous Catholics; and under their rule not only were the priests and monks expelled from the fort of Cochin, and their edifices for the most part razed to the ground, but the power of those in the country was as much curtailed as possible. The Dutch, however, ultimately allowed the Carmelite Bishop of Malabar to reside, on condition that he remained well affected towards the Dutch Government. His successors are still the representatives of the Pope on the Malabar coast.

The Dutch were also a busy people with their pens. The famous 'Hortus Malabaricus,' which was published towards the close of the seventeenth century at Amsterdam, was got up at Cochin under the auspices of the governor, Van Rheede. The flowers and plants were sketched by a Carmelite named Matthæus, and no doubt many hands were employed on it. Indeed we have every evidence that the Cochin Dutch were an eminently industrious and wide-awake people. This is not the opinion expressed by some local historians, but I hold it for the present, not-withstanding.[1]

The principal English residents at Cochin are a clergy-man, a doctor, a commandant, a magistrate and judge, and several merchants. There are also several Dutch families of some standing still remaining. The British Resident also has a fine house on the island in the Back-water, in which he resides some part of the year. There is a brisk trade going on during the dry season, and the place is anything but dull, though that is the character the English ladies, I find, generally give it. We joined the majority of resident Europeans in the evening at the regular evening rendezvous, a portion of an old Dutch bastion facing the sea, on which there are seats. We

[1] Major Heber Drury, of the Madras army, published in 1862 a trans-lation of interesting Dutch letters by a chaplain of Cochin named Jacob Canter Visscher, in which we have a picture of Cochin and Malabar as they appeared to a European in the early part of the last century. A MS. account of Cochin and Malabar by M. Adrian Van Moens, who was governor of Cochin about 1772, was also found by Major Drury among the Government records of Cochin. It is to be hoped that this may some day be translated and given to the world.

watched the sun set in glorious amber, and enjoyed the refreshing sea-breeze for more than an hour, discussing the politics of Europe, already six weeks old, with unabating vigour.

About half-past eight, after tea, we entered a cabin-boat again for another thirty miles' row to Cottayam. We arrived at about half-past five o'clock in the morning. We came southwards along the Backwater, and then about nine miles up a river towards the east. The early part of the night was dark, and the phosphorescence of the Backwater most striking. With every dash of the oars the top of the cabin was strongly illuminated, and on looking out we seemed to be ploughing through liquid phosphorus. This is always the case during, and especially towards the end of the dry season, when the Backwater is almost as salt as the sea. As soon as the monsoon freshes flow in from the interior the phosphorescence disappears, and the Backwater becomes as fresh as the rivers. Indeed for some distance along the coast at Cochin the surface of the sea itself is scarcely salt during the monsoon, the fresh water floating and not readily amalgamating with the salt. A friend of mine who had to procure salt-water every morning during one monsoon season for a bath for a delicate child, was often obliged to send out a boat more than a mile from the shore.

But now it is time that I made Cottayam, where I have

so long resided, my more especial theme. And how often, since Providence made this my home, as I have looked around, have I thankfully thought: 'The lines are fallen unto me in pleasant places!' The province of Travancore will, I think, yield the palm for beauty and fertility to few parts of the world. Even the far-famed Vale of Kashmir has been described to me by a friend who has visited it as being inferior to Travancore in luxuriancy of foliage. Rising in increasing undulations from the sea to the Southern Ghauts, Travancore is intersected by many rivers, which in the rainy season rush through avenues of noblest trees, often festooned to the topmost bough with creepers—here meandering by shady topes of palms, the fruit-crowned cocoanut, the queenly areca, and the huge talipot; and there expanding in beautiful lakes over alluvial valleys, and at last losing themselves in the Backwater or the sea. This little province is the garden of South India. You will not be surprised to learn that such a country is thickly populated. Wherever you go, along the rivers especially, you find signs of man. Here a broad flight of steps down to the water's edge tells of the abode of some wealthy landowner; there a still more elaborate flight perhaps indicates that a pagoda is not far distant. Here a succession of houses skirting the river's brink as far as the eye can reach, with a white church glittering in the sun, and perhaps in a more secluded spot a Mahomedan mosque, tell of a large and flourishing town. Traders with their boat-loads of merchandise, fishermen with their nets, slaves in the paddy-fields ploughing the ground, reaping the crops, turning the water-wheel, training the sugar-cane, or repairing the banks, meet the eye at every turn, and proclaim it a thriving and prosperous country.

I must, however, reserve a further description of Travancore for my next chapter, in which I shall not content myself with giving merely a general sketch of the different castes, but shall enter more particularly into the history of that most remarkable body of Christians that has for so many centuries existed on this coast, and amongst whom our first missionary efforts were made—the Syrian Christians, or Christians of St. Thomas.

CHAPTER IV.

In entering upon a sketch of the Syrian Church, which is
so interesting a feature in this part of India, my reader
will naturally first inquire as to the proportion this band
of Christians bears to the whole population of Travancore.
The caste, or race, of Syrians forms probably not less than
one-sixth of the population. But they are now divided
into Syrians and Syro-Romanists, the latter comprising
those Syrians who became Papists in the time of the
Portuguese under the terrible oppression of Menezes,
Roman Catholic Archbishop of Goa. There are at the
present time not less than 120,000 Syrians in Travancore
and about as many Roman Catholics, nearly all of whom

MAR ATHANASIUS, METROPOLITAN OF THE SYRIAN CHRISTIANS OF TRAVANCORE.

Page 26.

are Syro-Romanists. Among the nearly 10,000 Christians in the missions of the Church Missionary Society, probably not less than 5,000 are from the Syrians. The Christians of all denominations form not less than one-fifth of the population ; for we must add to the above about 30,000 converts from among the heathen in the missions of the London Missionary Society in South Travancore. I think we shall not be far wrong if we take the present population of Travancore as 1,400,000, of which 280,000 are professing Christians.

It will be perceived also that the province of Travancore, though small, being about 160 miles long by an average of 40 in breadth, is densely populated. It contains not less than 200 to the square mile. And if we leave out of the calculation the mountainous, and therefore very thinly populated portion of the country, the strip of land between the more hilly parts and the sea will be found to carry a population of from 300 to 400 to the square mile.

How was Christianity first introduced into Malabar? I have already hinted that I incline to accept the tradition of the Syrians themselves, that the gospel was brought to the coast in the first instance by the apostle St. Thomas, as at least as worthy of acceptation as anything that can be said against it. Mr. Hough, the most voluminous writer on Christianity in India, has given his verdict against the popular belief. And it seems to be the fashion of Church historians to follow in his steps. A great authority of the English Church said to me one day, ' Oh, it is only a legend got up by the Jesuits.' Sir John Kaye, in ' Christianity in India,' published in 1859, says, ' There is really no authority in its favour to divest it of all the attributes of fable.' But what is ' authority ' in such a question? There are, it is true, no historians of the Western Church who distinctly say that St. Thomas preached in Malabar; else there would be, probably, no controversy about it. But this is a case for the sifting of collateral evidence. And for this we summon the authorities of the west as well as the east. And if we can show on good authority that there is a high probability that St. Thomas did preach in India, it is all we need for the support of our legend.

The Roman Catholics have not *invented* the legend. Maffeus may indeed have added to the tale his embellishment of miracles, but the tale itself was Indian. The legend of St. Thomas's martyrdom in India was known in our own country so far back as the ninth century. The account, as given by Gibbon, of the visit of the ambassadors of King Alfred to the shrine of St. Thomas, we cannot blot from history. Sir John Kaye says, ' This story is related on such good authority that I am slow to pronounce it apocryphal. It would seem to be, at least partly true.' And even if we suppose, with some, that the ambassadors of Alfred never got further than Alexandria, where they 'collected their cargo (of pearls and spices) and legend,' the legend must have been in existence.

In the previous, that is, the eighth century, as acknowledged on all hands, Mar Thomas the merchant, called by the Syrians of Travancore, Knâu Thômâ, settled on the Malabar coast. He was a pillar of the Indian Church. And it has been supposed by some that the tradition of the advent of the apostle Thomas is to be traced to the fact that the merchant had the same name. But were Mar Thomas of the eighth century converted by the Syrians into the apostle Thomas, we should surely hear of but *one* Thomas in their accounts; whereas they tell us in the most circumstantial manner possible of the advent of Mar Thomas in A.D. 745, and *also* of that of the apostle Thomas in A.D. 52. Kaye admits, in a note, that ' it seems little likely that if the legend of the death and burial of St. Thomas in the neighbourhood of Madras really arose out of the fact of the death and burial of Mar Thomas (the merchant)—an event which took place only about half a century before Alfred's embassage—there should have been at that time, either in Egypt or Great Britain, any confusion of an incident which occurred fifty years before, with one that was at least eight centuries old.'

Moreover, there was a Church on the Malabar coast

long before the eighth century. Cosmas, a merchant of Alexandria, who visited India in the sixth century, bears witness to a Christian Church in the ' pepper country of Malabar,' as well as in Taprobane, or Ceylon. This is, I believe, the earliest mention of Malabar itself as being the seat of a Christian Church. But there are earlier notices of Christians in India. I would refer the reader here to Sir John Kaye's book for a most interesting account, derived from Socrates, or Sozomen, both of whom mention it, of the Episcopate of Frumentius in India, most probably on the Malabar coast, during the fourth century. There was also, as is well known, a prelate present at the Council of Nice, who subscribed his name as ' Metropolitan of Persia and the Great India.' Then, again, so far back as the second century, according to the testimony of Eusebius, Pantænus, the philosopher of Alexandria, ' advanced as far as India,' and ' found his arrival anticipated by some who then were acquainted with the gospel of Matthew, to whom Bartholomew, one of the apostles, had preached, and had left them the gospel of Matthew in the Hebrew ; ' which was also, he further says, preserved among them at that time. I shall have something to say about Bartholomew afterwards. But in the meantime let us observe that we have evidence here of an Indian Church existing within a century of the apostolic age. And there is the highest probability

that the Church Pantænus found was the same as Cosmas
found in Malabar. I know that many historians doubt
whether Pantænus ever went really to India; some
supposing that by India Eusebius may have meant
Arabia, or even Abyssinia. Thus Dr. Burton says,
' There is the same doubt concerning the proper
meaning of the term India, in another tradition,
concerning the apostles Matthew and Bartholomew. It
was reported, at the end of the second century, that a
Hebrew copy of the gospels, composed by Matthew, had
been found in India, which had been brought to that
country by Bartholomew. It is plain that a Hebrew
translation of this gospel could only have been of use to
Jews, who are known to have been settled in great numbers in Arabia; so that, if there is any truth in this story,
it probably applies to Arabia, and we may conclude that
one, or both, of these apostles visited that country.'
But why not let India mean India? And is there not
very good evidence that there were Jews, and probably
in great numbers, in Cranganore too at that very time?
Moreover, when Cosmas in the sixth century, and Frumentius in the fourth, and Solomon's sailors a thousand
years before (for I have shown in a former chapter that
Solomon's peacocks certainly came from South India) could
find their way to the western shores of India, surely
Pantænus could do the same in the second century? I

conclude, then, that the Syrian Church of Malabar existed so far back as the middle of the second century; and that they had at that time a copy of St. Matthew's gospel, left there by an apostle, in the Hebrew, or Syriac, language.

But what was the real origin of the Church? They say themselves that St. Thomas visited the coast in A.D. 52; and Eusebius says that Pantænus's report was that Bartholomew, an apostle, had visited them. Both reports speak of an apostle as having come to the coast. Did both come? or was it really Bartholomew who first preached in Malabar? And if so, how is it that, so early at least as the ninth century and ever since, it has been the uniform tradition of the South Indian Christians that St. Thómas founded their Church, and was martyred and buried near Madras?

Now I have been particularly struck with one thing in the history the Syrians give of themselves, and that is their early connection with *Edessa*: a fact, too, that harmonises with the bishop's designation of himself at the Council of Nice, which I have mentioned before. Many of the Syrian priests have accounts of the early history of their Church, which are handed down from generation to generation, and often copied. I have seen several. They are all very similar. One now in my hand, given me by a priest, commences thus :—'In A.D. 52, the apostle Mar. Thomas came to Malabar in the reign of Choshen. He was so successful in his preaching that seven Christian churches were founded by him there. For a long time after his death Christianity was in a declining state. But since India, as well as the rest of the East, was governed by the Patriarch of Antioch, in matters ecclesiastical, after the Nicene Council, he had authorised a Mapriana at Bagdad to see to the welfare of the Eastern Churches. This Mapriana, learning from Knâu Thômâ of the decline of the Church in Malabar, sent, by the authority of the Patriarch, the above-mentioned Thômâ and Joseph the Bishop, a native of Urahâi (or Edessa), and other bishops, priests, and deacons; and also a colony of Syrians, with their families. They landed at Kodungalloor (or Cranganore), in the reign of Cherman Perumal, A.D. 745.' I have just met with another and similar account, given 150 years ago by Mar Gabriel, a Nestorian bishop, who presided at that time over a section of the Syrian Christians, to the Dutch chaplain of Cochin, Jacobus Canter Visscher, whose letters from Cochin have been translated lately by Major Drury.

It runs as follows:—' Fifty-two years after the birth of the Messiah, the holy apostle Thomas arrived at Maliapore, on the coast of Coromandel, preaching the gospel and founding churches there. Passing from thence to Malabar, the holy man landed on the island of Maliankarre (situated between Cranganore and Paroe), preached and taught, and built churches in that island, and likewise at Cottacay, Repolym, Gokkomangalam, Pemetta, and Tierowangotta ; and, having finished his work in these parts and ordained two priests, returned to the land of the Pandies (as the natives of Coromandel are called) to teach the people there.   But whilst he was thus occupied the apostle was pierced by the heathen with spears, and thus ended his life.   In the course of a few years all the priests in Hindustan and Malabar died ; and many years afterwards, a *Tovenaar*, called Marmakawasser (probably Thomas the Manichee), an enemy to the Christian faith, arrived at Maliapore, performing many miracles to hinder its progress ; and, many of the principal Christians giving heed to him, forsook Christianity, and followed the false teacher Marmakawasser.   In those days certain persons came from Hindowy, or Hindustan, who were not disposed to abandon the people of Malabar, and who allied themselves with the believers—that is, the Christians who had remained   constant,   in   number   about   160   families   or tribes.

‘These men taught for many years in Malabar, but there were few among them who had knowledge, because they were destitute of pastors ; and therefore most of them ended in becoming heathens, and had all things in common with the other heathens.   This caused a second apostacy ; so that out of the 160 families 96 adopted the heathen superstitions, 64 only adhering to the true faith. Now in those days there appeared a vision to an arch-priest at Oerghai (Urahâi, or Edessa), in consequence whereof certain merchants were sent from Jerusalem by command of the Catholic authorities in the East to see whether there were here any Nazarenes or Christians. These persons arrived here with ships, joined all the Christians from Maliankarre, as far as Tierowan-gotta, treated them as brothers, and strengthened them in the faith.[1] And, having taken leave of the 64 families, set sail and returned to Jerusalem, and related to the Catholics in that place their adventures in Malabar.

'After this, several priests, students, and Christian women and children came hither from Bagdad, Nineveh, and Jerusalem, by order of the Catholic arch-priest at Oerghai (Edessa), arriving in the year of the Messiah 745, in company with the merchant Thomas; and, having made acquaintance with the 64 families, they became united, and lived in concord one with another. At that time the famous Emperor Cheram Perumal was reigning over the whole of Malabar. To him the new comers went; and, when they informed him of the cause of their arrival, the king was well pleased, and gave them pieces of ground in the territory of Cranganore to build churches

---

[1] Could this have been under the influence of the famous Jacob Albardai?

and shops upon, that they might pursue their trades. At the same time he granted royal marks of honour, and permission to carry on their trade throughout the whole country so long as the sun and moon should shine, as may be seen to this day in their documents written upon copper plates.'

Now we observe here that help is uniformly represented as coming to the early Malabar Church from Urahâi, or Edessa, and that the Edessens are supposed to have been *already acquainted* with the existence of Christians in Malabar. Did, then, the Edessens first bring the gospel to Western India? If so, they must have done so, according to what Pantænus found, at least by the middle of the second century, if not much earlier. There is only one other way of accounting for the early connection between Cranganore and Edessa, and that is by going back a few years, and supposing that both Churches were founded by the same apostle. That would account, in the readiest possible way, for the one Church being acquainted with and interested in the other. And who was the apostle of Edessa? According to Eusebius—and all historians agree here—it was St. Thomas.

Now Eusebius's account of Pantænus confirms the report of an apostle having reached the coast, but that apostle is said to have been Bartholomew. Here is a stumbling-block! I confess I have sometimes wondered whether

Pantænus, being a Greek, and being *possibly* imperfectly versed in Hebrew or Syriac, and much more being unaccustomed to the pronunciation of the Malabars, did not hear of *Mar Thômâ*, and translate it in his note-book by *Bartholomaios*. I fear that the reader will not accept this ' gratuitous supposition' of mine as an argument. Let us, however, remember that Pantænus brings an account from the Christians of Malabar that they had been visited by *an apostle*. From their connection with Edessa we should have expected that apostle to have been Thomas; and this would accord with the tradition of the Syrians ever since the ninth century. But here only we hear of Bartholomew.

The truth must lie in one of four suppositions : either that the Edessens brought the gospel to Malabar very early, and left the account of their own connection with the apostle Thomas to be adopted by the Malabar Christians as belonging to themselves; or that the apostle Bartholomew founded the Church; or that both Thomas and Bartholomew visited the Indian coast; or, lastly, that the present reading in Eusebius is, from some cause, a mistake, and St. Thomas was really the apostle who first preached in Malabar according to the tradition of the Syrians. The evidence, to my own mind, greatly preponderates in favour of the last supposition, especially as the name of Bartholomew nowhere occurs, either in tradition or Church history, except in that one passage of Eusebius and a passage in Socrates, which is manifestly a mere echo of it. Nearer to the truth than this we cannot, I think, get; but there is enough, surely, to make us regard the circumstantial account of the Syrians, that the apostle visited the coast in A.D. 52, with great respect.

It is remarkable that the Syrian Christians divide themselves into two classes, who do not generally intermarry, called the *Thekanbâgar* and the *Wadakanbâgar*. The Thekanbâgar state that they are descended from the colony of Mar Thomas; and that the other party, who are by far the more numerous, are the descendants of the converts from heathenism. The Wadakanbâgar, however, give a different account of themselves and of the Thekanbâgar. They say that the Thekanbâgar are the descendants of a native concubine of Knâu Thômâ, and that some of their ceremonies at marriages and on other occasions show that their progenitrix was of the Washer caste. They consider that they themselves are composed of the descendants of all the rest, both ancient colonists and the converts. It is not easy to decide which tradition is nearer the truth.

The Thekanbâgar consider themselves so superior to the Wadakanbâgar that they will not intermarry with them. It is, however, remarkable that the bishops of the Syrian Church have always been, so far as is known, of the Wadakanbâgar class. The terms Wadakanbâgar and Thekan-bâgar signify respectively Northerners and Southerners, and are said by some of the natives to be derived from the fact that, when the early colony resided at Cranganore, the Syrian colonists and Mar Thomas lived on the south side and the converts on the north side of a street. The real origin of the terms is, however, no doubt due to a wider separation than could be found in the same street. Whatever may have been the cause, whether jealousy of kindred or of caste, a separation took place, according to the testimony of Mar Gabriel, among the Christians of Cranganore in the year 823, when a party of them settled at Quilon, further down the coast. Hence, I suppose, the terms Northerners and Southerners.

There has been much dispute as to whether the Syrian Church in Travancore was ever Nestorian. No Syrian priest can now be found who would allow that this was the case. It is true indeed that sometimes Nestorian bishops have been in Travancore; but this is not much to be wondered at, when we remember that the Nestorian Patriarch of Babylon, and the Jacobite Patriarch of Antioch, who resides in the same neighbourhood, at Merdin, a little to the north of Bagdad, both claimed jurisdiction over the southern Syrian churches. Were the Syrians to apply to the Nestorian Patriarch of Babylon for a bishop, he would no doubt even now at once comply. We have evidence, indeed, that they did once so apply in the seventeenth century, during their thraldom under Rome.

At the present time their bishops are consecrated by the Jacobite Patriarch of Antioch alone. Nor can there be really much doubt that from the time when Jacob Albardai, in the sixth century, espoused the cause of the Eutychians, and enabled them to secure the sees of Antioch and Alexandria, the Syrian churches in Malabar owned the Eutychian patriarch, who was the most powerful bishop in the East, and were therefore Eutychians, or, as they are also called, from Jacob Albardai, Jacobites. This is confirmed by the early mention of Edessa in the Syrian narratives; for Jacob Albardai himself died Bishop of Edessa. Still there may occasionally have been divisions in the Church; and at these times it is not at all unlikely that one party may have applied to the Nestorian patriarch for a bishop, perhaps overlooking their doctrinal differences in their desire for a rival Metran. Such times of internal discord have occurred in the Syrian Church.

At the present moment, while there are two Metrans, both claiming supreme jurisdiction, both consecrated by the Patriarch of Antioch at Merdin—the second one, Mar Curillos, a Mesopotamian, having been sent, some years back, to depose the other, Mar Athenasius, a native, because many of the churches memorialised the patriarch against him—at this present moment a third Metropolitan, a native, is on his way back from Merdin, just consecrated, having been sent there from this country with letters from many of the churches, who will receive him as their Metran on his return, in opposition to the two others. These men, of course, are all Jacobites. But once at least, in a time of great urgency, when they must have a new bishop at all hazards, they applied simultaneously to the Jacobite Patriarch of Antioch, the Jacobite Patriarch of the Copts in Egypt, and the Nestorian Patriarch of Babylon, for a prelate.

This was about the. year 1640 or 1650, when they wished to emancipate themselves from the iron rule of Rome; for it is too well known to need repetition here that in 1599 Alexio Menezes, Roman Catholic Archbishop of Goa, visited the Syrian churches, and took the most urgent and violent measures to reduce them to subjection to Rome. He was for a time only too successful. After the memorable synod which he convened at Udazamparûr, near Cochin, where he burned all the Syriac bibles he could procure, and other documents, and, if we are to believe the Syrian report, caused not a few opposers to be put to death, among whom was at least one bishop, who was on his way from the Patriarch of Antioch—after this time, for upwards of fifty years, the whole Syrian Church was in abject submission to the Pope.

There were not, however, wanting those who were look-ing anxiously for a restoration of their ancient church customs; and then it was that, as though in despair, they applied to the three patriarchs above-mentioned for a Syrian bishop. None of these bishops seem ever to have reached their destination. The Syrians have a tradition that the one sent from the Patriarch of Antioch was drowned by the Portuguese at Cochin; and one at least of the other two, there is good reason to believe, became a victim to the Inquisition at Goa. At length the capture of Cochin by the Dutch in 1663 made way for the eman-cipation of the Syrian churches from Rome, for the Dutch banished the European Roman Catholic ecclesiastics from the coast.

And we are told that in 1685, one Mar Evanios, a bishop sent by the Jacobite Patriarch of Antioch, was instrumental in redeeming a large proportion of the Syrian churches from Popery, and restoring to them their old forms of worship and church government. Those churches that still remained in connection with Rome are now called Syro-Roman, and, as allowed by Menezes, still have their services in Syriac. On ac-count, no doubt, of the request sent to Babylon; as well as to Merdin, in 1640 or 1650, as before said, other Nestorian bishops were subsequently sent; and we find that from 1714 to 1730 there were two Metrans in

Travancore—Mar Thomas, a Jacobite, to whom twenty-two southern churches adhered, and Mar Gabriel, a Nestorian, whom I quoted above, who presided over the rest, and was buried in 1730 in one of the churches at Cottayam. But that the Nestorian bishops were the exception, and never the rule, is most probable ; and since that time no Nestorian bishop has had authority in Travancore. Much stress has been sometimes laid on the statement of Cosmas Indicopleustes, who was himself a Nestorian, that in his time the Syrians of Malabar were Nestorians also. But it must be remembered that his visit to Malabar was only in the sixth century, at which time Jacob Albardai's full influence may not have been yet felt in those distant churches. It is certain, too, that Menezes branded the Syrians as *Nestorian* heretics, and even the Abbé Dubois describes them as such; but when we remember the short acquaintance Menezes had of the Syrian Church at the time he wrote, and that the Abbé Dubois wrote merely from report, probably from Menezes' own account, we can hardly allow their testimony to invalidate the testimony of the Syrians themselves. It is just possible that the northern churches, which came more particularly under the cognizance of Menezes, were Nestorian, as in 1714.

That the Syrians are still Jacobites, or Monophysites, in doctrine, as regards the nature of our Lord's person, will be evident from a careful consideration of the following extracts from an account written during the present year, by one of the most respectable of the Syrian priests, of their doctrine and discipline. This tract is in the form of question and answer.[1]

'Question: How do the Syrian Christians believe in the Son?

'Answer: They believe him to be the only begotten Son of the Father before all the worlds, the true God, one equal to the Father; and that, for the salvation of mankind, he of his own will descended from heaven, and became man, having taken his body from the Holy Ghost, and from the Virgin Mary, *the Mother of God*,' &c.

'Question: What do they think concerning the union of Christ's divinity with his humanity?

'Answer: Not like oil and water, but like *wine and water*, they are joined together and *become one*,' &c.

By this definition perhaps alone, it would be hard to convict a man of Eutychianism; but it lurks under the expression, '*not like oil and water, but like wine and water*,' and is really stated in the words they are '*become one*.' And we shall see more clearly from the next extract that there is in the writer's mind a confusion of the two natures of Christ.

[1] Since this was written a translation of this tract has been published in England by Mr. Howard.

'Question : Let me hear a brief account of those who taught errors, and of those synods which established the true faith ?

'Answer :   *   *   *   *   *   * Nestorius, the Patriarch of Constantinople, erroneously taught of the divinity of Christ that the Virgin Mary brought forth only the human body of the Son of God, and not his divinity, and as he grew up his divinity would sometimes be absent from, and, sometimes only, present with that body ; and that there are two distinct natures and two distinct wills in the Messiah, and that, therefore, the Virgin Mary should not be called the *Mother of God*, but only mother of Christ, or of the Son of Man.   *   *

*   *   There is, however, only one nature, one person, and one will in Christ, and the Virgin Mary should be called the Mother of God.'

Here, as will at once be perceived, is a full exhibition of Eutychianism. In the ordinary Mass service the doctrine is clearly stated. In the consecration of the elements this passage occurs : ' Unus ipse Emmanuel, et non divisus, post unionem inseparabilem, in duas naturas.'[1] A stronger passage still is to be found in the service for Christmas Day, by Jacob of Urahâi (or Edessa), where, after the creed, are the following words : ' The only Son has *one nature*, and one person. He who imputes to Him

<hr>

[1] *Renaudotii Liturgiarum Orientalium Collectio*, vol. ii. p. 22.

two persons and *two natures is cursed.* Hallelujah! let him inherit hell.' The expressions—'Mother of God'—'who brought forth God'—(the very expressions that were at the root of the old Nestorian and Eutychian controversies) as applied to the Virgin Mary, are of continual occurrence in the Syriac Liturgies. It is true that the Church of Rome also retains the expression, 'Mother of God,' though not Monophysite in doctrine : but the Syrians use it in the Monophysite sense, stating that 'God' was born, died, and was buried. The doctrine generally professed by the Syrian Christians is, that the human nature of Christ is, as it were, *lost* in his divinity, as a drop of water is lost in the sea. I have heard a Syrian use this very illustration. The Syrians profess to abide by the decision of the Council of Ephesus on this question ; but they seem to misrepresent it, as no doubt they have done since the time of Jacob Albardai. The actual decision at Ephesus was, that Christ has 'one person,' in whom 'two natures were most closely and intimately united, but without being mixed or confounded together.'

The Syrians represent the decision at Ephesus to have been, that in Christ is only 'one person, *one nature*, and one will.' I cannot doubt that they have, as a Church, held this doctrine from at least the days of Knâu Thômâ, if not since the sixth century. Eutychus, as is well known, denied the two natures, and it was chiefly on account of his heresy that the Council at Chalcedon was summoned, where Eutychus was condemned. This fourth General Council is not acknowledged, as will readily be conceived, by the Syrians. They consider the canons of the first three only to be binding.

A few more extracts from the Catanar's tract will best explain in other matters too what the doctrines and practices of the Syrian Church are at the present time. And, first, as to the Mass :—

' Question : What is their belief concerning the holy ceremony of mass (*Kurubân*), and the bread and wine ?

' Answer : They believe the offering of the mass to be a holy sacrifice, and the bread and wine in it to be the real body and blood of Christ.'

Then, again, as to prayers to the saints : ' They pray to the saints to pray to God on their behalf, and they not only think that the saints will hear their prayers, and pray to God for them, but they also expect that God will help them for the sake of the saints.' They also pray for, and celebrate masses for the dead. They do not, however, *profess* to believe in purgatory, but in point of fact their belief is very little different from that of the Papists.

Such are the most serious of the doctrinal errors of the Syrian Church. An examination of one of the Mass services will illustrate still further what I have said. We shall find that the celebration of the Eucharist is regarded as *a sacrifice for the quick and dead*; moreover, the doctrine of transubstantiation is undeniably implied in the service, confirming what the Catanar says in his tract, that 'they believe the bread and wine to be the real body and blood of Christ.'

The first act in the consecration of the elements is the following invocation of the Holy Spirit, during the repetition of which the priest spreads forth his hands and waves them over the elements : 'O God the Father, have mercy upon us, and send down upon us, and upon this gift, thy Holy Spirit, who is co-equal with thyself and the Son, in being, power, and infinite essence, and who spake by the Old and New Testament; who descended upon our Lord Jesus Christ in Jordan like a dove, and rested upon thy apostles in the chamber, in the shape of fiery tongues.' During this prayer the deacon says, 'Bless, O Lord : my beloved brethren, how awful is this hour, and how dreadful is this time, in which the living and Holy Ghost, descending from the lofty heights of heaven, sits and rests upon this holy mass, and sanctifies it !' while the priest, still waving his hands over the plate, continues, 'That he may come, and cause this bread to become the life-giving body (here he marks the bread with a cross), the saving body (cross), the body (cross) of our God Christ.' Then waving his hands over the cup, he says, 'That he may cause this cup to become the blood (cross) of the New Testament, the saving blood (cross), the blood (cross) of our God Christ.'[1]

Shortly after comes the prayer: ' O Lord, we offer to thee this unbloody sacrifice in behalf of thy holy Sion, the mother of all Churches, and in behalf of thy Church in the whole world,' &c. Then follow intercessory prayers for the Church, various saints, the sick, afflicted, &c., when the following words occur: ' O righteous Father, behold thy Son, who is the sacrifice that appeaseth thee: receive thou this man who died for me; let me be made holy by Him; *receive this sacrifice from me*: remember not the sins I have committed against thy majesty.' This prayer is repeated while he divides the wafer and elevates it. Then, after further prayer, when the priest communicates, he says, taking a portion of the wafer with a silver spoon, ' O thou who inhabitest the upper regions of the world, I take thee. O thou that rulest the depths, I grasp thee. *O God, I put thee into my mouth.* O Lord, Lord God, may I be delivered from unquenchable fire, and be made worthy to receive pardon of sins, like the sinful woman and the thief.' He then puts the wafer into his mouth, and says, ' One sanctifying part of the body and blood of Christ, our God, is given to me a sinner, for the cleansing of transgressions and the pardon of sins.' When the ele-

---

[1] Compare Mr. Howard's *Translation of the Liturgies of the Christians of St. Thomas.*

ments are administered to a communicant, the wafer, first dipped in the wine, is given with the following words : ' It is given to the faithful believer for the atonement of his transgressions and the remission of his sins.'

I need not further multiply quotations to show that the Syrian Church holds the doctrine of transubstantiation, and the *opus operatum* doctrine of the Sacrament of the Lord's Supper.

If the Mass is for the dead, the soul of the departed is thus prayed for : ' O God, thou hast been sacrificed; a sacrifice is offered to thee; receive this offering from my weak and sinful hands for the soul of ——. O God, give comfort and good rest to —— in thy mansions of light, with all those who perform thy will.'

The Virgin Mary is invoked in several parts of the Mass service, and is constantly addressed as ' Holy Mary, *who brought forth God*'—' Mary, *Mother of God*' (Euty-chianism)—as thus—' Holy Mary, Mother of God, pray for us sinners now, and at the hour of our death.' It is gratifying, however, to be able to add that of late the prayers to the Virgin Mary and the saints have been omitted in several of the churches.

Not the least painful part of the Mass service is that in which the deacon proclaims the arrogated power of the priests to curse both body and soul: in this address these sentences occur : ' God has given to men two dominions, one to the king, the other to the priest: * * * the king has only power to kill the body, but the priest has power by his curses to destroy both body and soul: the prayer of him who is cursed is not received upon earth, and his supplication will not be accepted before God. * * O ye cursed! go and pray to the priest who cursed you; if he will, he can easily loose, as he bound you; when he bids you go in peace, the Lord will cleanse you, and the angels will spread their wings to receive you.'

Though the saints are addressed in prayer, the Syrian Christians happily have no images, nor are the pictures in their churches considered to be more than ornaments, and were no doubt painted chiefly, if not without exception, by Europeans in the time of the Portuguese, and since. They are generally of the most paltry description, and show abundant evidence, by the frequent occurrence of European articles of dress—*e. g.* a small representation of Judas in one of the churches at Cottayam habited exactly in the style of an English or French jockey— whence they have been derived.

It was with the hope of raising the Syrian Church from its long sleep, and rousing the priests from their apathy, that mission operations were first set on foot by the Church Missionary Society in Travancore. An interest among our own countrymen in this secluded body of Christians was no doubt first awakened by the researches of Dr. Buchanan, who in 1806 visited Travancore. Dr. Buchanan, however, partly no doubt through ignorance of their language, and partly led astray by the great urbanity of the ecclesiastics he visited, seems to have formed too favourable an opinion of the 'scriptural nature of their liturgy.' 'They have a bible,' he says, 'and a scriptural liturgy;' and again, 'The doctrines of the Syrian Christians are few in number, but pure, and agree in essential points with those of the Church of England.' It is indeed true that there is much of Scripture and much that is excellent in the liturgies commonly used in the Syrian churches in Travancore; but Dr. Buchanan evidently had not looked very carefully into them, or he would have detected, surely, such errors—and are they not grave errors?—as I have noticed above, namely, the heresy of the Monophysites, transubstantiation, the Eucharist a sacrifice for the quick and the dead, the worship of the Virgin Mary and invocation of the saints, the power claimed by the priests of cursing men's souls and bodies, a practical belief in purgatory, the administration of extreme unction, and performing the service in an unknown tongue. Remission of sins through the priests' sacrifice of the mass, and not justification through faith in Jesus Christ, who was once offered for the sins of the whole world, is the practical teaching of the Syriac liturgies. Hence the priests derive the largest portion of their income by saying masses for the dead.

The Syrian Church, on the whole, however, is far from being now in the same dark and degraded state that it was in when first visited by Europeans. Whatever difficulties and disappointments the European missionaries may have encountered, the wide dissemination by them of the Word of God in the vernacular, and the stimulus given to all educational measures through their influence and by their instrumentality, have not been without marked effect on the Syrians at large. In several of the churches now, in the face of opposition from the more ignorant party, the invocations to the Virgin have been expunged, the prayers for the dead discontinued, and the whole service is performed in Malayalim. Sermons too by some of the more enlightened of the priests, and even deacons, are preached in some of the churches every Sunday. There is indeed a stirring among the 'dry bones;' and there can be little doubt that the foundation of a Protestant party, in the original sense of the word, is already being laid in the heart of the Syrians, quite independent of those who have joined our own communion.

CHAPTER V.

Church Missionary Society's early work among the Syrians—General
  Munro—Dr. Buchanan—Early letters of the Secretary of the
  Corresponding Committee, Madras—Object of General Munro—
  Early difficulties—Mr. Norton first missionary, and a judge in the
  Allepie court—Mr. Bailey—The new College—The spirit that
  actuated the Church Missionary Society—Failure—Mr. Norton
  and the Metropolitan of the Syrians—Marriage of the Syrian
  priests—Causes of disappointment—Faith of the missionaries—
  Mr. Fenn—Mr. Baker—Syrian Synod—Letters of missionaries—
  Mr. Hough and the Metran—Caution of missionaries—Education
  in the College—No proselytism—Further history of the College—
  Mr. Tucker's questions—A change of plans—Interview with
  Metran and Dewan—Bishop Wilson visits Cottayam—His inter-
  view with the Metran—Preaches in Syrian Church—No result—
  Letters of Mr. Peet at that period—Synod of 1836—Division of
  Property—Open mission—Subsequent mission statistics.

I NOW address myself to a review of the Church Missionary Society's early work in Travancore. I have
wished, if possible, to track our work in all its vicissitudes, believing that thereby valuable lessons will be found
for future guidance.

This has been, in many respects, an arduous, though an
interesting task. Many an hour have I spent in ran-
sacking old documents, preserved happily by our predecessors, but well nigh forgotten; and in referring to the
published reports of the early missionaries, scattered
through many volumes. My gleanings will, I fear, take
some time to read; and the reading of extracts from

letters and reports may, perhaps, sometimes be rather dry; but I have thought that I ought to preserve so much, as I have said, for future, if not for present use.

The first decided steps for the improvement of the Syrian Christians of Travancore were taken by the British Resident, General (then Major) Munro, whose plans resulted in the establishment and endowment by the reigning princess of a Syrian College at Cottayam, for the instruction of both Syrian priests and laymen. Dr. Buchanan, indeed, led the way, by bringing the Syrians to the notice of Christian England, by carrying home the well-known Peschito MS., from which the present printed text that is in use amongst us was made, and by forming plans for the translation of the gospels into Malayalim. But with Major Munro rests the credit, under God, of having originated the measures which have since been worked upon for the education and improvement of the Syrian Christians. The Resident's wish was for an English clergyman to be located in Travancore ; and to this end he put himself in communication with Mr. Thompson, the secretary of the corresponding committee of the Church Missionary Society in Madras. We find him in August, 1815, writing as follows to Mr. Thompson :—

' I am more anxious than ever to attach a respectable clergyman of the Church of England to the Syrians in Travancore ; and I should wish that Mr. Norton might be sent to me for that purpose at the earliest convenient period of time. . . . He ought, perhaps, to be placed at my disposal; and he may depend upon receiving from me the most cordial support and assistance.

'During my absence from Travancore a considerable degree of animosity was manifested by certain Nairs and Brahmins against the Syrian Christians—a circumstance which I regard as fortunate, because it will convince these Christians of the advantage which they will derive from the presence and protection of an English clergyman.

'I propose to proceed to Quilon early in September, and I shall employ the best endeavours in my power to obtain a good translation into Malayalim of the whole of the Syrian Scriptures. I am now in communication with the Syrian Bishop on this subject: but the unfortunate difference between him and the Remban opposes many difficulties to the execution of all the plans which I have had in view for the benefit of the Syrian Christians.'

Mr. Thompson also wrote about the same time to the parent Committee on this subject.

'The mission to Travancore,' he writes, 'should not be delayed one day unnecessarily. We could greatly wish for an establishment there of three missionaries at least. Soon might we then hope, through Divine mercy, under their ministry and the patronage of the Resident, that the Syrian churches might revive, and Travancore not only yield a large increase of native Christians, but also supply missionaries, peculiarly qualified, above Europeans themselves, to a large extent of country, and gather in multitudes to the fold of Christ.'

Such were the bright hopes with which the mission to the Syrians was inaugurated ; hopes, however, which have been flickering, like the flame of a lamp in a gusty room, from that time to the present—for fifty years—sometimes bright, sometimes apparently extinguished, but still burning. May the time yet come when the Syrian priests *shall* become the ' missionaries ' of South India, ' gathering in multitudes to the fold of Christ.'

The object which General Munro had in view, and in compassing which the Church Missionary Society lent him all the assistance in their power, was indeed a noble one ; but the letter from which we have quoted above hints at the fact that from the very first these attempts were beset with difficulties. General Munro speaks of the ' difference ' between the Bishop and the Remban, and the consequent ' difficulties ' that beset all his plans for the benefit of the Syrians. The fact is, the Syrians seem never to have acquiesced heartily in the efforts made by the Resident on their behalf. We find such passages as the following in General Munro's early letters to Mr. Norton, the first missionary :—' The Bishop should take measures to collect teachers and students. I beg you will have a communication with him on this point, and urge him to carry into effect the injunctions which I have repeatedly conveyed to him concerning it. . . . I will also thank you to see to the progress that has been made in translating the Scriptures into Malayalim, and in examining a MS. translation of a part of the New Testament which I put into the Bishop's hands nearly two years ago. The Bishop is naturally slow, and will lose much valuable time unless he is stimulated by our advice.' This letter is dated July 22, 1816. Then again, on August 14 of the same year, he says:—'The Bishop should be particularly urged to employ all his exertions in completing the translation of the Scriptures into Malayalim; and may be informed that I am rather displeased at the little progress made in that work.' Then again, in 1817:—'I gave positive injunctions repeatedly to the late Metran to hasten by every means in his power the progress of the translation; and it appears that nothing has been done.'

Was this delay of the Metran's all supineness? Did the Syrians ever really cordially meet the views of the Europeans? It is true that some of the Metrans apparently appreciated what the Resident had done for the Church; but it would appear that no sooner did a Metran of doubtful character arise, than the whole Syrian body sided with him, whether secretly or openly, to the prejudice of all the good intentions of Europeans. Indeed difficulties and hindrances of various kinds beset the missionary operations then commenced, from the very first.

The Resident, however, was evidently not a man to be cowed by difficulties; and we cannot but admire the measures which he took, both for the temporal and spiritual improvement, not only of the Syrians, but of the whole country. His two great objects were to secure a translation of the whole Bible, and to have an English clergyman at the head of his new college at Cottayam. The study of the English language also he laid great stress upon. 'The translation of the whole Bible,' he writes to Mr. Norton, 'into Malayalim, is one of the most important and essential objects of our exertions.' And again : 'I have no hope of the reformation or improvement of the Syrian Church until an English clergyman is placed in superintendence over the college at Cottayam.' Accordingly, while Mr. Norton, who reached India in 1816, was located at Allepie, built a church and a mission-house on land granted by the Ranee, with funds partly raised by the Resident, and was constituted a judge in the Allepie Court (a rather questionable proceeding, but one which reflects infinite credit on General Munro's earnestness for the integrity of justice in the courts of law), Mr. Bailey, who reached India shortly afterwards, was placed at Cottayam, and was entrusted with the translation of the Scriptures and the general management of the college.

The principles on which the missionaries proceeded, and the object in view, were to influence the Syrian Church by educating the candidates for the priesthood, and a few of the laity, in the new college ; all their plans and arrangements being subject to the authority of the Metran, and without at all interfering with his rights as head of the Church, or with Church matters in any way at all. This was done with the hope that by means of a superior education an enlightened priesthood would in course of time see, and themselves expunge, the errors of Syrianism. On this plan the missionaries at Cottayam worked for eighteen years. While at Allepie and Cochin the English Liturgy was used by the missionaries Norton and Ridsdale, and missionary operations were carried on in the usual aggressive mode, at Cottayam Mr. Bailey and his coadjutors confined themselves conscientiously and exclusively to the translation of the Scriptures, and the education of the deacons in the college. They preached in the Syrian churches—all of which were opened to them—but in no way interfered with the usual services; even the college youths attended daily mass in the chapel. Thus they endeavoured to *influence* the Syrian Church for good, while carefully abstaining from any cause of schism.

The spirit which actuated the Church Missionary Society in thus dealing with the Syrians was very different from that which actuated the Church of Rome in her dealings with them two hundred years before. The Italian coerced, anathematised, and endeavoured to burn out the superstitions, to make way for those of

Rome. The Englishman came as a helper, a fellow-worker, with the gentle persuasions of the gospel of Christ, hoping that the corrupt Church would learn, and herself purge out the old leaven. We cannot but admire the sanguine hopes of these old and honoured missionaries, and the spirit of love and forbearance which influenced the Society under whose direction they worked; but at the end of eighteen years, although 153 Catanars (priests)—five-eighths of the whole number— had been educated in the college, not one of them, so far as we know, was found willing to abjure the errors of Antioch.

There was one redeeming character, in the Syrian Church, and that was the entire absence of any restraint on the study of the Scriptures. She is so far, and it is a great point, in advance of Rome. It was this, no doubt, that held up from the first the hearts of the missionaries amid all their other hindrances, and, above all other things, encouraged them in their work of patience, and labour of love. But the work of restoring a corrupt Church is one of no ordinary difficulty. Judaism is what it was, although the great Lawgiver Himself and his Apostles were the missionaries; Rome is Rome still, notwithstanding the sturdy eloquence of Luther; and can we wonder, though we admire the efforts that were made, that the early hopes of the missionaries to the Syrians are still unaccomplished? Indeed it was not until the mode of our operations was changed that any real fruits to mission labours were apparent.

It may, no doubt, still be considered an open question by many whether the missionaries should not have steadily pursued their original course of working as co-helpers, and in deference to the wishes of the Metropolitan, notwithstanding the discouragements of eighteen years' experience. Let us, then, see how matters stood during that period. Mr. Norton's introduction to his work may be best described in his own words, in a letter dated October 14, 1816, showing as it does his own views at the commencement, as well as those of the Syrian body.

'While I was at Quilon,' Mr. Norton writes, 'the Resident sent for the Metropolitan of the Syrian churches, that he and I might form some acquaintance with each other, and come to a right understanding with respect to the footing on which I should stand connected with him. I had, in consequence, several interviews with him. It appeared that some apprehensions existed in his mind, and much more in the minds of the clergy and people, lest we should innovate, and endeavour to do away with some of their legitimate rites, and bring them under English ecclesiastical power. Indeed this fear so possessed the minds of a few that they have actually left the Syrian, and joined the Romish Church, intimating that the Bishop was about to betray them to the English. I endeavoured, therefore, in the first place to convince the Metropolitan, in the presence of several of his Catanars, that we had no other object in view than the benefit of the Syrian Church; and assured him that it was our sole desire to be instrumental, by the Divine assistance, in strengthening his hands for removing those evils which they had derived from the Church of Rome, and which he himself lamented, and to bring them back to their primitive state, according to the purity of the gospel, that they might again become a holy and vigorous Church, active and useful in the cause of God. I have reason to be thankful, that, after a little conversation, I succeeded; and he received me, as he expressed himself, as sent by the Lord to be their deliverer and protector, and prayed that God would bless my efforts among them.'

In a subsequent part of the letter the marriage of Catanars is mentioned:

'In my conversations with the Metropolitan, one topic on which we touched was that of their clergy not marrying. The Bishop saw 'the evil of this practice, and wished to remedy it. One reason, among others, that was urged in its favour was their poverty; they were too poor to maintain a wife and family. To obviate this difficulty, the Resident immediately offered to give 400 rupees to the first priest that would marry; and promised so to arrange matters that the clergy, in general, might marry and support families.'

Now this letter unfolds to us one of the causes of subsequent disappointment to the missionaries. Led astray by Buchanan and Bishop Middleton, they had arrived at the hasty and incorrect conclusion that everything erroneous in doctrine and practice in the Syrian Church had been derived from their fifty years' subjection to Rome. Never was there a greater mistake. The errors of Syrianism were the errors of Antioch, not Rome. No sooner was the Roman yoke taken off her shoulders than the Syrian Church returned to her old liturgies, and her old faith, under the auspices of a bishop commissioned to this work by the Jacobite Patriarch of Antioch himself. The false teachings and customs of the Syrian Church were not mere excrescences, grafted on to an otherwise pure stock by Rome, and which needed only to be pointed out in order to their speedy excision; they were entwined amid the very vitals of the system.

The right of marriage among the clergy was indeed at once conceded, because the prohibition was not a necessary part of the discipline of the Church of Antioch. The Syrians had no objection to be purged from every stain they had received from Rome, and this probably was one; for though Antioch approved of celibacy, she did not enforce it upon the common clergy. They hated Rome—as well they might—but they had no idea of purging the errors of Antioch; and the missionaries only deceived themselves when they spoke of helping them to return to their 'primitive state, that they might *again* become a holy and vigorous Church.' The real nature of that primitive state to which the Syrians were entreated to return should have been more accurately examined. The whole history of the Jacobite Syrian Church should have been studied, and their liturgies understood, as a necessary preliminary to the establishment of a mission among the Jacobites of Travancore. Here, then, we can point out one cause of failure, which operated from the very first, and probably for some years. The early missionaries must have over-rated their own chances of success, by under-rating the difficulties, and misapprehending the real nature of the task to which they had applied themselves.

Still, though they seem to have been unconscious of the real extent of the difficulties that lay before them, we cannot but approve generally of the measures they took under the advice of General Munro, and the sanction of the parent Committee of the Church Missionary Society. They were men of strong faith, and knew that the stripling David had slain the giant of the Philistines with a sling and a stone. To endeavour to conciliate the Syrians, to educate an ignorant priesthood, to spread the Scriptures in the vernacular, to point out in the spirit of love the requirements of the pure gospel of Christ, and in doing this to become ' all things to all men, that they might by all means save some,' was but acting in accordance with that gospel. They proposed to conquer the Syrians by love, and by ignoring all claim to any authority over their Church matters. This was, no doubt, a laudable theory; but whether, when the theory was reduced to practice, there were not some unfortunate compromises, which resulted in the strengthening rather than the elimination of error, may well be questioned, and of which we may form a judgment as we proceed.

In 1818 Mr. Fenn joined the mission as principal of the college; and Mr. Bailey was enabled to give his time almost exclusively to the study of the language and the translation of the Scriptures. In the following year the mission was still further strengthened by the arrival at Cottayam of Mr. Baker; and for some years the work was divided between them, Mr. Baker having the superintendence of a number of schools which were established throughout the churches.

Mr. Fenn had not been long in the country before an assembly of Syrians was convened at Mavelicara. This happened on December 3, 1818, when upwards of 700 Syrians were present in the church, forty of whom were Catanars. The Metrópolitan took his seat in front of them, with Mr. Fenn and Mr. Bailey on either side of him. After the Litany had been read by Mr. Bailey, and the First Epistle to Timothy by two of the Catanars, Mr. Fenn delivered through an interpreter an address, in which he suggested many important measures for the benefit and restoration of the Church. Amongst other things it was now proposed that six of the elder Catanars should be appointed to define, in conjunction with the Metran and Malpan, the existing rites, ceremonies, and worship of the Syrian Church, in order that every part of them might be canvassed by them and the missionaries, and brought to the test of Scripture.

It does not appear, however, that very much was accomplished by this conference. The marriage of the clergy had been already approved of, and the objections to it gradually diminished; but, beyond this, few concessions seem to have been made by the Syrian body.

In 1819 the missionaries themselves thus describe their views and experiences :—

'We think we can safely assert that there is a gradual, though slow improvement. The mind of the Metropolitan evidently opens to a view of the real state of the Church over which he presides. Many hints of improvement are suggested by him, and he follows up warmly the plans proposed by us. . . . We will now mention two or three facts by which we judge of the improving state of things among this people. The first is the marriage of the clergy, and the few objections seriously made against it by any. . . . To prevent mistake, however, a little explanation is necessary. They attach great sanctity to a life of celibacy ; and derive a confirmation to their opinion from the epistles of Clemens Romanus, which they hold in high estimation. It is only from the present dissolute state of the morals of the clergy that the Metropolitan is so anxious for the measure. The number of Catanars now married is nearly thirty.'

Another favourable circumstance, adduced in the same letter, is ' the pleasure with which the Metran and several of his clergy received Mr. Bailey's present of the English Liturgy in their native tongue.' Not that the missionaries contemplated its use in the Syrian churches, but they considered it of great importance that they should have a ' model' set before them ' in their attempts at reformation.' Several of the Catanars, however, did read it in their own churches. It is worthy of remark here how careful the parent Committee was in guarding against anything like proselytism. The Report of the period tells us that 'the Committee conveyed to the missionaries their decided judgment that the Syrians should be brought back to their own ancient and primitive worship and discipline, rather than be induced to adopt the Liturgy and discipline of the English Church; and that should any considerations induce them to wish such a measure, it would be highly expedient to dissuade them from adopting it, both for the preservation of their individuality and entireness, and greater consequent weight and usefulness as a Church; and to prevent those jealousies and heart-burnings which would in all probability hereafter arise.'

The next year finds the missionaries deploring, in marked terms, the degraded state of the Syrians, and, not least, of the clergy. 'In themselves,' they say, ' they are sunk and degraded indeed. The total disregard of the Sabbath, the profanation of the name of God, drunkenness, and to a considerable extent, especially among the priesthood, adultery, are very prevalent among them. In our former statements about their moral character we have never, as the Committee will recollect, drawn highly-coloured pictures; and if at any time we have spoken of their virtues, it has only been in reference to the standard of human conduct existing in this dark and wretched land.'

The Metran was very cordial, and fell in with most of

their plans, which were always proposed with great circumspection; but whether his cordiality arose from any really enlightened convictions as to the errors of Syrianism may be gathered from the following conversation, which took place between him and Mr. Hough, who visited Travancore in 1820:—

Mr. Hough. 'Since by this time you will have been able to form an opinion of the object and plans of the gentlemen who are placed here, will you be kind enough to tell me whether you approve of what has been done?'

Metran. 'Yes; I entirely approve of everything.'

Mr. H. 'Have you any improvements to suggest in the college regulations, the mode of instruction, or in any other part of the measures now pursued?'

M. 'No; none whatever.'

Mr. H. 'Are these gentlemen understood when they perform divine service in Malayalim, and also when they converse with the people?'

M. 'Yes; perfectly.'

Mr. H. 'The English mode of worship is, you see, very different to that of the Syrian Church; what objection have you to that mode?'

M. 'I have no objection to it; it is very good.'

Mr. H. 'Do you perceive that any good effect is produced by what has been done hitherto for the benefit of your Catanars and people?'

M. 'Yes; a little improvement, both in their understanding and moral conduct. Formerly none of them could read, and they seldom or never heard a profitable discourse; and to this state of darkness are to be attributed the evil lives which they led; but now, by the conversation and instructions of these gentlemen, they have gained a little light, and their morals are proportionably improved.'

Mr. H. 'We are told by St. Paul that it is necessary to pray publicly in a language which all the congregation understand. But I perceive it is the custom of your Catanars to pray in Syriac, which is unintelligible to the people. Do you think that any portion of the public service might be translated into Malayalim? And, if so, what part or parts might be rendered into that tongue?'

M. 'There can be no objection to the whole of the prayers in which the people join being translated into Malayalim, for our Church has no canon against it; but such as belong peculiarly to the Catanars must always be used in Syriac.'

Mr. H. 'You have seen that it is customary for the ministers of the Church of England to conclude the service with a discourse to the congregation on some passage of Scripture: would it not be well to adopt the practice in the Syrian Church?'

M. 'This is done sometimes—always at an ordination

of Catanars ; and occasionally at other times, when a large congregation is assembled. There is no objection to the Catanars preaching every Sunday, when they shall be capable of doing so ; but at present they are too ignorant themselves to teach the people. That is indeed an important work ! '

The Metran never commits himself. He approves of what is done, but shows no inclination to go beyond the canons of his own Church.

Is it not, too, a little remarkable that the missionaries had hitherto, apparently, held their peace about the errors embodied in the Syrian liturgy ? In reference to the conversation recorded above, Mr. Hough makes the following observations :—

' I should remark, on that part of the above conversation which relates to the alteration of the customs and mode of worship in the Syrian Church, that the missionaries have never made any reference to the subject. Greatly as it must pain them to witness so much superstition and unmeaning ceremony among this interesting people, they have, as yet, with great wisdom and delicacy, refrained from interfering, in the slightest particular, on sacred matters. . . . They are too prudent to act with precipitation. At present they are expending their time and strength in preparing the people's minds for the reception of truth ; content to show them the light by degrees, as they appear ready to receive it.'   Were not the missionaries by this very reticence cherishing a worm at the root of their dearest hopes?   It is difficult to avoid the conclusion, from the records that remain, that a too timid policy shackled their early efforts.   The errors of Syrianism were allowed—nay, kept up—in the very college itself.   The missionaries, indeed, preached justification through faith in Christ alone; but, at the same time, the students in the college were not only permitted, but forced in the college chapel to see the priest put 'God into his mouth,' and to expect an atonement for their sins in the sacrifice then offered.

Another subject now presents itself to our notice, and that is the style of éducation in force in the college at that period.   We may be allowed to question whether it was exactly suited to the end in view, namely, the regeneration of a corrupt Church.   The subjects read by the first class in 1826 were Virgil, Horace, Xenophon, St. John's Gospel, Syriac (including instruction in the mode of performing mass, with the various crossings, waving of the hands, bowings, incensing, &c.), English, Euclid, and history.   A great attempt was made to cultivate the mind, but with little regard to theology.   The principal writes in 1825 : 'Catechisms, portions of the Scriptures, and homilies, they read and learn; but the study of theology, as a science, seems to me the last which should be taught, and not till the mind is a little enlarged, and emancipated from prejudice and passion.' But what was there in Virgil, Horace, and Xenophon to remove the 'prejudice and passion,' and pave the way for their seeing that the priest cannot make a sacrifice which shall atone for sin, especially when they themselves were instructed at the same time in the manner of offering the sacrifice of the mass for the quick and the dead? Was not such a course of education almost certain to result in failure?

It must, however, be conceded that the missionaries were carrying out well-studied plans, and in accordance with principles which had been carefully weighed both by themselves and the Committees under whom they worked. Their labours at first were an experiment, and an experiment so cautiously conducted, and with so much respect for the constitution of the ancient Church which they sought to benefit, that even the most rigid church-man can scarcely find anything to censure on the head of ecclesiastical interference. They were men of earnest prayer and faith; their example was a burning and shining light; while they did not shrink from holding up the reformed and Scriptural liturgy of the Church of England as a model for the Syrians to imitate in the re-form of their own, they received no proselytes; they diligently and successfully studied the vernacular language of the country; Mr. Fenn especially, by his careful study of Sanscrit, stood very high in the esteem of the natives, both Syrian and heathen ; and their names will long live in Travancore. Many missionaries who have come and gone are forgotten, but the names of Fenn and Bailey are still in every mouth.

And if, at this distance of time, we think that we can point out some of the causes which militated against the accomplishment of the great end they had in view, we must not be regarded as endeavouring to cast a slur on the work of these noble and self-denying men, but rather as sympathising with them in their experimental labours, and as wishing to gain from past failures experience for the future. We must not forget that their principle—a principle much dwelt upon by the Committee of the Church Missionary Society in all their instructions to these early missionaries—was to abstain from anything that might irritate or alarm, and thus at the first create prejudice in the minds of the Syrians. Their object was to *influence* them for good. There was much wisdom, no doubt, and much to be admired in such a determination—backed too, as it was, by a strong faith, leading them to hope that with increasing light error would disappear. What I would, however, endeavour to show is that other influences were at work as well, the real power of which the early missionaries did not and probably could not, well estimate at first.

The history of the college is, to a great extent, the history of the mission for some years, and we must still pursue it a little further. While Mr. Bailey laboured at the translation of the Scriptures, and superintended the working of the printing press, and Mr. Baker had schools at most of the chief Syrian churches throughout the country, the college was expected to furnish all the deacons required. To this end an agreement had been made between the Metran and the missionaries that he should ordain no one but those approved by the principal of the college. This was in accordance with the founder's designs, and was readily and apparently willingly conceded by the Metran. It was a rule, however, which was afterwards often wilfully broken. In 1826 Mr. Fenn returned to England, and was succeeded by Dr. Doran, the relations between the missionaries and the Metran remaining as before. At this period, Mr. Fenn, after nearly nine years' residence at Cottayam, speaks of the mission as a ' very peculiar one, and requiring in conducting it the greatest judgment and delicacy.'

With regard to the college, Mr. Fenn writes : ' It is the college of the Syrian Church, not of the mission. But the missionaries have identified themselves with the Syrian community, and have lived on that close and intimate footing with the prelates of the Church that all the affairs of it come under their notice. The missionaries have been anxious to avoid everything which might lead to schism in the Church ; and contented themselves with pointing out to the Metropolitan and superiors of the Church those things which appeared decidedly objectionable, without pressing an immediate correction of them. Many things have conspired to render the anticipated improvement very slow of approach.' Mr. Bailey also, during the same year, speaks of 'at present seeing but little fruit. We long,' he says, ' to see a spiritual revival take place in this ancient and interesting, but, at present, degraded Church.'

Thus earnestly for eighteen years the missionaries to the Syrian Christians laboured in Travancore ; but at the end of that period, in 1835, it became manifest, especially to the discerning scrutiny of the able secretary of the Church Missionary Society in Madras, Mr. Tucker, that something must be wrong. The older missionaries were still sanguine, but it became increasingly evident that no tangible improvement had resulted to the Syrian Church. Though five-eighths of the Catanars had by that time passed through the college, not one appeared in the light of a reformer, even in minor matters. Nay, it was stated by the missionaries themselves that the Catanars who had been educated in the college were, if anything, more inimical to them, and to any measures of reform, than the rest.

A new Metran had succeeded to the Syrian mitre, who, though friendly with the missionaries, was evidently adverse to change ; and continual, and apparently well-organised, attempts were made in the college itself, during the absence of the principal—who unfortunately lived a mile off—by the Malpans and teachers, to undermine all that the missionaries were teaching. This was discovered and exposed by Mr. Peet, who arrived in Travancore in 1833, and was for a time in charge of the college. On one occasion, led, no doubt, by some suspicion of what was going on, he returned unexpectedly to the college at an hour when he was usually at home, and there found the Malpan, surrounded by all the students, eagerly and violently contradicting all that he had just been enforcing on some matters of doctrine or Church history. The fact seems undoubted that up to that period the Syrians had never desired to reform their Church ; and, as Mr. Peet probably spoke more unguardedly and forcibly of the errors of Syrianism than his predecessors had done, the real state of their feelings became more evident. There can also be little doubt that the influence of the Metran, who was apparently much less disposed towards reformation than some of his fathers had been, had much to do with hindering the real object the missionaries had primarily in view.

At this time Mr. Tucker arrived in Travancore, and in

a long interview with the missionaries, Messrs. Bailey, Peet, and Woodcock, investigated all matters connected with the mission. He proposed no less than seventy questions to the missionaries; and had interviews with the Metran and several others of the Syrian body, as well as with the British Resident. Some of Mr. Tucker's questions, with the answers returned by the missionaries, were as follows :—

'What substantial reform has been effected in the Syrian Church through the direct or indirect labours of the missionaries from their first establishment at Cottayam to the present day?'

Answer 1. Rev. B. Bailey. 'I cannot say that any real substantial reform has hitherto been effected. The instruction of the youth in the college, &c., I trust has not been wholly in vain. The translating and printing of a portion of the Sacred Scriptures have been accomplished, and distributed among the Syrians, &c., which, I doubt not, will, through the blessing of God, eventually prove a means of bringing about a reform in the Syrian Church.'

2. Rev. J. Peet. 'I know not of any one.'

3. Rev. W. J. Woodcock. 'I am not aware that any kind of reform has been effected by the direct or indirect labours of the brethren at Cottayam. At the same time there is doubtless some general improvement among the

priests and people in and about Cottayam, by the diffusion of knowledge and the dissemination of God's Word.'

'What are the particular things in which a reform has been attempted ?'

Answer 1. Rev. B. Bailey. 'In answer to this question, I beg leave to refer to the reports of this mission forwarded from time to time to the Madras Corresponding Committee, where some attempts to reform the clergy by having a few to reside at Cottayam for a short time are mentioned; but this plan did not succeed. Some other reforms of less moment, such as putting a stop to many evil practices at their festivals, and correcting some abuses in Church government, were attempted, and for a time succeeded; but those practices, I am sorry to say, have again been introduced within the last few years.'

2. Rev. J. Peet. 'There has been an attempt to encourage marriage amongst the clergy; instruction has been communicated to the Syrian youth through the medium of parochial schools; and a portion of God's Word has been translated into the vernacular tongue, and distributed among the people.'

3. Rev. W. J. Woodcock. 'As far as I can learn, there never has been any direct attempt made to bring about a reformation in any one particular, excepting the marriage of Catanars by the offer of a premium.'

'Has the attempt to persuade the Syrians to have the

Scriptures regularly read in the churches in the stated services at all succeeded?'

All answer, 'No.'

'Is there sufficient evidence to lead to the conclusion that the Catanars as a body are more disposed to reform than they were at the commencement?'

Answer 1. Rev. B. Bailey. 'No. At the same time many of the Catanars are desirous to reform several things in the liturgy.'

2. Rev. J. Peet. 'No. I think there are a few; but how far they would be disposed to go is very doubtful.'

3. Rev. W. J. Woodcock. 'No. I think that there may be two who would be willing to reform in non-essentials, but know of none who wish a reform in essentials.'

Such were the opinions of the missionaries at that time, as elicited by Mr. Tucker's questions. Accordingly they unanimously agreed that the time was come for some more definite attempt to be made towards a reformation. And in considering to what extent the reformation ought to be attempted, it was their opinion that the things required as indispensable should be only such as are plainly contrary to Scripture; and that that attempt should first be made by means of the Church herself, lawfully represented in synod assembled. They therefore determined to urge the Metran to call a synod of Malpans, Catanars, and laity, where they should fully and freely discuss the state of the Church, and the conditions on which the funds for the college, &c., had been raised by General Munro. They at the same time considered it incumbent on themselves to abstain to the utmost from all actual interference, and in any commission or assembly to act merely as counsellors and helpers, without any right to vote.

In case of the failure of such an attempt, considering the light that had been, more or less, diffused throughout the Church, and considering that eighteen years had elapsed since the missionaries first commenced their labours, they were of opinion that they were bound, according to Scripture, no longer to bear with Syrian corruptions, but openly, and avowedly, to invite and encourage Catanars and people boldly to protest against the errors of their Church, and to refuse to read or join in those parts of the service which are plainly repugnant to the Word of God; and that, in regard to the college, they would consider themselves bound still to apply such part of its funds as were exclusively designed for it, as well as the income arising from Munro Island, according to what they are persuaded was the design of General Munro, for the especial purpose of promoting an entire reformation of the Church by means of education.[1]

---

[1] All properties connected with the college were held, from the first, jointly in the names of the missionaries and the Metran.

It is worth remembering also that the missionaries still disclaimed any desire to proselytise; they determined that, in case of a layman protesting, they should protect him, and, if necessary, admit him to the benefits of the Church of England, carefully, however, impressing upon his mind the duty of placing himself under the pastoral care of his own Catanars, so soon as any should have abjured the errors of their Church. In case also of a Catanar openly protesting, and seeking their aid, they considered that they should not regard him as belonging to the Church of England, but should encourage the retention of all such parts of the Syrian liturgies and ceremonies as are scriptural, and profitable for edification; and that they should encourage such an one in cherishing the hope that all such might be able to continue their orders through their own bishops.

Mr. Tucker now proceeded to Mavelicara, to have an interview with the senior Metran, who met him in the Syrian church there. The interview, however, was far from satisfactory. The Metran, indeed, agreed that a synod might be assembled, and after some trouble signed a declaration that he would not ordain more candidates without the necessary and previously arranged testimonial from the missionary in charge of the college. But everything in the interview indicated an unwillingness on his part to yield any point in the way of reformation, although assured that the time had arrived when the instructions of General Munro, in regard to the college, and the property generally, must be properly carried out according to the object of the founder.

Mr. Tucker subsequently visited the junior Metran also, at Annura. Mr. Tucker assured him that, being himself a priest, and he a bishop, he desired to pay him all due reverence. He found the junior bishop more affable and gentlemanly than the senior, but no nearer to reform. He spoke very kindly of the missionaries, and thought that he could see fruits to their labours. But when Mr. Tucker asked him more closely what one thing that was contrary to the Scriptures had the Church put away, he was unable to name one. Mr. Tucker further told him that the missionaries had no other wish than that the Syrian Christians should conform to the Word of God, and that there was not the slightest wish to introduce any English customs; that there was no wish to interfere with the authority of the Metrans, but suggested the desirability of calling a synod to decide fully upon what should be done. He approved of such a measure, and declared himself as ready there to take the side of the Word of God; but when the particular things in the liturgy that are contrary to the Word of God were set before him, he justified them by saying that they had existed from the beginning, and that it was impossible that men who were taught by the Holy Ghost could have erred in these things. He further said, much to Mr. Tucker's astonishment, that 'the Syrians, the Roman Catholics, the English, the heathen, the Mahomedans, and others, all thought their religion the true one, and who should decide which was right?'

I have been particular in recording what passed between Mr. Tucker and the junior Metran, as it will serve to show what amount of real enlightenment there was at that time amongst the best of the Syrian clergy. Had Church history and its lessons been studied in the college, instead of the etiquette of the mass service; and had a few other changes been made early enough in the course of reading, we cannot but think the result *might* have been different.

Mr. Tucker then had an interview with the Resident, Mr. Casamajor, in which the original design of General Munro and the Ranee, in establishing and endowing the college, was fully discussed. And, subsequently, the Dewan, Soobrow, met the senior Metran at Mavelicara, when he explained to him that the designs of the missionaries were to benefit the Church, but in no wise to interfere. The Metran stated, rather hesitatingly, as it appears, that some young gentlemen who were subordinate to Mr. Bailey showed their determination to abolish the established religious rites of the Syrian Church by the introduction of foreign ones in their room—a circumstance, he said, which prevented him from entrusting the education of his people entirely to them; adding, likewise, that 'Mr. Bailey's motives were very pure, and favourable to his cause.' By which we see that the Syrians were evidently, and perhaps had all along been, suspicious of the ultimate tendency of what was going on in the college under the English missionaries. They were, moreover, guilty of not a little duplicity.

At the close of the same year (1835) Bishop Wilson also visited Travancore. The Bishop's interview with the Metran is fully recorded in Bateman's second volume of the 'Life' of the bishop. With his usual love of pomp, he met the Syrian bishop in his robes, which may or may not have been necessary, and ultimately proposed six topics for discussion:—That the Metran should ordain none but those who had obtained certificates from the college; that all Church property should be looked after; that prayers for the dead should be discontinued; that more schools should be established; that the gospel should be preached in Malayalim; and that the prayers should be interpreted into the vernacular, selecting from the various liturgies in use in the Syrian Church such portions as would form a service of moderate length.

'We wish,' said the good bishop, 'that the Syrian Church should shine as a bright star in the right hand of the Son of Man, holding fast the faithful Word—the light of the Holy Spirit—the atoning blood of Christ—the pardon of sin through faith in Him—and the Holy Scripture as divinely inspired, and the foundation of all faith. I have longed to come here for three years past, and I shall represent to the Governor-General, and the Resident, and the Bishop of Madras, what has passed; and I shall do all I can to help, if the Metran and Church are willing.'

Metran. 'We will take it all into consideration.'

Bishop. 'If you think over what I have said, and imagine that it will tend to good, and wish for aid in carrying out the plan, I shall be happy to leave a sum of money.'

Metran. 'As may be most agreeable.'

Bishop. 'I shall leave 1,000 rupees out of love, and as a mark of love to the Church of Malabar, to be administered by the Resident, the Metran, and the Church missionaries.'

Metran. 'It will be as much as ten thousand, coming from you. All shall be taken into consideration, but it cannot be done in a day.'

But neither the bishop's entreaties nor the promise of the 1,000 rupees had power to change the human heart. The whole of the Metran's answers betray the real state of his feelings, and afford no token of any actual acquiescence in what the good Bishop of Calcutta proposed. The

Metran was polite, as a Hindu usually is ; but nothing was further from his intentions than a reform to the extent proposed. The description given by Mr. Bateman —who was present as the bishop's chaplain—of the Metran is no doubt as correct as it is graphic :—' He was a good-looking man, about fifty years of age, with a tendency to stoutness, the appearance of which was very much increased by the dress he wore—a cassock of figured lawn[1] over crimson satin, and a tippet of embroidered cloth stiff with gold. He had a mitre on his head of red and green velvet, tipped and edged with gold. A cross, studded with rubies, hung upon his breast ; an ornamented bag was held in his hand, and a silver crosier was carried and held by an attendant priest behind his back. The beard was long and grey, the moustache thick and black. The expression of his countenance was weak and feeble. He had a cunning twinkling eye, and a stiff, uneasy gait. He was evidently ill at ease, and doubtful " whereunto all this would grow." '

On the following Sunday the bishop was anxious to add his testimony to the gospel of Christ by preaching at one of the Syrian churches at Cottayam, as the missionaries had often done before him. Hundreds of people assembled, and as many as possible crowded into the church. Mass was said according to the usual form, the Metran

[1] Or an alb (?)—R. C.

being also present. ' The wafer,' says Mr. Bateman, ' was consecrated and elevated; but there was no prostration or adoration. On the contrary, the priests and the whole congregation joined in a chorus, or rather shout of praise, to which the large church bell, hung in this case within the building, added its loud clangour. The noise was deafening, and the bishop was much discomposed '—as well he might. The bishop's sermon after was from Rev. iii. 7, 8; but it is to be feared that those who heard it left the church with their convictions unshaken that their Church was pure enough, though humble; and that the Bishop of Calcutta would not have worshipped at the mass had there been in it such unscriptural doctrines as some had maintained.

It is interesting to read how sanguine the bishop was that, when the Resident should meet the Metran and senior missionary, his wishes would be realised. ' God only knows,' he says, ' what events may happen; but never in my life, I think, was I permitted to render a greater service than to these dear Syrian Christians. But hush, my soul! lest thou rob God of his glory.'

But the intensity and power of their ignorance and superstition had not been properly weighed; much less had it been faithfully combated. A portion of Mr. Peet's journal, written during the same year, will help to raise the veil, and to give us a glance at what was within the

shell of bishops, priests, deacons, and external worship :—
' In entering upon a detail of this part of my labours,
my object is to state a few circumstances that have taken
place in connection with my preaching at Cottayam
church, at which place I have for the last nine months
(with one exception on the score of bad health) preached
in Malayalim every Lord's Day morning. It grieves me,
however, to add that in the prosecution of this duty I
have met with every kind of opposition (short of personal
violence) from some of the leading men.

' They now tell the people, " that what the missionary
says about the Bible is partly good, but he wishes to
overturn mass-service altogether; but that it is highly
improper, and therefore the people ought not to listen."
However, the work is the Lord's; if He will, who shall
let ? The real cause of the above-mentioned opposition
seems to arise from the effects the preaching has upon
the people's minds. They are beginning to think for
themselves ; and I have been assured that fewer people
than usual go to private confession, and that now masses
are not so frequently made in the Cottayam church as in
former times. This is probably effected by the other
means I have adopted to disseminate truth there ; besides
preaching, I frequently distribute a large quantity of
tracts, and keep a man to read them or the gospels to
the people who attend that church ; and it is not un-

common to see fifty or sixty persons sitting in and about
the church porch, during the intervals of mass, listening
to the reading of some printed tract or chapter of the
gospel.

'*Sunday, April* 13.—Being Sunday before Easter,
preached in the Cottayam church on the subject of
Christ's entering into Jerusalem; and afterwards, wishing
to see the ceremony usually performed on that day, I was
forced to remain till all the people present had been to
auricular confession. During the time I was staying in the
verandah I had an opportunity of conversing with many
of the more respectable people on the all-important topic
of religion, and the necessity there was of purifying their
Church from its corruptions. In conversing on the subject of vital godliness, I was truly shocked at their utter
ignorance of Divine truth, and the levity with which they
treated religious subjects. After asking whether I should
be offended if they spoke their minds plainly, they said,
" that as to the Bible, it was all very well, but of no great
importance, being but the words of ministers; that they
concluded all sects to be equally right; and that all that
was required was, that each party should follow the rules
of its own body, and the precepts of its ecclesiastical
rulers; that many, and perhaps the majority, of the
wealthy Syrians would long ago have embraced heathenism,
but that they would not be received into the society of

Brahmins, and therefore their condition would not have benefited by the change," &c. Upon expatiating on the corruptions found in their Church, and the evils connected with their Catanars deriving their subsistence from the performance of unscriptural rites, &c., they replied, "the Catanars must live, and ought we not to support them?" "Yes," I replied, "it is your duty to love, honour, and provide a suitable maintenance for your clergy; but you should encourage them to become good and faithful, and pay them for teaching you and your children the truths of God's blessed Word, and not permit them to be obliged for a living to have recourse to falsehood and to the open commission of acts of transgression against God's truth, to the injury of Christ's honour, and the ruin of all your souls, as I have witnessed this very morning (in allusion to the private confessions then going on), when your Catanars make you repeat the ten commandments taught you, and to omit the second and add to the fourth, by saying that in the fourth commandment God taught you to remember the Sabbath days and feast days, to keep them holy." N. replied, "Yes, it was true; it would be well to devise some other means for the support of their clergy, but, however, they wanted no changes."

'*Sunday, May* 24.—Preached this morning at the Cottayam church; congregation numerous and attentive; several Catanars present, on account of some marriage ceremonie*s*, and because a chettam upon three thrones was to be celebrated (*i.e.* mass was to be peiformed by three priests upon as many altars, at the same time) for the soul of the late Metran's brother. Lord Jesus, when shall thy Church be purified from such abominations?

'*Sunday, May* 31.—In consequence of a marriage to be celebrated between the Pepper cash-keeper's son and the daughter of an ex-judge, the church was crowded to excess. My subject was the Fall of man, chosen in consequence of having the four first chapters of Genesis printed as a tract, 200 of which I took with me for distribution. During the former part of the discourse the people were attentive, but we were afterwards disturbed by the coming of the bride, accompanied by the shouts of a mob, and the horrid din of what here is denominated music. This continued for a considerable time after the bride and company had entered the church, and it was with the greatest difficulty I could gain a second hearing, which, having achieved, I changed my subject into a sharp rebuke on the evil of Sabbath-breaking and desecrating the house of God, &c., and in conclusion called their attention to the contents of the tract, which, at the close of the service, I distributed among them.

'*Sunday, June* 14.—Having to wait in the church verandah till the conclusion of their mass-service, a number of persons came about me, one of whom requested me to procure a grant of timber from the Government for the repair of the church. I replied as usual in such cases, "You quite mistake the nature of our business here; I am simply a Catanar, and have not the slightest influence with the Government; besides that, my sole business among you is to instruct you in the knowledge of Christianity. If, however, I can help you in this particular, I shall be happy to do so."

' This led to a conversation, in the course of which Iwas gravely asked, what was the use of having a church? I replied, " Seeing the use you make of your churches, I am not at all surprised you should ask such a question; and, in order to put you right in this matter, I will answer the question first negatively, and then positively. First, the church was not made to spit or eat rice in, nor for people to meet together to transact their worldly business; neither should the congregation be disturbed by noisy women and brawling infants; but, secondly, a church should be a place especially and exclusively dedicated to the service of the Most High God; so that when we enter its walls our minds should be solemnized by the reflection that this is the house of God, and that our business here is to think of religion and our immortal souls.' This brought us to the subject of heart religion, and the necessity of worshipping God according to his own appointments, &c. Some of them replied, " Our worship is pure, and agreeable to the Bible—agreeable to the Word of God!" I replied, "What! is it agreeable to the Word of God to worship saints or pictures?" "Yes," rejoined one, who had been educated at the college, "I will prove it from your own books. You say that the second commandment forbids the worship of anything in heaven, &c. This is the neuter gender; but the representation of a saint or the Virgin is not the likeness of a thing, and therefore, even upon your own showing, to worship them is not contrary to the Word of God."

'I replied, "It grieves me much to find one who can so abuse the advantages of education; but as the stopping to reply fully to such grammatical quibbles would only tend to do as you wish, viz., to keep the unlettered people in darkness, I shall only refer to one part of your worship, to convince the most un-learned of us how futile your argument is, and how greatly the Syrians err from the truth once delivered to the saints. Now please to answer me the following question:—" Do not all the Syrians, from the Metran, fully profess to worship the cross?" "Yes," was the answer. "Now," I said, "what is a cross like? Is it like a man, or a beast, or a thing?" At this the man looked chagrined, and the people laughed. After a little pause I added, "The Bible tells me I must answer a fool according to his folly, to prevent him becoming wise in his own conceit;

but as for you, my dear people, beware; for unless you repent of the evil of your doings, and cast away every false mode of worship, God will reject your spurious services, and you may lose your souls."

'*Thursday, Sept.* 15.—Hearing that this week had been set apart to observe an especial fast in honour of the Virgin, and that it was customary for the people to live in the church, and to abstain from certain food, and bathe every day, with the full assurance that by that oblation they were made perfectly holy, I resolved to try as much as possible to stop such an awful delusion, and for that purpose proceeded to Manucattee Church, where were more than 2,000 persons assembled in and about the building; and as that church was honoured with a large image of the Virgin, it was considered as a most holy place. As I entered within the church doors, they fled from me as from a tiger. Upon going to the church and looking about, a scene presented itself which baffles all description. Some with the greatest fervour were praying before the image of the Virgin, others preparing their food, some playing, and others conversing aloud on ordinary subjects; while the apparel of all was in the most wretched plight, and the ground was strewed with broken cocoanut shells, rice, plantain leaves, &c., and, from the people frequently coming in with muddy feet, had the appearance of the pavement in a city after a heavy fall of rain. After I had sat down for a little time, a man came within three or four feet of me, and asked me very gravely whether as I came in I had touched any person. I replied, " Why ?" " Oh," he rejoined, " we are all holy, and if you have touched any one you have defiled him." " Man," I answered, " how can you be so foolish ? But tell me, are you holy?" " Yes, surely I am," was the reply, " for I have bathed in the river." " That appears very strange," I said, " since the water has not been sufficiently efficacious even to cleanse your clothes."

'After a little time I arose, with a view of preaching to them, but they all (and I regret to add were led by an individual who ought to have known better) immediately began their prayers to the Virgin in so loud a tone of voice as to prevent my being heard. This was repeated as often as I endeavoured to gain a hearing. At length, finding they would not hear, I offered to distribute some tracts among them, but these they would not so much as touch. Finding this, I said to them, " I heartily grieve for you ; and since I cannot preach to you I will pray for you." Accordingly I kneeled down, and poured out my heart before God for their salvation and deliverance from such a wretched thraldom. On coming out of church they all, as before, fled from me, lest I should perchance touch them.'

It will not now surprise my reader to learn that when the

various proposals for reform, which, as we have seen,
originated with Mr. Tucker, and were agreed upon by
him and the missionaries, were laid before the Syrian
body with the sanction of the parent Committee, backed
by the authority and approval of the Bishop of Calcutta,
they were rejected.   A crisis had now arrived ; and for
the cause of God's truth and the welfare of the country at
large, no doubt, it was a happy one.   It was indeed
painful to think that all that had been done in a spirit of
the greatest Christian kindness and forbearance for the
Syrian Church had been spurned; but it left the missionaries now unfettered to disseminate the truth, and
more unreservedly to expose the errors of the corrupt
Church in whose midst they were placed.   In a synod assembled at Mavelicara in the next year, 1836, the Syrians
went so far as to refuse any longer to recognise the rela-
tionship which had existed between themselves and the
missionaries.   It became impossible, therefore, for the
missionaries any longer to work in the college, and for
the benefit of the Church at large, in conjunction with
the Metran.   Their services, as they had hitherto been
rendered, were altogether repudiated.

The first thing, therefore, that was necessary was a
division of property: this was a delicate matter.   It was
ultimately accomplished by arbitration in the hands of
three of the most respectable gentlemen in the country,

who had no connection whatever with the missionaries or
the Syrians. They were Conrad, Baron D'Albedyhlle, John
Scipio Vernede, Esq., and William Henry Horsley, Esq.
These gentlemen were appointed as arbitrators by the Corresponding Committee of the Church Missionary Society,
the Metropolitan of the Syrian Church, and the Travancore
Government, respectively. Nothing could have been
more just than the award then made, though there
are those still among the Syrians who would deny
its impartiality. The great cause of difficulty was, that
much of the property was held in the joint names of the
missionaries and the Metran, while other properties were
granted solely to the missionaries, and some belonged to
the Metran alone. The difficulty lay in justly awarding
what had been held in the joint names of the missionaries
and the Metrans. Such property, evidently, could not
now be held by those parties as before, since the Metran
had refused to act in concert with the missionaries any
longer. It remained, therefore, for the commissioners to
determine which of the parties was entitled to a continuance of such trust; and to enable them to do so, they
referred to the object of the endowment of the college.
'The grand object,' they write, 'contemplated by Colonel
Munro, through whose influence solely this money was
obtained, was the political, moral, and religious renovation
of the whole of the Syrian people through the instruction

of English missionaries, and there is not the shadow of a
reason to suppose that the benefactions then and subsequently granted by the liberality of the Travancore
Government, and of private individuals, for a specific
purpose, to be attained by specific means, would ever have
been conferred on the Syrians irrespectively of those
means, viz.: the instruction to be afforded by the English
missionaries. In this opinion we are fully borne out
by the whole tenour of Colonel Munro's autograph letters,
which have been produced before us. The Metran having,
in synod assembled, positively determined on having no
further intercourse with the English missionaries, and
having thus refused to execute the duties of the trust
jointly with them, we have no alternative but to substitute
a trustee in his stead. We therefore award that the
future management of the said property be entrusted to
the Reverend the missionaries at Cottayam and their
successors; the secretary, *pro tempore*, of the Corresponding Committee of the Church Missionary Society,
and the British Resident for the time being, to be held by
them in trust for the exclusive benefit of the Syrians.
Such property as evidently belonged to the Syrians
alone was awarded to them, together with the college
buildings; and such property as was held in the
sole names of the missionaries and their successors,

as, for instance, the Munro Island, was awarded to them still for the exclusive benefit of the Syrians, as originally designed.

The missionaries were now free to carry out their own plans untrammelled. A new college was built by the Church Missionary Society, which was endowed by the funds above-mentioned, for the education of Syrians alone, and which endowment still supports about fifty youths of Syrian parentage in the college; others, the sons of heathen converts, being maintained by an especial grant from the society. With this exception, that the endowment of the college was exclusively appropriated to the education of the class for whom it was originally intended, the style of missionary operations was altogether changed. The missionaries now established at Cottayam an open mission; the gospel was equally preached to all classes; and while the instruction of the Syrians was still provided for, the missionaries carefully abstained from anything like a compromise of principle; the new college was, *bonâ fide*, a Church of England institution. Mr. Bailey soon built a noble church 128 feet by 64 feet, which, though not strictly classical Gothic, such as a Gilbert Scott would turn out (and where is there such an one in South India?), is yet of excellent, and indeed elegant, proportions, and is one of the best examples of good building to be found in the country.

It reflects infinite credit on the Rev. B. Bailey, as indeed does every work of his in Travancore—his bible, his dictionaries, his printing. The Rev. J. Peet established a mission, in the face of great opposition from the heathen, at Mavelicara, and built there also ultimately a substantial church. The liturgy of the Church of England was appreciated by not a few far and wide; and in a few years after 1836, there was a goodly number of professing protestants gathered out from among both Syrians and heathen.

Thus the year 1836 was memorable in the history of the mission to Travancore. The preceding eighteen years, though uncrowned by the specific object of the system adopted at Cottayam, in accordance with the designs of General Munro, had yet laid some foundation for future work. Not a few Syrians at the separation remained by the missionaries, and for the most part, though with many exceptions, have, with their descendants, remained in communion with the English Church.

The succeeding eighteen years (from 1836 to 1854) told very differently on the country at large in a mission-ary point of view. At the end of that period the number of protestants gathered from among both Syrians and heathens were—

Cottayam	.	.	.	.	.	745
Pallam .	.	.	.	.	.	1100
Mavelicara	.	.	.	.	.	1020
Tiruwilla	.	.	.	.	.	873
Allepie .	.	.	.	.	.	534
Trichoor .	.	.	.	.	.	564
			Total	.	.	4836

This is copied from the statistical returns of 1854. Three of these missions were at that time comparatively new; Pallam had been divided off from the Cottayam district, which had been previously worked by the Rev. H. Baker, and was now a new mission, under the charge of his son, the Rev. H. Baker, jun.; Tiruwilla was commenced in 1847 by the Rev. John Hawksworth, some of the congregations having previously belonged to the Mavelicara district; and Trichoor was a recent mission, commenced by the Rev. H. Harley, in the kingdom of Cochin.

Subsequently two other missions have been opened: Mundakayam, where the work has been chiefly among the hill tribes; and Kununkulum, in the Cochin territory, near Trichoor. And to show numerically—though let us remember that *numbers alone* give us but a poor idea of missionary success, or otherwise—what has been done since, during the next twelve years the numbers were nearly doubled; the subjoined statistical account of the missions for 1866 may be immediately compared with the one above.

Cottayam	.	.	.	.	.	521
Pallam .	.	.	.	.	.	1858
Mundakayam	.	.	.	.	.	909
Mavelicara	.	.	.	.	.	2631
Tiruwilla	.	.	.	.	.	1676
Allepie .	.	.	.	.	.	421
Trichoor	.	.	.	.	.	520
Kununkulum .	.	.	.	.	.	137
Cochin .	.	.	.	.	.	420

Total .   . 9093

There can be no question that the missionaries were now in their right sphere; they were no longer bound to sanction by their silence things of which they could not approve, or to be parties in proceedings which violated their consciences. They were free to rebuke error, and fully to unfold the whole mystery of God, without compromise. The pure and scriptural liturgy of the Church of England was used in their churches, and many were they who were thus enabled to worship in sincerity and truth. What they did, in the matter of their separation, was, in fact, scarcely a matter of choice. They had, indeed, no alternative; the Syrians had rejected their aid in the way in which it had been proffered, and they could only then establish an open mission. And now God seemed more abundantly to bless their labours; the fire which, when thrust into the midst of the fagot, seemed to be smothered and powerless, now when kindled on the outside soon caught the propitious winds of heaven, and spread its flames around. As the early Church only grew after its founder was removed, and his work was revealed *as a whole* by the Spirit, so the Church in Travancore only seemed to increase when the missionaries could pitch their tabernacle outside, and exhibit a pure example of the worship of the Most High.

Since that time God has given us many witnesses. We have now fourteen ordained clergymen, thirteen of whom are of Syrian parentage, two of them having been deacons in the Syrian Church when young. The remaining one is a Brahmin convert. And, numerically, with regard to those in communion with our own Church, I have spoken. But the question will be asked—and that, no doubt, pointedly—what has the result of the *open mission* been on the Syrian Church as a Church?—for the first object of the mission to Travancore was the renovation of this ancient institution. Is the Church, as a Church, any nearer a reform than in 1836? The answer, I think, is undeniable, that the system of the last thirty years *has told* on the Syrian Church.

The preaching of the missionaries (and by preaching I mean the whole of their teaching as ministers of the gospel), the example of a pure ritual, the lives and teachings of the native clergy and other agents, increased education, and, above all, the dissemination of the Word of God in the vernacular, have moved the Syrian Church to the centre. A reforming party is growing up, already so far developed as to be known by that distinctive title, who are beginning to read their liturgy in Malayalim, refuse to acknowledge the validity of prayers for the dead, to worship the Virgin Mary and saints, and to engage in other superstitious observances that have long polluted their religion. They are found chiefly in the southern districts, where, of all places, the missionaries, Messrs. Peet and Hawksworth, never gave any quarter to Syrianism. And if further proof were needed of the sincerity of the movement, the following fact stands out prominent among the rest: that Syrian deacons are in increasing numbers seeking their education in the Church Missionary Society's college, at their own expense. Thus it would seem that the very opposite of the methods at first pursued, in the management of the mission to the Syrians, is gradually producing the very results then so earnestly desired.

May our Society be ever guided by the Spirit of God in the choice of missionaries for this field, that they send out none other than those who are wise in their generation, men of sound learning, and, above all, men 'full of the Holy Ghost;' for this is indeed a field which needs the most skilful and most devoted of husbandmen—men 'wise as serpents, and harmless as doves.'

SYRIAN PRIEST IN EUCHARISTIC VESTMENTS IN THE ATTITUDE OF PRAYER.

Page 143.

CHAPTER VI.

Present state of Syrian Church—A midnight service—Hint to ritualists—Syrian ignorance rather than bigotry—Mission instrumentalities—The College—Its religious aspect—Two brothers—Religious tone in College—Protestant results—Disappointments—Causes of failure—Unmanageable boys—High pay—Attitude of a dominant race—Native capacities not developed—Foreigners and evangelism—Power of national sympathy—Our present agency—Cottayam Church — Other congregations — The printing establishment — Electro-plating types—Rev. George Matthan—Butler's 'Analogy' —*Marumakathdyam*— Rev. Koshi Koshi—Our Timothies and Tituses—Leaders in the native Church—The slaves of Travancore — First efforts on their behalf — College boys as teachers — Baptism of slaves – The slave and the Brahmin—Testimony of masters.

I HAVE already mentioned that there is a decided movement towards reform in certain quarters amongst the Syrian body. But I lately witnessed a scene which furnishes an example of what the Syrian Church, as a whole, really is still. One evening a deputation from one of the churches (of which there are two) at Cottayam waited upon me to ask if they could borrow two hanging lamps from my verandah for the night, as they were going to have a grand 'entertainment,' and they needed an unusual amount of illumination. The members of the deputation were all well known to me, so that I found it difficult to say them ' nay.'   But my curiosity was excited, and I made inquiries as to the ' entertainment.'   I found that it was the commemoration of the death and burial of Mar Gabriel, whose account of the early history of the Syrians I quoted in a former chapter.   In the morning masses were to be said for the repose of his soul, and at midnight there was to be a preparatory service, which many hundreds of Syrians were expected to attend.   This midnight service was to be in commemoration of the bishop's burial, as his mortal remains lie in the chancel of the church, and it was to conclude with a funeral procession. I asked permission to witness it, which, I need scarcely say, was at once allowed. Accordingly a little after eleven o'clock I set out for the church.   I found the church and churchyard already crammed with people. It was with no small difficulty that I worked my way to the west door of the church, aided though I was by many who knew me, and at last established myself under the west gallery.   The church was brilliantly lighted, hung with a galaxy of lamps, among which, not, I confess, without some feeling of shame, I recognised my own.   Through a friendly feeling towards some of the members of the church my own verandah had been plunged in unwonted darkness, in order that, perhaps, very questionable orgies might be the more fully illuminated.

But when I lent the lamps I was hardly prepared

for what was to follow. And, perhaps, when this is read
—in the contemplative quiet, it may be, of the study
—the question will arise, whether, if I saw anything that
I felt to be derogatory to the honour of God, I should not
have lifted up my voice for the ‘true light.’ I did not.
I was there only by permission. There were few who did
not know my sentiments, and to many I could speak
afterwards. So I stood, though sometimes ill at ease,
in what I thought my wisdom and my patience. My
object was simply to be an eye-witness of the ‘entertainment,’ for what I thought to be a not unworthy
object. And that the assembled multitudes desired an
‘entertainment,’ and nothing more, was evident from
the merry shouts and incessant roar of the hundreds of
people, chiefly men and boys, who filled the church
and churchyard, and crowned the high wall that surrounded it. I was surprised, after standing for some
time in the church, to see a number of men about the
door with the ashes of Shiva on their foreheads.' What!
Hindus amongst the company. Yes, indeed; and each
one with a musical instrument in his hand, or under his
arm. We were to have music, then, as a part of the
entertainment. Had I not been forewarned of this by
what I saw, my ears would soon have undeceived me, for
at about a quarter to twelve o'clock the combined bands
of three or four of the neighbouring pagodas began to

beat their drums, and rend the air with their hautboys and flageolets. Strange sight. The men whose daily employment is to honour the idols of Vishnu, or Shiva, or Bhagawathy, in their daily processions round the temples, were here engaged to do honour to the spirit of a Christian bishop. Here is a subject for contemplation. It is not that the heathen musicians are thereby brought to see anything more noble or true in Christianity than in Hinduism, in a Mar Gabriel than in a Shiva, but that everywhere Christianity, when degraded by superstition and ignorance, degenerates into mere idolatry. Metaphysicians may see a difference, but the common man sees —aye, and suspects none.

But now the priests began to flit to and fro before the altar, coming up the chancel steps in their ordinary white dress ; and as they come up one by one, the deacons help them to robe. Ten priests there are, when all have assembled, and each puts on a differently coloured and differently patterned cope. All are of the richest silk. One with a huge scarlet cross at the back, another with a yellow cross, another a crimson, another a white ; some with only a small cross at the shoulder, and the rest broad stripes of scarlet and yellow or scarlet and white. And then they arrange themselves in a semi-circle before the altar, their heads slightly inclined, and behind them, in a wider circle, are from fifteen to twenty deacons, also beautifully clad in a kind of figured cassock, and each swinging a censer. Then there was a hush: the temple bands were still: the voices died out: and a chant arose from the chancel. I scarcely know how to describe it. One who has been in a Jew's synagogue may form some idea, perhaps, of its effect. Instead of Hebrew, the Syrians use its sister Syriac, and the mode of chanting is very similar. This chanting lasted about ten minutes, and consisted of invocations of the Virgin Mary and saints, and among them Mar Gabriel himself. The chanting concluded, they formed in procession, each having in his hand a taper, and the deacons still waving the censers. As they reached the west door of the church, I perceived that the leading priest—an amiable and intelligent young man, who says he has no sympathy with these travesties of religion, but has not courage to make a determined stand against them, and who is well known to me, as he helps me occasionally to spell out a little Syriac—was bearing a silver image of the Virgin Mary. A grand canopy was ready outside, under which he heads the procession round the church. His stepping under the canopy was the signal for Shiva's bands to strike up again with their deafening 'tom-toms' and shrieking pipes; and immediately an enormous rocket was fired just in front of the procession, and for a moment displayed the mass of heads swaying to and fro in the churchyard, as it went rushing up

towards the beautiful stars. Then presently there was a
cessation of the frantic beating of the tom-toms, and
a chant was again raised by the priests, which sounded
like a verse from the *De Profundis*, while for a short
time they halted. Then again in the front of the procession there sprang up another brilliant light, this
time an exquisite fountain of fire, something similar to
what, when I was a schoolboy, we used to call a
'flowerpot.' In India they are great adepts in the
manufacture of fireworks. Then the procession moved
slowly on again to the music of Shiva's bands, and then
again halts. Another rocket hisses from the front, and
soon explodes in beautifully coloured balls. Then there
is another pause for chanting, and then another rocket,
and then another tremendous clash of tom-toms and
cymbals, and 'all kinds of music;' a few yards of progress for the procession, more fireworks, and so on,
with an alternation of music, fireworks, and chanting;
till in about an hour the circle of the church had been
completed, and the ceremony was ended. I left before
the conclusion, having witnessed all that I needed to
enable me to say that I have seen Syrianism now
under, I think, every aspect.

The Syrian system itself is as bad as bad can be.
It is, however, more the result of ignorance than
bigotry. The Syrian priests are certainly, as a rule,

not bigoted; they are in no way afraid of or prejudiced against the Protestant labours of our missionaries. The best of them send their sons to us for their education. There is, so far as I can perceive, no feeling of distrust towards the efforts of Englishmen, as there was when the missionaries were associated with their bishops in the government of their college. They have no 'Index Expurgatorius.' They accept, for the most part, everything we do. And, above all, they are not afraid of the influence of the Bible. Notwithstanding, therefore, their superstitions, they are not separated from us by the exclusive fanaticism of the Roman Catholics. They are open to the influence of kindness, education, and the Word of God. But the ignorance of the masses, and even of the great majority of the priests, as regards scriptural knowledge, is still dense. This is because their system leaves them ignorant. Their religious services, even were they ever so pure and scriptural, could never send one ray of light into the darkness of the human heart; for they are in Syriac, a language that comparatively few even of the priests understand. Our duty, then, is to try to expel the ignorance, while we take advantage of their friendly feeling towards us. Education—and it cannot be too good for a decidedly intellectual people like these—and with it the Word of God in the vernacular, are manifestly the two great instrumentalities for us to wield.

Such were my thoughts as I traced my way homewards. And as the clamour of drum and cymbals, and the shrill tone of the hautboys, and the rush of the rockets, grew fainter in the distance, I could not help wondering whether I should ever see the day when such follies should become the exception, instead of the rule, amongst the Syrian churches, and should likewise die away in the distance of time, a mere echo of an ignorant and superstitious past.

How far are we using the proper instrumentalities aright? The answer is to be found in the present state and working of the missions; in the college, the printing press, the mission churches and schools, and last, but not least, the status of our native agency.

Let us begin by a review of the college. I have often wished that the friends and authorities of missionary societies could *visit missions*; that is, not give us merely 'pop' visits to examine our schools, and look at our churches, and assemble conferences—which are often, after all, more or less a sham—but stay with us a month or two, or even a year or two, and, by taking themselves for a while an active share in our work, obtain an insight otherwise impossible. But as this is for the many impossible, I must try to describe our work as well as I can. How far does the education in the college act evangelistically on the country, and particularly on the Syrian body?

It is evident that it ought to exert a very powerful in-

fluence, for the college endowment allows of its accommo-
dating (at the present time) about eighty boarders, each
one of whom must be of Syrian parentage, besides about
fifty day boys, who are drawn from both Christians and
the higher-caste heathen. The education given is such
as to fit the young men for almost any position in life;
and, at least so long as I was connected with it, considerable attention was given to divinity. The first
class, consisting of young men of from 18 to 21
years of age, read each half-year a gospel or an
epistle in Greek, as well as Church history (of which
I made a great point), and Evidences of Christianity.
Great pains was also taken, as you would suppose,
in the explanation of Christian doctrine, and in ex-
posing the errors and superstitions both of the Syrians
and the Roman Catholics—of whom, as I have told
you, there are great numbers on the coast. The secular part of the education is exactly such as is required
for matriculation in the Madras University, to which
the Cottayam College is affiliated. The 'Syrians are
intellectually a superior class of people. I have had a
boy under nineteen years of age reading as high in
mathematics as the elements of geometrical conic
sections and statics; and, judging from themes and
essays I have had, they are in vigour of imagination,
I think, above the average of Anglo-Saxons.

Religiously too, the college bears gratifying fruits.

And to God alone the praise is due. Of several of our number who have died in youth, I have had most satisfactory, and in one or two instances most affecting evidence of real simple-hearted piety. One dear lad, who had reached the head of the second class at an unusually early age, and was from his striking skill in mathematics and vivid imagination almost another Kirke White, when dying at the early age of sixteen wrote with his dying hand on a card, and sent it to me as a last memento, ' To me to live is Christ, and to die is gain.' His father gave it to me with many tears, and said with choking voice, ' Sir, I used to fear death ; it was one of my weaknesses, of my burdens ; but now that I have seen how my John died, I can fear it no longer.' Another, who died at seventeen or eighteen, after a lingering dysentery, was, I was told, a true evangelist on his sick bed, both through the consistency of his patience and his words to those about him. A third, who died suddenly of cholera in the midst of an examination in one of the large towns of the Carnatic, at a distance from his home, left his friends, who urged him to delay attending the examination on account of the prevalence of that fell disease, with these words, ' I go in the strength of God, because I believe it to be my duty.' His brother, who is now in a prominent position as an inspector of schools, under the Madras

Government, wrote to me in the most touching manner about the poor lad's death. I cannot help feeling almost as much attachment for many of these lads as though they were my own children. And these two brothers I really regarded almost as sons.

Their short story is worth telling. Their father, who was a village schoolmaster in one of our out-stations, and had a little property, died when the eldest son was about fourteen years of age. They were in the third class in the college. Their widowed mother in her desolation came to me, and wished to take them away to protect her, and see to her little property. But they were boys of considerable intelligence, and I felt what a pity it would be for them to leave the college so young, and degenerate perhaps into nobodies. I don't know that I expected anything very extraordinary from them, though the eldest has turned out one of the most remarkable, I think, both for intelligence and consistent character, of any boys that have left me. I urged upon the widow the advisability of their staying in the college. But she could not see her way to it; she could not pay their fees, and she had no one to look after their few paddy-fields. At last, after some days' hesitation, and when I had almost begun to fear that I should lose them, circumstances led me to make an offer of a position to the widow, which was finally accepted. My wife had a small girls' school, chiefly the daughters of some of the native clergy, and just at that time it happened that we wanted a matron to sleep with them, and cook for them, and so forth. It struck me to propose to her that she should become the matron, with a small allowance every month, and for a time let her little house and fields; that she should bring her own little girl with her, a bright little laughing lass of six years of age; and that I should pay the fees for her boys till they had reached the first class in the college. She accepted the proposal.

The result was that the eldest boy in the course of time became schoolmaster in the German mission school in Palghaut. He rapidly won the good opinion of the missionaries; and when, after a year or two, they were obliged to give up the school for want of funds from Germany, they offered him the schoolroom rent free, if he would take the school on his own responsibility. He did so. The pupils, all heathen, increased. He got it put under Government inspection. The inspector ranked him as one of the first teachers on his beat. And then came a strong trial of his Christian character. He had always given his first hour every morning to the Bible. But this did not suit the English Government. The Bible must no longer be a class book. He might teach anything he liked privately, but no

Bible in school hours. His boys, observe, had never taken any exception to his Bible lesson, and he had already several interesting inquirers. Here he made a noble stand. 'My principles,' he said, 'force me to teach the Bible, as I have done before; I do not thereby neglect the prescribed secular work of the school.' But the Director of Public Instruction was inexorable. The Bible must not be taught in school hours. He wrote to me, I remember, fearing that perhaps he must give up the school. Still nothing daunted, he then went up himself to Madras, to lay the case before the Director of Public Instruction in person; and, contrary to all expectation, at last obtained permission to teach the Bible, as he had done before, on condition that he should teach an hour longer in the afternoon, so as to secure the proper number of hours for secular work. He did so, his school still prospering. His quiet determination evidently lost him no favour, for he was subsequently appointed to a more important post in a higher Government school, and from that became an inspector. Of many others who have gone out into the world I have the most gratifying evidences of their God-fearing lives.

The religious tone, too, of the college, as a whole, is much higher than anything I remember myself as a schoolboy in Christian England; and that without,

I think, any of the cant and mushrooms of what I feel inclined to call a hot-bed religion. I mean that there is an evident acknowledgment of the reality of religion in many of the boys. I have been struck with the general truthfulness and honour among them, so different from what report generally speaks of Asiatics. Report, by the way, often speaks as though England, in contrast, were a happy nest of angels! Active religion too has its manifestations in a way that, I think, you would scarcely find in a public school at home. I was surprised one Sunday morning, about eight o'clock, when I was walking in my garden, about a year after I took charge of the college, to hear singing in the large room at the end of the college farthest from my house. It was evidently a hymn, for it was sung to a well-known old English tune. I peeped into the verandah, and found it empty; there were no boys about, all were apparently in the room. Presently I heard a voice praying, and finally a voice evidently giving an address. I afterwards made cautious inquiries about it, and found that it consisted of some of the prayers of the Liturgy, and a chapter, read by one of the elder boys, and a short sermon delivered by another. There being no morning chapel on Sundays, as we attend the ten o'clock Malayalim service in the mission church, besides having our English service in the college chapel in the evening, this service had been agreed upon by some of the elder boys, the initiative having been taken, I believe, by an excellent young man, who is now a native minister.

There is something, I think, extremely gratifying in this. There is nothing whatever of the 'please master' air about it. Indeed it had existed some time before I knew anything about it. And ever since I have carefully abstained from taking more than a silent notice of it. No one is obliged to attend ; and occasionally I observe some of the more careless boys hanging about the verandah, but the great majority are always there for the short time it lasts. It seems to have become an institution of the college, for it goes on without intermission from half-year to half-year. I look upon it as a most decided index to a genuine religious feeling among the lads.

Another thing I cannot resist mentioning, and that is, that I find the vast majority of the sons of Syrians— indeed I can point now to no one exception, though no doubt, as years pass on, some exceptions will manifest themselves—leave the college either as professed Protestants in communion with the English Church, or as decided members of the Reforming party in the Syrian Church; the few deacons, who have been my pupils, forming no exception, so far as I can judge at present. Two of them, I am informed, are already earnest gospel preachers during their holidays, though still young deacons.

Now here, you would suppose, is at least an approximation towards the required instrumentality for penetrating the ignorance and superstition of the masses, both of Syrians and Hindus. And so, indeed, in a certain measure, there is. The college acts directly on all educated in it; and they indirectly, to a greater or less degree, on their homes and kindred. But you would expect much more. You would expect the college to furnish, in the course of years, some Chrysostoms, and Luthers, and Melanchthons for our missions. Here, however, is my disappointment. Here, from some cause or other, is a failure. There seems to be some fatality in our missions, by which the brightest spirits, and the largest hearts, and the best capacities in the college, fail to be assimilated by our mission system. The best boys are too often lost to us, though no doubt they exert a certain influence for good elsewhere. This is the weak point in the Travancore mission of the Church Missionary Society.

There is a great possibility; but it is not able to struggle to power. And, indeed, how often under the contradiction of human opinions do the noblest opportunities, uses, resources, remain at a standstill for years! All history is full of it. The same poisoned arrow runs through all time. Galileo, Sir Isaac Newton, George Stephenson, have all been in turn transfixed by it, and pinned to the ground for a time. The Cottayam college is no exception. Now I regard this as a most serious matter. To myself personally, of course, it is an intense disappointment: but that is a minor matter. Good work, after all, is not to be done without disappointments. In the 'evening time,' at least, we trust 'it will be light.' But I do not see that therefore we are to sit content with present darkness. What, it may be asked, is the real cause of this failure? It is, I think, that under the present system there is not provision made for utilising the best intellects. There are differences of opinion, in the first place, as to the nature of the agency required for evangelistic work.

For instance, while a German missionary in North Malabar writes to me to ask if I could possibly supply him with a native teacher, saying that they can find no boys like the Cottayam college boys, and offering forty rupees a month to such a boy as —— (the highest pay *possible* in our missions for such a teacher is from ten to fifteen rupees), one of our own dear and earnest friends writes thus: ' Could you make up your mind to allow me to choose one or two boys out of your second class as schoolmasters, and to be hereafter, if found suitable, associated with me in my mission in more direct evangelistic work ?

for I find that when once a boy enters your first class he becomes somewhat unmanageable.' I do not pretend to account for such opposite states of opinion : but there are the letters before me. Boys 'unmanageable' in one direction appear to be perfectly manageable in another.

One of the unmanageable youths (never, by the way, unmanageable in the college, where, whilst he stood high in the first class, he was one of the most modest, unassuming young men I ever met) found, as he expressed himself, 'more peace' as the head-master of a Government school in Malabar; where, to his great honour, he found time also, notwithstanding his heavy work, to read for the matriculation examination of the Madras University, which he passed. Nor have I ever heard from the inspector, whom I know well, that he has exhibited any particular restiveness.

I have often, again, been told that the high pay in Government and other schools is too much for the weak human nature of the college boys. Well, human nature is much the same in the breast of the Hindu as it is in the impliedly more self-denying Englishman. But this much I must say, that the young men I have educated have, for the most part, entrusted me with the choice of the positions they should fill, and have gone to the posts I have myself chosen for them. Now, many will be surprised to learn that the pay offered in our missions to a young man of twenty-one, who may have been at the head of the first class in the Cottayam college, is less than I give to my cook ; and less than many of us give to our horse-keepers, who often have to sleep in the stable, and are supposed only to be able just to keep body and soul together. We cannot, it is said, employ a highly-paid native agency. But are we, then, to understand that the Government pay of a schoolmaster is unnecessarily high? that the members of Government deliberately intend to make their teachers rich? If so, they commit a crime against all India. The funds of a missionary society are, of course, limited; the closest economy is expected by all at the hands of those who administer them. Perhaps they will soon reach their maximum; perhaps even diminish. But what we do should surely be done well. And one centre of missionary effort in India, well worked, will do, ultimately, infinitely more for the country than many crippled ones. If we cannot pay the world's price for the world's goods, we cannot get them. We should, I think, be very jealous lest evangelical Protestantism, when too far removed from the check of public opinion, degenerate in some points into what may be very like Popery. That 'poverty and obedience' are necessary parts of an evangelistic agency, is a doctrine that has apparently been taken to be a corollary of Christian zeal, more or less, in every age of the Church.

But it is a perversion of true judgment: it is rank Popery; and has never provided anything better than poltroons.

But the real weakness of our system, the real reason why we do not utilise the resources of the college to the full, do not arise so much from the relation of the mission to the outer world as from the nature of the system itself. The European in India is in a peculiar position. He is a member of a conquering people. The attitude of a dominant race is naturally to keep all power in its own hands, to leave no room for independence of action in the conquered; but to use every capacity to be found among them subordinate to itself. This may be all very well for a secular Government; but is it the proper attitude of the missionary? My own verdict is, 'No.' We do not come to set up an *imperium in imperio*, but simply to develop the religious capacities of the people. We come, not to set up the authority of the English Church, or of any other Church; but to incite the people to search the Scriptures 'whether those things are so.'

But, it will be said, there must be authority somewhere. True: and there is in every Christian body, who may send out evangelists to India, the necessary authorities in spiritual matters. But we do not want one party in authority over another party in the Church. Now, the European missionary too often puts himself practically in this false position. He settles down, for the most part, as a pastor of a large district, where he uses the native agency entirely in subordinate capacities. The native minister is placed in charge of a small congregation, already gathered out from the masses, to act there always under the missionary in whose district he is. The catechist and reader are, by virtue of their office, of course subordinates. And so, in every phase of mission progress at present, the European is the only aggressor. It is so even in literature. The natives have done very little independently, so far, in that direction; though it is by no means from incapacity. Now all this is natural in the mere infancy of a mission set on foot by Europeans; but to remain half a century in this state is to keep the Church in swaddling-clothes. It can never develop its limbs. It will finally, like the Chinese lady's foot, fill only a tenth of the space it ought to fill; and will at last be next to useless. Our duty is to develop the native character; and I believe we shall never do that till we give them wide spheres of action, and leave them to feel the weight of responsibility on their own shoulders. A great capacity is never developed in a subordinate position. So long as a man is a servant, he is only half a man; he remains a Moses in the wilderness, when he might be a Moses the leader and lawgiver. There are capacities that live undeveloped and die undeveloped in the midst of the stupendous mission-fields of India. "'The harvest truly is plenteous, but the labourers few.'

Are the Christian Churches of Europe to find all the labourers? Or are they only to pave the way? We want to employ, at least in Travancore, the resources we have amongst the educated Christian natives in a different way from what they have yet been employed. We want positions, in which men of mark can be placed, *to take the lead* they are, many of them, well capable of taking. We want native missionaries, native evangelists, a native literature; and we have neither. Nay, our present system is leading us further and further away from the possibility of having these. I am convinced that a large portion of the funds of the Church Missionary Society would be better spent in developing a more perfectly-organised native agency than in providing so extensive a one from Europe. It is not *many* Europeans that we want; but a few men of real power in bringing forward the native youth. Travancore is quite ripe for this, both from the large number of intelligent Christians already existing, and from the real resources of the college at Cottayam.

There is another reason for putting the necessity for a highly-educated native agency before a multitudinous European one, and that is that the native of the country is its natural evangelist. It will, no doubt, be objected that the early evangelists in almost all countries have been foreigners. True; but only the very first. The older missions ought to have got past that stage of their history. The foreigner comes to break the ice; but now we want to draw the water. The first grand missionary day in the Church points out to us what is the true condition for successful evangelistic work. Why was *the* gift of Pentecost the ' gift of tongues,' but that it is a *sine quâ non* of success in preaching the gospel?

The absence of this gift is one of the grand barriers, to success in the case of the European missionary in India. A clever man may, indeed, do much by industry to make up for the want of the gift; but he will be still the foreigner; and I am certain, from some years' close observation, that often great talents and most noble purposes have been left nearly powerless through the halting of the tongue. God gives to every man the gift of one tongue—his mother's tongue. The natural gift fits him for his work, just as the miraculous gift fitted the apostles for theirs; the absence of the gift (and the more, of course, in proportion as it is not made up for by industry and a constitutional aptness) leaves a man unfit, as the apostles were unfit before the miraculous gift came. And should we not bear ever in mind that this is not the age of miracles, but of ordinary means? The deputation from the Christian Churches of the West has no longer the miraculous gift; but the native Christian has the gift by nature. It seems almost childish to point out so simple a fact; but it is because we are not acting up to it. The Churches of Europe will still send out *preachers,* instead of sending *teachers;* they will send out *pastors,* instead of sending out *leaders;* they will send out an agency destitute of a necessary gift, instead of raising up an agency in the country itself which has the gift already to perfection.

One word more as to a native agency. It commands the immense power of national sympathy. A man can touch the susceptibilities of his own race; he can reach their idiosyncrasies; he can feel the national pulse, and speak to the national heart; he is *en rapport* with his own people. But all these subtle influences, which are everywhere the secret power of the orator and the revolutionist, forsake him when he stands before an alien race. He may be Sampson still, but he is Sampson shorn of his might. John Wesley was a feeble instrument in Georgia, though he revolutionised the slumbering Church in England. Luther would not have been Luther in England, nor Wickliffe Wickliffe in Wittemberg. We must study more our resources for raising up a superior native agency in India than we have yet done.

I shall not be understood to say that we are without a

native agency in Travancore. We are not. We have what is, in many respects, a fine agency. But it is too much subordinate—too cramped—too much drawn from the half-educated and less powerful of our converts ; and that too often for the sake of a timid economy, as well as because the more feeble are supposed to be the more ' manageable ; ' two motives altogether unworthy of Christendom.

But let us turn to look at what has really been done with the style of agency we have. I wish my reader could first of all spend a Sunday at Cottayam. I shall not soon forget my own first Sunday morning in the large mission church. The building itself is a worthy monument of the Rev. Benjamin Bailey, the father of the mission. It is, like all our edifices, constructed of the laterite of the country, covered with a lime made from shells something like large cockles. These shells form a lime of great purity ; and when it is polished it looks almost like marble. The six lofty arches and five pillars on each side of the nave are of this polished white *chunam*, as we call the shell-lime, and are scarcely inferior to the pillars in the Madras Cathedral. And then the congregation. It is to a stranger a most imposing sight to see a large church like this gradually filling with men, women, and children, all in purest white cloths ; the men throwing their muslins gracefully round one shoulder, and the women with muslin veils on their heads, often of great elegance, and not unfrequently trimmed with gold thread.

All sit on the ground, which is covered with mats, the men filling the church halfway down from the pulpit, and the women the western half. The decorum and attention are perfect. The stranger is at once struck, as Buchanan was at Tanjore, by a scratching kind of noise going on frequently during the sermon, not unlike the nibbling of rats or mice. Several of our visitors have been puzzled to know what it was. It proceeds from Mrs. Baker's large and interesting girls' school. They are taking notes of the sermon on pieces of the palmyra leaf, the paper of the country, and as the writing is accomplished by means of a sharp iron style, it is heard at some little distance. I have not unfrequently had the leading thoughts of my own sermons reported by these same young ladies with great accuracy. This good old custom—would it not be a good one in schools at home?—has been brought by Mrs. Baker, who was a Miss Kohlohff, from Tanjore, and originated, I believe, from Swartz himself. Cottayam being the central station, and therefore containing several establishments, the college, the Cambridge Nicholson Institution, the printing office and book depôt, besides four missionaries' residences, and three girls' schools, the congregation is larger than any other single one in the district. There are, however, no less than fifty congregations assembling each Sunday in the different stations and out-stations. Where there is no ordained native minister, the service is conducted by catechists and readers, and the European missionary preaches and administers the Lord's Supper in all as frequently as possible.

Not the least interesting part of our mission system is the printing establishment. When the missionaries first came into the country there were no means for printing the vernacular. Mr. Bailey commenced the work under difficulties. The first fount of type was, I believe, made in Madras, but was so unsatisfactory that it could not be used. Mr. Bailey then had the punches made under his own eye by a clever native blacksmith. A fount of type was cast on the spot. A printing press was constructed by the help of the 'Encyclopædia Britannica.' Compositors, printers, and bookbinders were soon elaborated through Mr. Bailey's sagacity, and the all-important work of printing the vernacular commenced.

The primitive press, which was built of wood, and is now kept as a curiosity and trophy of early missionary zeal and talent, has long since been superseded by American ones, three of which are hand presses, and the fourth a wheel press. I am myself now acting as superintendent of the printing establishment, as there is no resident superin-

tendent there at present; and while I write I have before
me on the table a galvanic battery, with which I am
making some experiments in electroplating the type with
copper. Our letters are composed chiefly of fine lines, and
the consequence is the type soon becomes worn out. I have
thought that if it has a copper facing it might wear
much longer, and save a good deal of the expense of cast-
ing new type, a work that is at present continually going
on. I think I shall be successful, for a few of the types
I have coppered were yesterday put into the press, and
worked to perfection. A year or two will tell whether
the coppering of a whole new fount, which is now being
cast, will be really a work of economy. A missionary,
indeed, must be a thorough Jack-of-all-trades, or else
must leave things much as he finds them.

The Press is a great mission power, and no pains should
be spared to make our mission printing establishments as
perfect in every branch as possible. With clever management too, they may be made a source of considerable
income. We print here all the Bible Society's work in
Malayalim, as well as books belonging to other societies.
I am now putting a new quarto edition of the whole
Bible through the press, the fourth edition the Bible has
reached in the vernacular of Malabar. Several valuable
books have also lately been printed, among them a translation by the Rev. George Matthan of Butler's ‘ Analogy.’

It is surprising how many of the more intelligent of the people read this book. It is just the style of evidence suited to the subtile mind of the Hindu. Historical evidence they are hardly yet ripe for. They do not know enough yet of history to believe in it; but reasoning like Butler's they thoroughly appreciate. The translation, when we consider the difficulty of the task, is admirable. Indeed, George Matthan has a mind capable of almost anything; and I think that it is a matter deeply to be regretted that his literary powers were not much earlier brought forward. Our great want is books in the vernacular; but when I came out to India, and found George already a middle-aged man, he had printed only one tract. He has, however, used his pen more lately. Among other things he has printed a clever grammar of the vernacular, besides contributing valuable papers to our ' College Magazine.' One of his papers on what is here called *Marumakatháyam*—that is, the right of inheritance through the female line, by which a man's property descends to his nephew instead of his own son—so attracted the attention of the Dewan that he proposed to make George Matthan director of all the vernacular school literature under the native Government. I always thought it an immense pity that he could not see his way to undertake that work. It would have given him great influence at the native Court, where he was already a favourite, owing to his evident superiority in every way.[1]

This custom of *Marumakatháyam* is peculiar, I believe, to the heathen castes of this coast. The object of it is to keep property in the same family. This may be thought strange, but it arises from the peculiar marriage customs of the Hindus of Malabar. In fact, there is no legal marriage except for the eldest son in a Brahmin family. He marries, and his sons by his married wife inherit his property. His younger brothers are not allowed to marry, though they themselves have a right to the enjoyment of the family property as long as they live. Their sons belong to the family in which they are born, and inherit from their mother's eldest brother.

This custom of inheritance obtains through all the heathen castes. The origin of the custom is of great antiquity, and cannot now be traced; but it is probable that the Brahmins first prohibited legal marriage, except for their eldest sons, in order to enforce an entail of property. The practical result upon the different castes is that, as a woman is not legally bound to one husband, she may have many successively, and their children would be unprovided for unless they inherited from their mother. They do thus inherit, by having a share during lifetime of her eldest brother's property, the eldest child by the eldest sister

---

[1] The Rev. George Matthan has since died.

being the heir-at-law, and being under obligation to share
the enjoyment of the family property with his brothers
and cousins in the female line. Hence cousins are almost
always called brothers and sisters. The custom is very
distasteful to many of the more intelligent men. My
own Munshi, who has always lived honestly with one wife,
one day brought a fine, handsome-looking lad, of twelve
years of age, to see me, his only son. 'Look there,
Sahib,' he said; 'did you ever see a finer lad than that?
He has already learnt the *Sidharupum* off by heart from
one end to the other, and will be a better Sanscrit scholar
than I am; but not one *pice* of my property can I leave
to him; my heir is that great gawky boy you have in the
college, who hardly knows his right hand from his left.
This is a *waleja Tankardam*, a great grief.' The late
reigning Prince some time back showed his fine children,
with some demonstrations of pride, to a missionary friend
of mine; but soon, with tears starting from his eyes, he
said—for they had been talking of the *Marumakatháyam*
—'but these children, though mine, are nobodies; they
are not even princes; the princes are my nephews, and
they, not my own children, are my heirs, and one of them
will sit on my throne. It would be well should this
custom some day die out.'

But this chapter is becoming a medley of digressions. I
must remember that I wish to show what kind of work we
are enabled to carry on particularly through means of our

native agency.   Besides a large number of catechists and readers, we have now fourteen ordained native ministers. They are for the most part located as pastors in some of the principal out-stations of the missions.   I may take the out-station of Olesha as an example of the rest. It is two and a half or three miles from Cottayam. A neat little church was built there some years ago, and more recently a small but compact house for a native pastor.   The pastor at present is the Rev. Koshi Koshi, an able and well-informed young man, and an excellent English scholar.   He is placed over a small congregation, gathered out chiefly from among the Syrians, but containing also converts from some of the heathen castes.   Now Mr. Koshi is an earnest worker, and the Olesha congregation has received several fresh members from some influential families during his pastorate.   He is of a more aggressive disposition than some of his brethren.   He is also very active amongst some Christian congregations that have been lately gathered out from among one of the lowest castes in the country, and of whom I shall have more to say hereafter, the ground slaves.   But still I have always felt that there is a good deal in Koshi in the way of missionary power that remains latent.   His mere pastorate of a small village does not seem to develop all his capabilities. He is esteemed by the natives as being endowed with an unusual aptitude and elegance of speech, and as being a

man of remarkably clear judgment, as well as being con-
ciliatory in his manners. Would not these qualities point
him out as one of nature's leaders? as being capable of
exerting a wider influence than that circumscribed by his
little pastorate? as capable, in short, of being an aggressive missionary in a larger sphere? as well fitted to be
a 'worker together' with the European missionary, instead of being subordinate to him?

These little pastorates are very beautiful features in our
mission system. They are everywhere the proper result
of missionary effort. Here and there a little band of converts is gathered together—a church; and the ministerial
office must be supplied. But I very much doubt whether
our Timothys and Tituses—such men as George Matthan
and Koshi Koshi, and some others—should, where the
gospel has to be preached for a witness to the millions of
India, have their energies circumscribed altogether within
such narrow bounds.

But at the same time it is undoubted that wherever the
gospel takes root, it is true *leaven.* It will spread because it
is possessed of a *divine* imperishable power. We need
not doubt it. We ought not to doubt it. God's Word
must accomplish that whereunto He has sent it. The only
thing we have to remember is that the sowing of tares by
its side is thick and constant; and what the Church has
needed in all ages has been to guard the true plant. This

must always be done by men who are capable of being *leaders* in the Church. If the Church in India is to remain healthy, we must have men capable by education of grappling with the modern gnosticism of the Brahmo Somáj, and all other travesties of the truth : and these men must be in the *right places.* Were we to leave India to-morrow—and who knows how far or near that to-morrow may be?—should we leave such men in the infant Church? In the meantime, we must allow that the influence of the Word is spreading through means of its own divine energy; and as an illustration of this I may close this chapter with an account of its spread among the slaves that I mentioned before.

The people of which I speak are the serfs of Travancore. They no doubt belong, by almost pure descent, to the Turanian race that peopled India before the Aryan invasion. I have observed that some casts of faces of the Himalayan tribes which are in the Madras Museum exhibit exactly similar features to those of many of the Travancore slaves. Until very lately they have been the property of the owner of the soil, just in the same sense as his dog or his bullock. They could own no property themselves, and could obtain no redress in a court of law. Their masters could buy them or sell them, feed them or starve them, pet them or bully them, just as their own objects or disposition dictated. Such a state of things, however, could scarcely face the light of a rapidly developing civilisation. And the Government of Travancore has at last given them the privilege of being at least ranked amongst human beings. They can now hold property, and have a right to legal protection. Still they are at the very bottom of the social scale. They are not yet suffered by the high castes to walk in the highways. As they go along they are obliged to cry out, that the high castes may be warned of their polluting presence. They are not allowed to come within sixty paces of a Brahmin, and if they should be caught too near to such a holy presence they would stand a good chance of being well thrashed.

When they approach a court of law, where the high-caste man sits to distribute justice or injustice, as the case may be, they are obliged to stand at the same distance from the door, and to shout out their petition. The defendant, who is most probably of a higher caste, has bribed the reporter to give a garbled account of the matter; and so the law court seldom benefits them much. If they purchase a little rice, or a little oil, or a little tobacco, at the shop of a higher-caste man, they must equally stand at a respectful distance, shout out their wants, and put their money down where they stand; they must then recede to a like respectful distance while the shopman sallies out to replace the money by his wares.

N

Christianity has now begun to work a great change amongst these oppressed slaves. In the earlier days of the missions no special efforts had been made on their behalf, till, I believe, at the suggestion of good Mr. Ragland, when he once visited Travancore as secretary of the Corresponding Committee in Madras, a school was commenced among some of them, under the joint superintendence of Mr. Hawksworth and George Matthan, at Mallapalli. This was the only work among the slaves when I first came to Cottayam, unless there was, perhaps, already a Sunday school opened for such of them as were employed in the plantations of the Mundakayam mission. A more extended effort for their improvement in a Christian point of view originated from the college. I was walking one evening, soon after my arrival, with my wife, by the side of some of the Cottayam paddy-fields, when we came across the first slave hut we had seen. It was built, so far as I remember, of five sticks, four of which were stuck into the ground, two in front and two behind, and tied together so as to form two little forks at the top, on which was laid the fifth : over all were tied some leaves of the cocoanut palm, which forms an excellent thatch. Two naked black children were crawling about, making mud puddings, just after the fashion of their brothers and sisters in Europe ; and a woman was boiling some rice in an earthenware pot, here called a *codune* or *chatty*, which was supported over the fire upon a few pieces of stone. The picture was garnished with two or three fish that lay about, and which had been caught by means of a fishing basket in the little canal hard by.

My wife at once proposed that we should make an attempt to teach them ; and that we should endeavour to raise subscriptions in the college for the purpose. We returned home, and mentioned the subject to one of the teachers and some of the elder boys. The result was that we got promises of monthly subscriptions to the amount of six rupees. The collection of money in the college for this novel purpose interested the people in the printing office also ; and there Mr. Paul Schaffter, the superintendent, son of one of our Tinnevelley missionaries, raised three rupees a month in addition. Our first nine rupees we took to Mr. Baker, senior, at that time the missionary in charge of Cottayam ; and he built three schools in different parts of the mission, and used our subscription for the monthly pay of the three schoolmasters, paying each man three rupees a month. Of course it will be understood that these schoolrooms were simply made of mud walls, bamboo poles, and cocoanut leaves for the roof. For a long time we had immense trouble with these schools. The masters of the slaves were chiefly adverse to their learning anything. Many were prosecuted. The schools were burnt down. The children were forbidden to go, and when they attempted, were waylaid and beaten. Then we had trouble with one or two of the schoolmasters. One of them we found had in a few weeks got his school full of Chogans (the same caste as the Tinnevelley Shânârs) instead of slaves. The slaves however, many of them, when a beginning had once been made, seemed determined that their children and themselves should be taught. And in the face of many difficulties and much opposition, they and we at length carried our point. I then had a slave school built in my own compound. The funds were found by Mr. Paul Schaffter. It was intended to be a model for such buildings. The roof was supported on stone pillars, nicely chunamed; and the whole was surrounded by a well-chunamed wall three feet high; and its cost was seventy rupees. It was quite a cathedral for the poor slaves. It was used as a day school for any slaves, children or adults, who liked to come; and on Sundays a little service was conducted by some of the elder boys or teachers in the college. The Rev. Mr. Andrews, when he was located at Cottayam, took particular interest in this school, and often went there to superintend the teaching, and to teach himself. Its influence soon began to be widely felt; and the greater part of the slaves who attended it living at some distance, themselves set up a school at a place called Velloor, about three miles away, and nearer to their homes. This nearly emptied my

A SLAVE CHURCH IN THE RICE FIELDS, TRAVANCORE.

school; and the building was ultimately removed by the Velloor people to be their church there. Thus the school in my compound was the origin of what is now a flourishing slave church at Velloor. The other schools also resulted in the establishment of a congregation at Komarum, a place about seven miles to the south-west of Cottayam. Mr. Andrews took charge of these two congregations, which both increased and flourished under his care; and for a time four boys from the college went, two and two, to them every Sunday morning. At eight o'clock they came, as they voluntarily offered themselves to my study, whence I dismissed them for their work of love with prayer; and sometimes I heard them read the notes of their sermons, the subjects of which were generally remarkably well chosen.

This movement among the slave population has proved to be of very great interest and importance. I went to Pallam some time since to witness the baptism of upwards of seventy of them by Mr. Andrews. The scene was most impressive. As the more solemn parts of the service were read—and never did I more appreciate its beauty—there was scarcely a dry eye among the adults. Whole families were in some instances baptised, father, mother, and children; and the parents afterwards consecrated to God in their union by the marriage service. On a later occasion I went with some of my first class boys to Komarum, where about fifty were similarly admitted into the visible Church by Mr. Hawksworth. The faith and earnestness of some of them were singularly tested. One man, for instance, as is not uncommon amongst them, had three wives. He felt that if he became a Christian he could only have one wife. What should he do? Such questions as this are often very perplexing to the missionary, as might be supposed. The oldest of his wives was a broken-down, sickly woman; the other two were fine, handsome-looking, healthy young women as you would wish to see; and it was understood that he was very fond of them both. He, however, decided for himself that, as the oldest was his first, she was his proper wife; and to her he remained faithful after his baptism.

These poor people have, of course, by becoming Christians gained a great step socially and politically, as well as religiously. They are by no means slow to discern this, and on this account the greatest wisdom is needed in leading them. Some of them have perhaps thought more of their advance as citizens than as simple Christians. And so we begin already to find not a few of them rather 'cheeky,' and given to self-assertion. They feel— and it would be strange if they did not—that they are no longer mere beasts of burden, but men. One consequence is that, following the example of their higher-caste brethren, and relying on the protection of the

European, they are beginning to be too much given to litigation. Nor are they willing any longer to be deprived of the use of the highways.

A short time since an amusing conversation was overheard by a friend of mine between two slaves and a Brahmin. The slaves were walking along the highway, when the Brahmin, meeting them, stopped at some distance, and cried out in a very authoritative manner the usual '*Po! Po!*'—English 'Go! Go!' But the men were not willing to go, and marched onwards with a rather determined and careless air. The Brahmin raised his '*Po! Po!*' with a still higher and more angry tone. 'But,' said the slaves, 'we are not going to go; we have as much right now to the road as you; we are Christians.' ' Ho, ho!' exclaimed the Brahmin, softening his voice a little, ' but it has not quite come to that yet, that I should have to get out of the way for you; times are changing, it is true, and perhaps before long we shall be obliged to yield to another state of things; but for the present, while the custom lasts, you had better move out of the way.' The slaves laughed, but did not move out of the way, and the Brahmin was obliged to go into the hedge himself, while they passed, though quite respectfully, by on the other side.

With some drawbacks, however, which must be expected while human nature remains what it is, this

Christian movement among the serfs of Travancore is really a grand one ; and while it developes many truly noble characters among this long down-trodden people, it is influencing the higher castes too to a great degree. The masters are beginning to acknowledge that the Christian slaves are much the best and most honest work-men ; and their opposition to the schools seems almost to have ceased. Indeed one of the wealthiest land-owners near Velloor, a Syrian, who had long shown a determined opposition to his slaves being taught, asto-nished Mr. Hawksworth one Sunday morning by coming into the slave church, and joining in the worship, and afterwards bearing testimony to the good that had been effected among his own slaves. Pointing to one man in particular, he said, 'That man was once the terror of all his neighbours, but now that he is a Christian, he is a gentleman.' This Syrian further showed his change of mind by giving a portion of land, that the slave church might be enlarged. The testimony—and it is not a solitary one—of such men as this, who was once 'a persecutor and injurious,' is of the utmost value as to the reality of the influence of Christianity on the slaves.

CHAPTER VII.

I HAVE lately returned from a trip to several of the principal mission stations. I generally spend my holidays away from Cottayam, if I can; and often find it a pleasant change from the monotony of school work to visit my missionary brethren. The day after the college broke up for the Christmas holidays, I started with Mr. Hawksworth in his fine cabin boat for Tiruwilla. We had a splendid row and sail for about seven hours. Through the lovely river scenery we rowed, and as we got into more open country by the Backwater we put up the sail, which took us along at about six miles an hour, the boatmen entertaining us with their peculiar songs. One man leads off by singing the first line, and then all the rest sing it after him in chorus; and so on for every line of the song. Sometimes they extemporise in a very amusing manner. Not a few of these songs, I am sorry to say, contain passages hardly consistent with good taste and propriety. Here, however, is an example of one of the better sort, and the tune they sing it to:

A free translation of part of the song follows:

Once upon this earth of ours
    A bee flew out at evening hour;
And as he hasted here and there,
    It chanced he spied a beauteous flower.

The flower it was a moon-faced lotus;
    Glad he was to enter in;
Waiting not he sipped the honey;
    He cared not for the world a pin.

He knew not that the sun was setting,
    While he sucked the nectar pure;
And if we know not what is doing,
    We shall find misfortune sure.

Then that fair flower too closed its petals,
    And the bee was roused at last—
Alas!—But soon the hours will hasten,
    Soon the night that's come be past.

Soon will the day again be dawning,
  The sun will flood the eastern sky,
And this fair flower that's now my prison
  O'er the tank will open lie.

'An elephant, while thus he mused,
  The tempting lotus chanced to see ;
With hungry maw he cropped and ate,
  And crunched the too presumptuous bee.

Of course it ends at length with a moral, that we must not presume on the future, but always take time by the forelock.

Many of their tunes are in the minor key. Here is one.

The Tiruwilla mission is now without a resident missionary, so that our living there was very primitive. It was almost like picnicing. The deserted mission bungalow is a witness to the changing and uncertain nature of everything European in India. Mr. Hawksworth commenced this mission in 1847, built his bungalow, and had half built a large church near, when his health compelled him to return for a time to England. On his coming out to India again, he was requested to build and take charge of a new institution at Cottayam for the express training of mission agents, chiefly through the medium of the vernacular. He was also put in charge of the Cottayam mission ; but as no European had been appointed to Tiruwilla, he had charge of that mission also. He was now come to visit his old flock; and extremely interesting were the few days we spent there. In the evening after our arrival, we had a large company of natives in the bungalow, the hearts of all of whom Mr. Hawksworth had evidently won by his great amiability and tact. Nor were they all members of the mission congregation; several Brahmins and others were among them. They all stayed for some time, while we showed them, among other things, a magic lantern, the slides being chiefly scenes in the Holy Land: some of them were astronomical ones. Many were the questions asked as to eclipses, the tides, the seasons, and so forth; all of which gave an opportunity for many a word in season. The next evening I endeavoured to amuse the people who came to the bungalow with an electrifying machine, which at Mr. Hawksworth's request I had taken with me from the college. Numbers afterwards came to see it, hearing the report, which spread rapidly, that the Sahibs could bring lightning from the heavens by turning a handle and a plate of glass. 'Yendê ammê!'—literally 'My mother!'—'it stings!' exclaimed a rather loquacious Brahmin, as he took a spark on his knuckle; and when I gave him a pretty sharp shock, in company with some others, his eyes almost started out of his head, and the perspiration stood on his forehead, as with a prolonged 'Yo-ho-o-o!' he gave vent to his astonishment, and declared that he did not want any more of the 'lightning.'

One morning we went to call on a petty Rajah who lives near. We passed the pagoda on our way, one of the largest in this part of India. It was the first time I had seen it; and I sketched it, while Mr. Hawksworth spoke to some of the people who were about.

As we stood there the mid-day procession of the idol round the inner precincts of the temple took place. We could not of course see anything of it, as the whole place is surrounded by a high wall, but we heard the accompanying music. The chief instrument is the hautboy I have mentioned before. This is accompanied by a number of horns, some of great length, all of which sound the *tonic*, sometimes in concert with the *dominant*, the only attempt at harmony I have ever heard in Hindu music. The effect is not unlike the drone of the bagpipe. Indeed the whole character of the Hindu music decidedly reminds one of the national music of Scotland. For domestic music a flageolet is much used, and is generally accompanied also by a drone. One in my possession is of a most ingenious and beautiful, though in some respects perhaps rude, construction: it is formed of bamboo, and is on the exact principle of a reed pipe in an organ. The reed is cut neatly at the end of a *calamus*, one end of which

is stopped with wax, and the other inserted in a larger
pipe of bamboo about nine inches long and half an inch
in diameter, pierced with six holes like a flute; the reed
end is then inserted in a still larger pipe of bamboo
fourteen or sixteen inches long, and so arranged that the
holes of the smaller pipe are exposed, that by them the
tone may be modulated. The appearance of the instrument
when completed is this—

The tune, *râjum* as they call it, is handed down from
generation to generation.   They have no method of
writing music, so that each musician learns from his
betters by ear.   It is impossible to tell how far the
râjums may become changed in course of time: but no
doubt many of them might claim a very high antiquity.
An accomplished Brahmin musician once favoured me
with a visit, and sang a portion of the 'Râmâyana' to me.
The râjum that he used, as nearly as I can write it, is as
follows—the first semibreve being the reciting note, as
in an English chant:

There is a peculiar slur between the C and G, which I can only express by writing semitones, and the last D is often dwelt upon with closed lips.

I may take this opportunity of endeavouring to give some idea of the nature of the worship performed in a Hindu temple. The daily rites which I shall describe are those belonging to the temples of Shiva, the principal object of worship in most temples on the Malabar coast. In a large temple, like that of Tiruwilla, for instance, which covers several acres of ground, there are fanes to more gods and goddesses than one: there is probably one to Bhaga-wathi (also named *Kâli*), the wife of Shiva, another to Ganesa or Ganapatlu, the son of Shiva, another to Krishna, or even Vishnu. But the principal shrine, in nine cases out of ten in this part of India, is to Shiva. The shrine, or temple proper, consists of two rooms, in the inner of which the idol is placed. It is very commonly roofed with copper, and surmounted by a finial of some handsome device cast in the same metal. No bloody offerings are, I believe, ever made in these temples, except in the case of a temple dedi-cated to Bhagawathi alone; and then no Brahmin officiates, or takes any part in the proceedings. The blood shed is commonly that of a cock. Nairs, Chogans, and the lower castes only, engage in this offering. Bringing their cocks in their hands, they cut off the head at an altar placed before the temple of Kâli, and then take the bird home and feast on it. This is no doubt a remnant of aboriginal worship.

The object of adoration which stands in the inner room in a temple of Shiva is a plain conical stone, cut out of granite. It is the *lingam,* the same emblem as the phallus of ancient Europe. At daybreak, and before the sun rises, the first act of worship is performed. The Brahmin who is the officiating priest for the time being commences the day by anointing the lingam. This is done by pouring over it ghee (clarified butter). A portion of the bark of one of the *sapindaceæ,* which is commonly used among the natives instead of soap when they bathe, is then taken, and with it the greasy stone is well scrubbed. Water is then poured over it by means of a *shankha,* the sacred conch of the Hindus, and the resulting water is most carefully kept: it is the *tìrthum,* or sacred water of the temple. The priest then takes a portion of sandal wood (*Santalum album*), and rubs it with water on a stone, till he obtains a certain amount of paste from the ground wood. This is placed on the top of the lingam, and remains there till the next morning. It is removed before the anointing, and is carefully kept. A garland of flowers is then placed round the idol, the *Michelia champaca* (one of the *Magnoliaceæ*) being in much esteem for this purpose, when they can procure it, as also one of the *Ixoras,* and the *Poinceana pulcheriena,* often called ' The

'Peacock's Pride.' Offerings are also made of cocoanuts, palm sugar, ghee, and other things, among which the chief is a portion of the food prepared for the morning's meal in the temple, generally consisting of parched rice and sugar. During all this time the priest repeats his *manthras*, portions of the Vedic hymns. After this a small gold, silver, or brass image of the god, according to the wealth of the establishment, is carried round the temple with music. A somewhat similar service, with the exception of the anointing, is performed at noon, and again at sunset. Sometimes a burnt offering is made, called *hômam*, or *hômabali*, when ghee, rice, and other things are thrown into a fire, kindled, not in the shrine itself, but in the open space. But this is not, I believe, a daily offering; the Hindu who wishes to perform his devotions in the temple generally does so during the morning. Having bathed, and marked his forehead, breast, and arms with the ashes of sandal-wood, which they call *bhasmam*, he presents himself before Shiva. If a Brahmin, he stands on the upper step of the shrine; if a Nair, below. Here he probably repeats the *gayatri*, the most sacred verse of the Vedas, and makes his requests, whatever they may be—most likely for riches.

But a Hindu will not tell you what his private devotions are. When I once asked a man, whom I had known some time, what he said before the shrine, he immediately repeated some words in imitation of our prayer book, which he knew, '*Yenāe dévamê, yenóda rakshikénamê,*' 'My God, deliver me.' But the chief object of appearing in the temple is to receive a portion of the ground sandal wood of which I spoke above. On presenting himself before the fane, the worshipper is sprinkled by the priest with the tîrthum, a portion of which he may also receive in the palm of his hand to drink. He then receives a small portion of the sandal-wood which had been placed on the idol the day before, and having moistened that with the tîrthum, he makes a circular mark with it by the forefinger of his right hand on his forehead, just above the nose, on his breast, and on his two arms near the shoulder. This is to signify that his intellect, his heart, and his strength are his god's, and also to show to the outer world that he is a good Hindu, and attentive to his religious duties. Two or three hundred Brahmins are daily fed in some of the larger pagodas; and although many of the pagodas have considerable landed property connected with them, the sum expended by the Government of the country—that is, the native Government of Travancore—in these religious establishments is enormous. From £50,000 to £60,000 of the revenue is yearly expended in Travancore on pagoda expenses—a larger sum than is allotted to any other single item in the budget.

The Rajah received us in a most elegant little reception

room in his compound. It was in a tope of cocoanuts, palmyras, areca palms, mangoes, and jack trees (*Artocarpus integrifolia*). About the size of an ordinary English room, the floor raised on three or four steps, the roof supported by handsome wooden pillars, open on three sides, it was a very cool and comfortable resting place after our walk through the hot sun. There was a handsome rug on the floor, several chairs, a magnificent silver *betel* box in the middle of the rug, and the universal brass spittoons, of elegant shape, but to European taste nasty associations. Betel and tobacco were offered to us, which we of course politely declined. The Rajah himself, a man of about fifty years of age, is remarkably fair, very handsome, and intelligent; he wore nothing higher than his waist, round which a cloth of purest white was wrapped in the country fashion, and reached down to his ankles. Mr. Hawksworth had long known him, and had reason to believe that he has privately studied the Scriptures for some time. He conversed unreservedly before a good number of people who were about him on Christian topics; and I was particularly struck by his saying that, whatever of truth there might be in the Hindu religion, when it was freed from the fables and other follies that had grown up about it, it was inferior to the Christian religion in one thing, and that was the absence of any direct revelation of a Mediator. He quite admitted, he said—for it was his conviction—that the strong point of Christianity is its doctrine of an atonement. We were very much struck when he added that the Hindu system also admits, or supposes, the *necessity* for a mediator between God and man; only there Shiva, Vishnu, and Brahma have been substituted for Christ. When speaking of the doctrine of the Trinity, he quoted verbatim from our translation of the Athanasian Creed, showing that he must have taken some pains in studying the Christian religion.

There appears to have been a very decided spirit of inquiry among several of the high-caste people in the neighbourhood during Mr. Hawksworth's residence at Tiruwilla. One man, a leading Brahmin near, was so interested in his private study of the Scriptures, a copy of which he had purchased of Mr. Hawksworth, that on one occasion he was actually discovered reading a portion of the Bible in the temple, where he was obliged to be present. This was iniquity of the first degree in the eyes of the temple authorities, but I believe it was hushed up, as he was a man of considerable influence, and generally liked. But he was very bold to go so far, for many a man of influence has been put out of the way, even by his own relatives, for a less glaring breach of orthodoxy; such cases are perhaps commoner than is often supposed.

A chaplain whom I know, who resided many years in a

large and important city in this presidency, was very intimate with a wealthy and most intelligent Hindu, who was
in a very high and influential position, and, if I remember
rightly, a judge in one of the courts. This man used
often to pay my friend a visit; and their conversation
generally turned on the doctrines of the Christian
religion. But he still, though an enlightened and earnest
inquirer, like Naaman went for the sake of appearance to
worship in the temple. He had not summed up resolution
to openly declare for Christ, but his sentiments were
well known. One afternoon he drove up to my friend's
in his carriage, and from thence went to the pagoda,
saying that some important ceremonies called him there,
which he was bound to attend. Judge of my friend's
astonishment, when he learned on the following morning
that the judge was dead and burnt; for the Hindus burn
instead of burying their dead. The man was taken suddenly ill in the pagoda, was carried away in a dying
state, was hurried off the moment life was extinct to the
burning ground, and all by his relatives. His eldest son
put the torch to the funeral pile; and the body was consumed before an inquest could have been held, or indeed
any inquiry could possibly have been made. I need
scarcely say that my friend had always strong misgivings
as to the cause of this mysteriously sudden death.

The mission bungalow at Tiruwilla is very pleasantly

situated on a hill; and is within easy distance of the river—rivers being the highways of this part of the country. The situation is remarkably well chosen. As we sat out of doors enjoying the sea breeze the first evening we were there, Mr. Hawksworth gave me an account of his first experiences there. He had been residing at Mavelicara for several years during Mr. Peet's stay in England on sick leave; and on the eve of his return was requested by the Madras Corresponding Committee to look out for a site on which to build a new mission house, as the centre of a new district. He accordingly set out on a tour of exploration. Proceeding northwards, about fourteen miles from Mavelicara he came to a large Syrian village; a little further on stood one of the largest pagodas in Travancore, with a teeming population of Brahmins, Nairs, and Chogans, in the surrounding district. He continued his walk about a mile beyond; and after passing another smaller pagoda, he at length came to some rising ground, the very spot on which we were sitting, then covered with jungle, with the exception of a few small gardens, which had formerly been occupied by Syrians, but which they had deserted on account of the depredations of the Sircar petty officials, and other neighbouring thieves. On looking round, Mr. Hawksworth thought that this was the very spot for his new mission-house.

In this choice he was supported by Mr. Chapman, who was at that time principal of the Cottayam college. How to obtain the ground was the next consideration. He at once made application, through the British Resident, as was usual, to the Sircar, for permission to hold the ground for mission purposes; and at the same time purchased the little deserted gardens from the Syrians. It could not be expected that such a site could be obtained without much opposition. The Brahmins belonging to the adjacent temples, dreading, no doubt, the light that would be cast over the place by the proximity of a mission station, even though at the distance of a mile, sent in counter-applications, stating that they wished to have the ground for the purpose of building a pagoda upon it. And when that plea did not answer, they put forth their mightiest argument, that their idol would be defiled on his progress to and from his bathing operations in the adjacent river, if the hilly ground were occupied by Christians. Sircar officials were sent to measure distances, which proved to be greater than were usually allowed for such purposes. So after much delay the foundation stone of the new mission bungalow was laid in 1848. But before the building could be completed, Mr. Hawksworth was relieved of Mavelicara by the return of Mr. Peet; and he and his family lived for some time, and that in the hottest time of the year, in a small wooden house, which was in fact a paddy granary, while the bungalow was being finished. Scarcely, however, had they entered it, when Mr. Hawksworth, partly, no doubt, through the unhealthy atmosphere of Mavelicara as it then was, and partly through the insufficient protection of the wooden hut in which they had lived at Tiruwilla, became seriously ill; and they were ordered off to Coimbatore for change of climate and scene. But already the hearts of some of the high-caste men about had been won.

Among those who followed them to the boat, to bid them farewell, was a respectable heathen, the owner of a large temple in the immediate neighbourhood. 'Sir,' he said at parting, 'I shall pray for you during your absence.' 'I could but reply,' says Mr. Hawksworth, 'how delighted I should be when he should have learned to pray to the true God, and Jesus Christ whom He has sent.' And but a few days before another high-caste man, the chief Brahmin in the neighbourhood, who was very wealthy, and possessed great influence, most obligingly made over to Mr. Hawksworth a piece of ground, saying that he should have more if he wished it, gratis; or, if otherwise, he must fix the price. Indeed the prospects of the mission on its opening seemed unusually promising. Never before, Mr. Hawksworth says, had he such opportunities for distributing the Scriptures among the higher classes of the heathen.

After a stay of seven months at Coimbatore they were permitted to return to their station in health. Great were the demonstrations of joy among the people who had already joined the mission; the bell of the temporary mission church was not allowed to be silent; fireworks were seen on every hand, guns were fired, and more grateful to them than all was a device worked in flowers— the simple word 'Ebenezer'—a proof, as Mr. Hawksworth expressed himself, of a far higher and better feeling than a mere wish to please master. Many of the heathen too came about them, and evinced unmistakably their sincere pleasure to see them back again.

A marked success attended Mr. Hawksworth's efforts at Tiruwilla. By the close of the year 1854 those who had joined the mission numbered upwards of 700, and rapidly increased to more than 1,000. Twenty-five families by that time also had settled on the hill in the neighbourhood of the mission-house. Several new out-stations had also been formed, and small temporary churches built, as it was thought the distances were often too great to allow of the people walking in all weathers, sometimes up to their necks in water, to the head station.

He now also began to think of building a larger and more substantial church near his bungalow. But here again he had many difficulties to face; the Brahmins, for instance, of the adjacent temple, which was on the opposite

hill, fearing that the rising sun would cast the shadow of
the church upon their holy place, opposed the site being
granted.   The Sircar officials and authorities lent only too
ready an ear to their objections, and much consequent
delay was the result.   Mr. Hawksworth however was not
to be foiled ; he chose a site to the north, instead of the
south, of his bungalow; the difficulty was thereby
removed, and the church commenced.   It is not even
yet actually finished ; but it was sufficiently complete by
the end of 1855 to allow of its being opened for service.
Very soon after this it was that Mr. Hawksworth's health
obliged him to return for a time to England.   And, alas
for Tiruwilla! there has never been a resident missionary
in charge there since.

One day during our stay we visited a wealthy and prominent Syrian family, at a place about twelve or thirteen
miles from the bungalow.   They had been long very
steadfast friends of Mr. Hawksworth's, and one or two of
the family are members of our Church.   This was one of
the places that Dr. Buchanan visited in 1806, and I there
saw an old priest who remembered his visit well.   He is a
fine, venerable old man, and very liberal in his views; a
Syrian, but by no means bigoted.   Mr. Hawksworth's
friends lived in one of the finest native houses I have seen
in this part of India ; and as I have no doubt the reader

will be anxious to know what a first-rate house among these rich Syrians is, I insert a ground plan of it, as nearly as I can remember it.

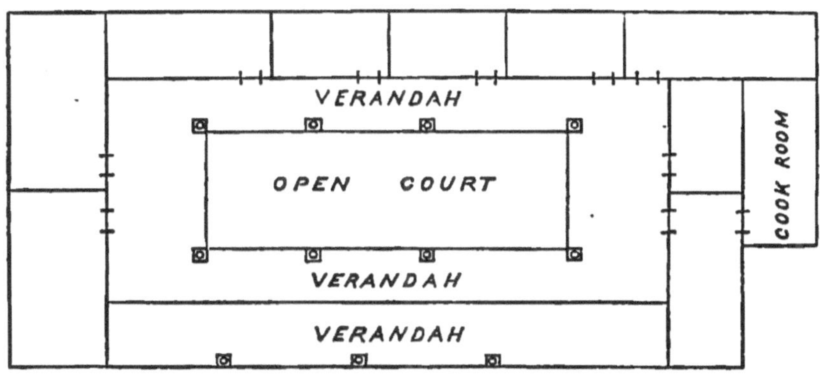

The rooms are ranged, as will be seen, round a small court; and the whole, except the verandahs, which are built of stone, and well *chunamed*, is of wood, and in many places prettily carved, according to the established designs of the country. In many of the houses, and the churches in particular, the beams, and other portions of the woodwork, are most elegantly carved—are often, in fact, quite works of art. No expense had been spared on this house. The entrance is, as in all cases, by a verandah about two yards in width, and through a wooden screen, which separates the outer from an inner verandah of the same width. This inner verandah runs round the court, and is raised about two feet from the ground. At the ends it is very wide, and is the reception-room, sitting-room, and bed-room in fine weather, for, I believe, the greater part of the family. A very handsome cot, on which the master of the house takes his rest, stood in one corner of the verandah while we were there. The legs were of turned wood, coloured with blue, green, yellow, and red, very pretty in effect. This colouring is done on the turning-lathe, with sealing-wax of the different colours, which they make by beating vermilion, orpiment, and other colours with lac. It is then polished with a piece of teak. The rooms of the house are chiefly used as store-rooms, though some of them are also used as sleeping-rooms. This is the style of the better houses, I believe, throughout India. The smaller houses consist of one, two, or three rooms, without a court, and surrounded by a verandah, parts of which also are frequently divided into rooms, the main rooms being generally used for keeping household stuffs, rice, and so forth.

The father-in-law of one of the young men of this house has earned our great esteem by his readiness to engage in every good work ; he has distinguished himself by taking a marked interest in the slave congregations, especially, of course, among those that work on his own lands. He not only frequently teaches in a slave-school on a Sunday, but remains to worship with them, too.

Few of the wealthy Syrians would stoop to such a service as this.

Many notable instances of much more than an outward profession of Christianity cheered Mr. Hawksworth's heart during the few years he was at Tiruwilla. Here is the death-bed testimony of a man who, less than ten years previously, had been a worshipper of Shiva. He was at the point of death when one of the mission people went to see him. The sick man, recognising him, said, ' I want to send a message to master. You must say I shall not see him again in this world, because I am about to die; but we shall meet very soon in the presence of Jesus. I expect that I shall die to-morrow at noon ; but I have no fear, I am happy. I am a sinner, but Christ has died to save me. That is sufficient for me. Tell master what I say.' He remained sensible, speaking about the Saviour to all around him at intervals till noon the next day, when he died. His conduct when in health, and during his sickness, was in keeping with his last hours. No man was ever more keenly alive to the communion of that joy, which our Saviour tells us thrills through heaven at the news of a sinner repenting, than Mr. Hawksworth. He is, spiritually, one of the most improving companions I ever met. ' What unutterable joy,' he writes, in one of his letters, referring to the man I have just mentioned, ' if permitted to meet such men in eternity, and then unite in singing, " Not unto us, O Lord, not unto us; but unto Thy name give glory, for Thy mercy, and for Thy truth's sake." '[1]

I may turn aside for a moment to tell what I know will interest many—that Mr. Hawksworth was very intimate with, and no doubt owes much to, two clergymen, one at least of whom was well known in England. He was a member of the Rev. Hugh Stowell's congregation, and a teacher in his Sunday School. He also read for a year, before entering the Church Missionary Society's Institution at Islington, with the Rev. Robert Frost, another Manchester clergyman, who was afterwards secretary to the British and Foreign Bible Society. When a young man, he once called upon a poor but pious woman, whom he had often seen before, and their conversation turned on missionary objects. He had attended a missionary meeting the evening before. The old lady asked him what was most wanted, and he replied that the speakers pleaded hard for men; upon which she said at once, ' Why don't *you* go ? ' These words rested with him. He was always hearing the question, ' Why don't *you* go ? ' And at last it came to this : that his conscience could not rest until he could find for himself a satisfactory answer. He sought the answer, I need scarcely say, on his knees ; and the result was that, with the advice of Mr. Stowell,

---

[1] Mr. Hawksworth has since died at the early age of forty-seven.

who encouraged him, he offered his services to the Church
Missionary Society. And a true missionary he has been.
What an apparently small thing often turns the whole
current of our lives for ever! It looks like chance; but
we know better. And how unconscious we are often of
the real mission of our lives! God had a great mission
for this secluded and humble old lady; but how little she
may have suspected that one unpremeditated word of hers
could do more than all the deliberate speeches at the
missionary meeting!

From Tiruwilla we went to Mavelicara. The missionary and founder of this mission is the Rev. Joseph
Peet. I have mentioned his name before, and given some
extracts from his published letters on the subject of his
preaching at Cottayam. From them it will have been
already concluded that he is a man of undaunted determination and unwearied energy. His success at Mavelicara,
in the face of great opposition on the part of the heathen
population especially, is most remarkable. The members
of his different congregations now number more than
3,000. He is a man *sui generis*—one of that good old
school which seems now fast wearing out from the missionary field. He is truly apostolic in this—that nothing,
I think, would 'move him,' if he set his mind on accom-
plishing anything, however difficult; and here no doubt,
humanly speaking, lies one great secret of his success.

He is a man who, if he has anything to do that he feels ought to be done, will do it, with all his heart and soul. Most of our great accomplishers have been made of such stuff. I was amused, the first Sunday I spent at Mavelicara, with this trait in his character, in the simple singing of the hymn at church. It is not by any means easy to get the Hindus to sing, or even to like our English tunes. For this reason in Tinnevelley they use many of the native tunes in public worship. But the Travancore missionaries have always honoured the old English tunes of their own child-hood. The hymns that we use here have been all, so far, written by the missionaries, chiefly Mr. Baker, senior, to English metres. Never shall I forget the first time I saw Mr. Peet in his pulpit, giving out and singing the hymn before the sermon. Long used to the difficulty of leading the natives, he sang the well-known 104th Psalm with a stentorian voice, that thrilled through the building. Every voice was raised through the church—but not to the tune. A great sound truly as of 'many waters,' such a Babel of discord as I have nowhere else heard, began as soon as he had given out a verse; but ever, high above all, the determined voice of our dear friend Mr. Peet ringing out the tune true to a semitone. And so he was ever; if a thing was to be done, Mr. Peet knew no answer but ' do it.'

I remember that he took me out on the Monday morning before breakfast to see his church. Pointing to

two ornaments that crown the angles at the ends of the
nave and chancel, he said, 'Thereby hangs a tale. When
I had built the church, I still wanted some kind of a
finish there. I often wondered, as the building grew,
what I should put; but could not make up my mind.
But at last the roof was on, and something must be done;
the roof looked so bare. I could not put a cross—I
would not—and yet I did not know what to put. So I
gave a day to study it. I went to bed late, but had not
got it; when in the night I dreamt that I had at last
made a design. When I awoke in the morning, I remembered the design of my dream; got a piece of paper and
drew it out; sent, after breakfast, for a carpenter, and had
it cut in wood most carefully, according to the dream;
and there you see it in stone. Don't you admire it?' I
am afraid I was ever so near saying what was not strictly
the truth. But I could not very much admire it; I don't
think the Society of Arts would have given a prize for the
design. To me it suggested the idea of an antediluvian
pine-apple—if there were such things then—not quite developed. In short, it looked like a pine-apple in an early
stage of the ' struggle for existence,' as we may suppose a
swan has struggled from a Plesiosaurus. But the thing
was *done,* and to his satisfaction. 'And so,' he concluded, ' you are a young man. I will give you a piece of
advice—never give in ; you'll always do it at last.'

Mr. Peet was proud of his church; and no wonder, for what had he not gone through to build it where it was! It is always a difficult thing in a native State, as with the bungalow and church at Tiruwilla, to obtain a site for a mission building. He had after long thought fixed upon the spot on which his church now stands, and the Sircar gave their consent. But it was near a small building on the river's brink, belonging to the pagoda, the very spot where they yearly brought the idol to bathe. The temple people said the idol would be polluted by being brought so near to a Christian church and the low-caste people who would probably become converts. In short, they put every obstacle in his way in the most persevering manner—so much so, that, on account of the prominence of the Mavelicara pagoda, and the fact that some of the Maharajah's relatives who resided at Mavelicara worshipped there, the authorities at Trevandrum lent for a time only too ready an ear to them. Mr. Peet, however, was a match for them, and ended the matter by purchasing the building by the river's side, and the plot of ground on which it stood, from the river up to his churchyard; and there the building still stands on the mission premises, kept in good repair by Mr. Peet, and used by him as a shelter from the sun or rain on entering or leaving his boat, the landing-place being close by. He looks upon it as a trophy for the ' Church militant.'

The Brahmins now bathe their idol in another part of the river.

Among the many interesting episodes in the history of the Mavelicara mission is that of the reception lately into the Christian Church of a Brahmin family. Such cases are comparatively rare amongst us. The very high castes still illustrate the Saviour's words, 'How hardly shall they that have riches enter into the kingdom of God.' Moreover, the higher the position of a man, the more sure and terrible is the persecution to which he is liable. Thus it is an undertaking, the full import of which we can hardly perhaps justly appreciate, when a high-caste man openly professes Christianity. In this instance, the first member of the family to investigate the truth of Christianity was the mother. She was, for a Hindu, a highly-educated woman, having been originally, I believe, trained as a temple musician. Hence she could read—a privilege enjoyed by but few of her sex—and was conversant with much of the Hindu mythology and religious obligations. She became anxious, while still in her heathen state, about her soul. She especially studied the Shasters to find a place of salvation; she followed their directions as to good works, meditation on the deity, pilgrimages to holy places, bathing in holy streams, and everything that Hinduism could suggest, but without effect. She was still wondering and uncertain, when she met with a portion of the sacred Scriptures. Here at last she thought that she had found the thing she sought for.

She was thus led to seek an interview with a native minister, the Rev. Mr. Tharien, who lived at no great distance from her home; and he and his wife, like Aquila and Priscilla of Bible times, were enabled to ' expound unto her the way of God more perfectly.' Her eldest son was the first of the family to be influenced by her; and ultimately all the rest allowed the truth of the new religion which she was ready to embrace. They then sought Mr. Peet, and asked for baptism. He kept them for a time under instruction, and being fully satisfied as to the purity of motive that brought them to him, he consented to admit them into the Christian Church by baptism at Mavelicara itself. As regards this world, however, it was a most serious step that they were taking. They were threatened with the loss of all their property, as well as an entire separation from their relatives. And the eldest son was in great distress on account of his wife. Though tenderly attached to him—influenced, no doubt, greatly by her own family—she left him rather than join in his apostacy. It appeared as though if he became a Christian he must lose her for ever. This weighed greatly on his mind; and Mr. Peet has described to me a most affecting scene he had with the young man in his

study a few weeks before he was baptised. The idea of
this separation unmanned him, and it seemed at one time
as though he would not have been able to surmount the
obstacle thus thrown in his way. He came at last to un-
burden his mind to Mr. Peet, who said that the struggle
in the young man's mind was so severe that he himself
could not refrain from shedding tears with him, as they
were both on their knees in his study laying the matter
before God.

Well, God was better to him than his fears—and
is it not ever so for the earnest and trusting? Before
the day fixed for their baptism came, his wife returned to him, overcome by her love to him, and it is
to be hoped by convictions also as to the truth of the
religion he was about to profess. She was baptised with
the rest, and appears to have made him a first-rate wife.
He is now an ordained clergyman, and a more worthy one
we have not got amongst us, nor perhaps a more able
one. He has not long been ordained, but I heard him
preach a few Sundays back a most eloquent and well-
thought out sermon. He has also already learned English
enough to understand most books; and I had the gratifi-
cation, after hearing him preach, of giving him a volume
of Dean Close's outlines of sermons, which he is well able
to use. What a change is here! From being born a
priest of a heathen temple—for all Brahmins are priests

by caste—to being a priest in the temple of the one Jehovah! After having been dedicated to a heathen god at his birth, and called by his name, and having been one of the *bhudevangal*, as the Brahmins call themselves, or *gods of the earth*, and having the right to be addressed as *Twammy*, which really is *God*, he is now a δοῦλος Ἰησοῦ Χριστοῦ, a slave of the Lord Jesus Christ, and is well named Joseph, after him who was 'added' late to Jacob's family, and ever 'feared God.'

Some time before Joseph was ordained, a little incident occurred at Cottayam which was full of meaning, and to my own mind of promise for India's future. It had been my good fortune to have a proposition that I ventured to make to my missionary brethren unanimously accepted by them, that once a year as many as possible of the mission agents should meet us all at one of our annual gatherings. At one of these gatherings, at Cottayam, when we were all assembled for a kind of missionary meeting, Mr. Peet suddenly came forward, and taking one hand of his Brahmin convert, and one hand of a Christian slave of the Komarum congregation, named Poulúsa, he joined them, and holding them together said, 'See what Christianity can do for us; it makes us all brethren. Christianity, like its founder God, is no respecter of persons.' Its effect was electrical. It gave a tone to all the addresses of that night; and

I am convinced that there was not a native present who did not both feel and own the reality of what Mr. Peet thus happily brought forward as the most prominent fact suggested by our gathering.

The separation that caste causes between class and class is, in more ways than one, a blight on everything like national progress in India. Though to write the word 'national' is hardly fair; for there is no such thing in India as nationality. There are as many nations as there are languages; nay, practically as many in any district as there are castes. A national movement in any one direction is impossible in India. It is the disintegration of the people, by caste especially—though, of course, in no small degree by the differences of speech— that renders India so easy, as it has been so constant, a prey to foreigners. It is caste that makes our own rule so easy. The force of the old saying 'Divide et impera,' was never, I suppose, more fully illustrated than in India. It is because the people *are* so divided that we are what we are among those 200 millions. But in the meantime there is no native expansion, except in European directions. And nothing can produce it until there is union. Whatever has the power of uniting the peoples of India will help to transform a most heterogeneous multitude into a nation. The two greatest powers at work in this direction at present are the English language and Christianity; the English language, because it brings the educated all over India into communication with each other; Christianity, because it is gradually undermining caste. Caste is the greatest of all barriers to progress, because it keeps men from combining. In this view of the case, perhaps, the statesman might see in the spread of our language and our religion in India the greatest danger to the continuance of our rule. But with questions of this kind the missionary, and even the philanthropist, has nothing to do. His work is simply to be instrumental, as far as possible, in putting each member of the human race in possession of those privileges to which he is entitled as man, and especially the privileges which come through the gospel of Jesus Christ.

The greatest care, however, is required in dealing with caste from a European standpoint. The caste question, as it affects our missions, is a decidedly complicated one, and is a matter that should be well studied by every missionary. From a misapprehension of its true bearings harm has, I think, not unfrequently been done, and the progress of Christianity checked among some of the infant Churches of India. From an attempt to put it down 'vi et armis'—for instance, by inducing a high-caste convert to marry a convert from a low caste, or making it a *sine quâ non* of Christianity that the converts from high and low should eat together, or forcing a high-caste youth to sit on the same form with a low-caste in a school—an unnecessary and violent prejudice has often been raised against Christianity. But what is the real state of the case? Caste is but an exaggerated form of what is found in all countries where one race has conquered another, or made another to serve.

There is as great a separation between the white and coloured races in America, as between the Brahmins and low-castes in India; and the separation is originally of precisely the same nature. The white man in America tells you that the blacks are an inferior race, that they have a peculiar odour, that they have tender shins and thick skulls; and observe, the Brahmin tells you exactly the same thing. Caste in India dates from the time when the Aryan of the north subdued and oppressed the Turanian of the south. The Aryans descend upon India as 'gods of the earth;' and in their annals and songs, as we find in the Vedas, and other of their poems, they speak of the Turanians as black demons, hideous giants, and apes of untold cruelty, treachery, and deceit. But upon this fundamental race difference were grafted most jealous social distinctions, as the race became more mixed, such as will always be found where anything of superiority, especially class superiority, can be asserted. Civilisation, too, will always multiply class distinctions; and the Aryans of India were early civilised, and that probably far beyond any other nation. It is absurd to suppose that caste distinction in India is peculiar to the soil. It is in its essence nothing but what we have full-blown among ourselves.

It possesses indeed a peculiarity, which, as it happens, has greatly intensified its baneful influence-; but that is a second thought altogether; and it is of great importance to remember that: I mean its religious aspect, of which I shall speak presently. But the thing itself is the child of what we call civilisation. Is there no caste among Europeans? for instance, in India? Those who have seen, even at a dinner table in India, the jealousies of rank between the major's wife and the captain's wife, the collector's wife and the assistant collector's wife, the 'covenanted' and the ' uncovenanted,' have seen that phase of human nature among their own race which is the parent of the many caste distinctions among the Hindus. In its most exaggerated form you see it, as I have said, between white and coloured in America; and perhaps scarcely less between '*pukka*' Europeans and country-born in India. Now jealousies in the matter of social rank may be bad, and may indicate that human nature is very far from what it ought to be:

but the distinctions of social position will exist; and so long as human nature is what it is, the assertion of such distinctions will be accompanied with more or less of acrimony. Nay, amongst ourselves the breach of caste distinction in certain ways is regarded as scarcely less than an offence against morality. We should hardly expect the most liberal minded of evangelical clergyman in England to sanction the marriage of his daughter with his butler's son, on the ground that all men are of one blood.

And the European in India who should marry a native woman would inevitably lose caste among his own race and could never introduce his wife into society. Now if there is right in these distinctions—and I do not say whether there is or is not, but the world seems to acknowledge the right—why should we deny to the Hindu the same social principles that rule ourselves? I believe we often err in India in this respect: that we look upon all the natives of the country as of the same status; to us, in fact, they are but *one* caste. The (shall I say thoughtless?) European is scandalised when he sees people, as he supposes of one class by natural rights, possessed of such marked class distinctions. To him it is as absurd for a Brahmin to refuse to eat with a low-caste man as it would be for one ploughboy in England to refuse to eat his bread and cheese from the same table as another ploughboy, on the plea of some imaginary social superiority.

But the Brahmin sees the matter in a very different light; and he sees as wide a social gulf between himself and the lower caste, as the English clergyman does between his daughter and his butler's son, or, even in some cases, as the white man in the West does between himself and his negro dependant. Class distinctions of this kind we can never remove from India any more than we can from England or America.

On this account we should be chary how we offend Hindu class prejudices, which are perfectly natural. On the ground of social distinction and habits alone, for instance, it is unwise to precipitate marriages between the members of different castes; though it has often been done under the idea that *everything* about caste distinctions is bad and unchristian. The greatest unhappiness has often followed such marriages amongst our converts. As a case in point, a servant of my own, who, though as respectable to European eyes as a high-caste servant could have been, was nevertheless a pariah by birth. Being a Christian, he was united in marriage to a girl who was from a much higher position, but also a Christian. The marriage was advocated from the best of motives by the European friends of the girl, who had in fact brought her up. But the whole thing was a mistake. The girl's relatives made the lad so unhappy that he soon fled. After a time he returned and his wife rejoined him; but twelve months after that he was in his grave; and the symptoms of his illness were such as to suggest most painful suspicions in my own mind. We cannot ignore the social distinctions that are at the foundation of the caste divisions in India. The attempt to do it has caused the most serious perplexities in the management of some missions. It has often been laid at Swartz's door that he erred in being too lax in the matter of caste among his converts. He had, no doubt, and every missionary has, great difficulties to deal with. But I feel convinced, were he able to answer for himself, he would tell us that he felt that the social distinctions of the Hindus could not be rudely infringed by Europeans with impunity; and that, if anything of heathen superstition still lingered among his converts in the matter, it must be a work of time to remove it.

But there are *two* aspects to caste: and in another aspect there *is* something about it which is eminently bad, and which nothing can purge it of but a pure religion. It can never be got rid of by encouraging people to 'break caste' by eating with others, and inter-marrying with others, or any such violent measures, that will only offend the social feelings of the people; but it must be a work of simple Christian principle. I refer, of course, to the religious aspect of caste. The Brahmins— and other high castes have followed them—have fortified their position, beyond what we find in most other nations, by preaching up for themselves a *moral* superiority, as well as a social one. Never has priestcraft in this world's history excelled theirs. They have for ages insisted that they are of a different mould altogether from the rest of mankind; they are the chosen of heaven, the favoured of the gods, the receptacles of the divine oracles, and entitled themselves to divine honours. They have done what the Pope of Rome alone probably of all other men ever thought of doing, they have surrounded their dignity with a religious inviolability; and that of so strict a nature, that the very touch of a lower-caste man means *moral* defilement, and in some cases even the very presence of a man within certain bounds. And this idea of moral defilement has been taken up by every succeeding caste; so that even a blacksmith, or a stonemason, will not touch a pariah. The Institutes of Menu, though perhaps the oldest writings in the world next to the Vedas, contain already the germs of this state of things. For instance, we there read that—

'When a Brahmin springs to light, he is born above the world, the chief of all creatures, assigned to guard the treasury of duties, religious and civil.

'Whatever exists in the universe is all in effect, though not in form, the wealth of the Brahmin, since he is entitled to it all by his primogeniture and eminence of birth.

'A Brahmin may seize without hesitation, if he be distressed for subsistence, the goods of his Sudra slaves; for as that slave can have no property, his master may take his goods.'

With regard to some of the low castes, the same authority says :—

'Let no man who regards his duty, religious and civil, hold any intercourse with them; let their transactions be confined to themselves, and their marriages only between equals : let food be given them in *potsherds,* but *not by the hands of the giver.*'

Now to allow a vestige of such doctrine to remain in the minds of any of our converts from heathenism would indeed be a blot on the very name of Christianity. But what we should do is to be careful that we direct our efforts solely against the religious element of caste, the idea of *moral defilement.* To treat caste as though it were altogether from beginning to end a matter of religion is to make a great mistake. The social differences will remain, even when the superstition is gone. An attempt has often been made to force low-caste boys into a high-caste school. It has also been done with a certain amount of success. But I see nothing to be gained by it. It is simply analogous to thrusting a lot of street Arabs into Eton or Westminster; the other boys would at least turn up their noses. It is just so in India, quite independently of the idea of moral defilement—though that of course remains among the heathen. I do not object to the different castes mingling in a school, if they will do it : but I cannot see any principle sustained by forcing it, except Socialism, and that is not approved of in England.

It is the religious element of caste that is the great curse of India—the idea of moral pollution by touch. It separates men that live on the same soil, and in the same village, in a way that no other influence on earth, I suppose, could do. It keeps the slave, as I have told you, from entering a court of justice; were military power desirable it would make it impossible; and there is no kind of progress to which it is not a barrier. Nothing but Christianity can undermine it. And our exertions to this end cannot be too earnest or too wise. Hence, when I saw Joseph the Brahmin grasp Paul the slave by the right hand, with a smile of true Christian love on his face, I recognised an earnest of a better day some time for the sons of India, whom for their many noble qualities I love so well.

The numbers that have rallied round Mr. Peet—now upwards of three thousand—are a splendid testimony to his unwearied zeal and love in his work.[1] For several years those who joined his mission were almost exclusively Syrians. In time, however, several congregations were

---

[1] Mr. Peet died in 1865, aged sixty-five years.

gathered out from among the heathen.   I believe the first converts in any number from heathenism were received during the time Mr. Hawksworth was in charge while Mr. Peet was in England.   The influence of the Bible is often being felt, where and how the missionary knows not.   At Krishnapoorum, a place about six miles south of Mavelicara, there was an old man who had for some time been earnestly reading the New Testament in Malayalim.   He one day made his appearance at Mr. Hawksworth's study door, and asked for instruction for himself and his family. His daughter and her husband were with him.   They and several others received the instruction they needed, and after a time were baptized.   These people were *Chogans*, the same caste as the *Shânârs* of Tinnevelley.   Thus the nucleus was formed of what is now a flourishing Church amongst that class.

It is remarkable how missions vary as regards the numbers of converts.   While in Travancore we number our people by hundreds, and in Tinnevelley by thousands, in Bengal in comparison they count only by tens, and in Bombay by units.   While no doubt much of this diversity is due to the different methods of evangelisation followed by individual missionaries—the European bazaar and street preaching, as a rule, failing in drawing out numbers, as it appears to me from a want I have already mentioned, of the gift of tongues, and the absence of nationality on the part of the preacher—much more is due to the condition of the people themselves to whom we preach. For some classes of people it is a much more easy matter to become members of a Christian congregation than for others. Some are in danger of losing everything in this life, and even life itself; others are gainers, and that often to a very considerable degree, as regards this world's matters. This world, for instance, offers I suppose but little, if any, resistance to the Syrian Christian joining the English communion, if he prefers it. The Travancore slaves who have lately become Christians, though suffering persecution at the hands of their employers, have not suffered much, if at all, from *their own body*; moreover, their position even in this native State has been much raised. The Shânârs of Tinnevelley have also, no doubt, in many cases been gainers in no small degree, for this world. Whole villages have sometimes adopted Christianity at once. And it is a matter for immense rejoicing that so many are brought under the constant means of grace, and that their children and children's children will, it is to be hoped, have thus the privilege of being not only born, but trained, as Christians. But the case is very different when a man must necessarily suffer persecution from those of *his own household*. And this is probably the case in Northern India to a far greater degree than in Travancore or Tinnevelley. There only the

sincere, strong-minded, earnest believer will separate him
self. Thus in Benares, for instance, the numbers who
have openly ' put on Christ ' are comparatively few ; certainly few when compared with the thousands of Tinnevelley : and though the mission numbers some hundreds,
more than half are orphans, who have been humanely
rescued by the missionaries from starvation and death in
the streets, during the influx of pilgrims, and have been
brought up in the orphanage.

Still it is quite possible that in many fields, where now
the numbers are few, but where there has been real scriptural work carried on, there may some day arise a harvest
more copious even than those of the south ; for the *good
seed* has been sown, though now it still lies apparently
dormant. Thus we must not judge, now at least, of
missionary results by numbers alone ; much less
must we thus only judge of missionary earnestness and
zeal.

Then, again, when we hear of a mission of many years'
standing containing three or four thousand Christians, we
are not to suppose that each individual of such a number
has been directly brought over from the enemy's ranks.
A vast proportion of that number, and the more the older
the mission be, will of course have been born in the
Church. And I have observed that the Christian families
of our missions, like the Israelites in Egypt, increase more

rapidly than the heathen about them.   There are several
reasons for this. 'Godliness hath promise of the life
that now is,' as well as 'of that which is to come.'   First,
the lives of the Christians are more moral than those of
their neighbours.   I have heard a missionary, who has
had a large accession of converts from heathenism, say
that many married couples, who had no children in their
heathen state, had subsequently large families.   Secondly,
while vast numbers of children among the heathen die from
ignorance and carelessness, so that frequently only one or two
in a family attain to maturity, the children of our Christian
people are much better cared for, and are reared in much
larger numbers.

On our way home we turned aside to call at Allepie, a
sea-port town on the narrow strip of land that lies between
the Backwater and the sea.   As we passed along through
the low lands before reaching the Backwater, numbers of
slaves were still engaged in pumping the water out of the
paddy-fields, preparatory to sowing the rice, though it was
late in the season.   This is done by means of a large wheel
without rim, the spokes of which are wooden blades that
work through a trough, and drive up the water into the
canals.   The slaves sit on a framework of bamboos, and
propel the wheel by the foot.   When the wheel is large,
three or even four slaves are perched one above the other,
and work night and day at this agricultural treadmill.   A

good number of hands—or rather feet—is required for this service, as the work is very heavy, and each individual can only work for a short time at once..

There is something very grand even in these great wildernesses of water that lie for miles around the deeper Backwater, interspersed, as they are in the season, with tracts of green paddy. Each portion of land is sown only once in five or six or even more years, so that a great proportion of the low country is always under water. Thousands of water-fowl of all kinds and sizes wade about fishing, or stand in their dreamy way on one leg on the banks. As we rowed along we saw ibises, cranes, herons, marabouts, and numbers of other birds whose names I know not, and specimens of which I have never been fortunate enough to get, though I once employed a native to shoot birds for me : he always made out that the paddy-field birds were very shy, and that he could seldom get at them.

Crocodiles are very numerous in these low lands : we counted a dozen lying with their mouths open on the river bank in as many miles. On the shores of the Backwater lurking among the mangroves (*Rhizophora conjugata*), we find immense alligators, three times the size of the common crocodile of the rivers, and different from them in several particulars. A friend of mine shot one of these monsters some time since, and in the stomach he found quite a collection of rings, bangles, and beads, chiefly such as are worn by the slave women. Whether these were the remains of recent victims, and with how many such holocausts this monster had filled his terrible maw, or whether such substances may lie for some time in an alligator's stomach, are matters about which we can only guess. It is generally believed among the natives that these alligators are very long lived. As we sailed along under a delightful evening breeze into the Backwater, which at its southern end is nine miles across, skirting the shore, dark with the tangled growth of the *Cereops candolliana*, the *Kandella rheedei*, the *Bruguieria malabarica*, and occasionally others of the mangrove tribe, we found even that, too, instinct with life, for myriads of teal, startled at our approach, rose here and there in perfect clouds. These teal are a great addition to our table when we can get them; and they are not unfrequently brought to us by native sportsmen. A gentleman at whose house I once stayed has what he calls his tealery, in which he has always a supply for the table. It consists of a pond through which fresh water is always flowing, and a house in which the birds can find shelter. His stock is replenished from time to time by natives whom he employs to catch the teal for him. They do it in a rather novel way. Each man ties on the top of his head a bunch of grass and reeds, cleverly managed so as to imitate a natural growth. He then seeks a place where the teal abound, and having stepped into the water, he craftily approaches them with nothing but his head above the water. The innocent birds, supposing the grass and reeds indicate a natural mound of earth so covered, are sure ere long to approach it ; and no sooner does one alight than the man's nimble hands are raised, and the bird is caught.

Allepie is our oldest mission station. The father of the mission was the Mr. Norton of whom I wrote in one of my former letters. He was there for many years, and had a fair measure of success, so far as we may be permitted to judge. Latterly, however, I could hardly say the mission, as a whole, has prospered: this has arisen, probably, chiefly from two causes—one that the leading men there are for the most part Mahomedans, and they are very inaccessible to the influences of the Christian religion ; the other that since Mr. Norton's death there has been so frequent a change of missionaries—the place often having been, moreover, without a missionary at all. Mr. Hawksworth succeeded Mr. Norton. A sad scene awaited them when he and Mrs. Hawksworth for the first time entered the mission compound on the evening of August 5, 1840. They found the once active missionary after twenty-four years of anxious work at death's door ; he lay on a couch in the verandah of the mission bungalow, where he had been carried, that he might welcome his new brother, before himself bidding adieu to earth. Some of whom he had hoped great things had grievously fallen, and trial and disappointment had broken his heart. A week passed, and he was buried in the mission church, the first English church that had been built in Travancore, and he the first missionary that had set foot on its soil. The melancholy aspect of the Allepie mission at that time was further enhanced by the appearance presented by the churchyard. The original church had just been pulled down that it might be rebuilt on a larger scale. To the eye everything wore the appearance of ruin. The rebuilding of the edifice fell to the lot of the new, and as yet inexperienced, missionary. He began his work with his hands full indeed.

While at Allepie we were invited to be guests at a Mahomedan marriage feast; not that we were invited to witness the actual ceremony—that would have been, I suppose, impossible. The feast lasted a week, and we were invited to visit the bridegroom's father's house the evening before the ceremony took place. The bridegroom elect and his father, after having first, according to Eastern etiquette, asked permission, called upon us to deliver the invitation in person. The father is a hadji, that is to say, he has been on pilgrimage to Mecca. Hundreds of Mahomedans yearly embark at Allepie on this pilgrimage, and when they return are hadjis, or saints, and receive in consequence the honour due from those who have not yet been able to afford to undertake so important a journey. Both the young man and his father were perfect gentlemen in their manners and appearance. And whatever may be the cause, there is no doubt of the truth of what has so often been said, that Englishmen in the mass present an unfortunate contrast to Orientals in this respect. There is, as a rule, too much of self-assertion, and too little regard for the feelings of others about most Europeans in their intercourse with our Indian fellow-subjects.

When will Englishmen learn that, if they were to show themselves to be not only men, but gentlemen, they might soon have the world at their feet? If there is any hatred of Europeans lurking in the hearts of Hindus or Mahomedans, it is not so much hatred of our rule, as many seem to think, but hatred of our manners. England's rule is liked ; the brusqueness and too frequent licentiousness of the Englishman are hated. I am not sure that they may not some day cost us an empire. We went to the hadji's as invited, and were served with tea in European style, our own servants being consulted as to the proprieties. Afterwards some ladies of our party were taken to visit the apartments of the ladies of the house. In the meantime we had abundance of music of all kinds : there was a band of East Indians who played English airs and dance music very respectably on violins and violoncellos ; when they were tired we had an old white-headed Hindu with his hautboy; then there was a *wena,* the Hindu guitar, very well played; and lastly we had some of the most extraordinary dances I ever saw, some of them Arab war-dances, the mode and method of which I could not describe, for in fact they beggar description. One incident I took particular note of as illustrative of St. Luke xii. 37—'He shall gird himself, and make them to sit down to meat, and will come forth and serve them;'—the bridegroom elect opened the feast by coming round himself and offering sweetmeats to everyone, even the servants. On the following evening the bride was brought to her new home. About midnight we saw the procession approach, the house in which we were staying lying by the road on which they must come, and being very near the bridegroom's. The procession was a very long one; torches and fireworks and music were distributed along the whole line, and in the midst of it were the bride and groom, the latter on horseback, his turban glittering with jewels, and his coat with gold and silver lace and ornaments, and the bride in a palanquin with closed doors. They halted for a moment before our house, and honoured us with a short but brilliant display of fireworks. When the drums were first heard in the distance, one of our servants ran up into the room where we were, and in the most natural way possible exclaimed, '*Kettiyawen warunnu,*' ' The bridegroom is coming,' reminding us, as we are so often reminded in the East, of the extreme fidelity of Scripture language, and the force of our Lord's illustrations. A minute afterwards there would be the same cry in the bridegroom's own house among his ' waiting ' servants, with the addition of ' Go ye out to meet him.'

CHAPTER VIII.

Missionary success among Âryan and un-Âryan castes—Âryans the 'once bidden' but 'not worthy!'—Aboriginal tribes, men of the 'highways and hedges'—Their worship—Hindu Pharisees—Missionary instrumentalities—The agency required—The gift of tongues—Theological literature in the vernaculars—A well-educated native agency—Doctrine of compensation—The Arayans of Travancore—Village of Mundakayam—Deputation of Arayans—Their desire for protection—Visit to the east—The tope—The primeval forest—The bungalow—The elephants—Primitive men—The Ullâdans—Sunday at Mundakayam—The physical type of the Arayans—The converted devil-dancer—The ghaut—The burnt timbers—The table-land—Advance of cultivation—Deserted village—The Roman Catholic sculptor—A Syrian church as a bedroom—Kununkulum—Conclusion as to general principles in missionary matters—Able men for difficult work—Prejudices as to Hindu capacity—Reaction on the native.

ALTHOUGH I have incidentally alluded to converts in our Travancore mission from among the heathen, and especially to the case of the slaves, my remarks have been chiefly directed hitherto to the Syrian element in our body. I shall therefore speak in this chapter more particularly of the former.

It is a fact which I have before mentioned, and a very significant one, that the success of missionaries, as regards numbers, has been immensely greater among the un-Âryan, and what, for want of previous knowledge, we may regard as the aboriginal races of India, than among the Âryans. The Shânârs of Tinnevelley, the Santhals of North India, the slaves of Travancore, and the Arayans of Travancore, of whom I shall write presently, are all aboriginal tribes. In fifteen years we read of seven or eight hundred Christians from among the Santhals; the Christians of Tinnevelley are numbered by thousands; and the slaves and Arayans of Travancore already number some hundreds. In Benares, for instance, on the other hand, the numbers are still small, though the mission is forty years old.

Now this is suggestive; there must be some very definite cause for this most remarkable difference. Can we not discover it?

First, there may be some cause in the secret counsels of the Almighty. Indeed we know that nations are judged as well as individuals, and that their judgment must take place in this world. And I have often asked myself whether we do not see signs that the Sanscrit-speaking conquerors of India are still, as has been the case with the Jews for 1800 years (and, may we not add, with some Christian Churches for a period almost as long?), suffering the terrible retribution of a judicial blindness in Divine things. I cannot but think that the Âryans of India, probably before they migrated from the plains of Central Asia, once possessed in a signal manner a knowledge of the Divine will, either by direct revelation, or by retaining above other tribes the religion of Noah. No one can read carefully the Institutes of Menu without being struck with the feeling that there is much there that looks at least very like the remains of a revelation. Among much that is indeed utterly and grossly human, there is not a little that is eminently wise and good ; that reminds one, moreover, of the particular directions given by Jehovah to the Israelites under the Mount. There are even some of the *peculiarities,* as we sometimes perhaps think them, of the law of Moses to be found in the Code of Menu. For instance, the peculiar law as to the childless widow of a brother, found in Deut. xxv. 5, is found also in the Code of Menu.

Then there is the peculiar and most mystic Vedic sacrifice of a goat or a lamb. Then there are the unbloody offerings : as amongst the Israelites the sheaf, so amongst the Hindus the daily offering before the idol of the rice eaten in the temple. Then there is the anointing of the idol, called the *abhishagam ;* whence, we ask, derived ? Then there is the very form of the Hindu temple itself, of which it is not too much to say that it is after the exact plan of the tabernacle in the wilderness, or Solomon's temple at Jerusalem. The fane always consists of two rooms—the holy place, where no one enters but the ministering priest, and the holy of holies, in which the idol stands, this fane generally standing in a large court surrounded by a wall. This marked similarity of the Hindu to the Jewish temple was long a puzzle to me, till it occurred to me that it might possibly be that it was a stereotype of a once Divine appointment as to the externals of worship among the early inhabitants of the world.

The form of the tabernacle given to Moses may not have been then given for the first time; it may have been a renewal of an eastern command, as was, for instance, the command to keep the Sabbath-day holy. Then, again, the fact that the Hindus have got interwoven with their religion the doctrine of incarnation of the Deity causes us to ask of this too, whence has it been derived? These things may not strike everyone in the light in which I have put them: but they appear to me to point at least possibly, if not probably, to a past state of Divine privilege under the immediate revelation of God himself, which the Âryans of India have wilfully corrupted. If so, it may cause us to wonder the less that they are, like the Israelites, still slow to believe. Are they examples of the 'once bidden,' but 'not worthy?' Nor has light been denied them in later times, if I judge rightly; for in the history of Krishna, their most recent incarnation, we have an undoubted parody of the life of Jesus Christ.

But if we look at the religious state of the aboriginal

tribes, we can find no such marks of privileges degraded and betrayed. They strike us at once as being the men of the 'highways and hedges,' who late in the world's history are bidden to the marriage supper of the Lamb. Long since cast upon the desolate wilds and primeval forests of India, they seem long since to have lost almost every trace of a Divine law. They do, indeed, acknowledge a Supreme Spirit, whom they originally named Kô, or Kôn, *the King*; but whatever the case once, they now offer him no worship. While the Sanscrit language is rich in theological terms, the aboriginal language, of which our Malayalim is a branch, contained, or retained, scarcely any. The religion of these ancient tribes consists in the worship, if it can be so called, of their ancestors, which is an offering made yearly, on the anniversary of death, before a rude image, generally of bronze, or brass, the effigy of the ancestor; and they worship demons, through the intervention of a devil-dancer. The man who is to perform this unenviable office, generally the head man of the village, puts on a brazen belt covered with a number of small bells, and hollow bangles, with pieces of copper inside to rattle, round his ankles. With a staff in his hand, also hung with small bells, and other parapher- nalia, the man then begins to jump and dance to the increasing sound of tom-toms, cymbals, and like noisy affairs; sometimes even lacerating his flesh, till he is apparently in a frenzy, and is thought to be—perhaps is—possessed by the demon; when a terrific shout is raised by the people, and he is supposed to be able to give an oracular response to any question that may be put to him. As I said, these are markedly the men of the 'highways and hedges,' and therefore, on Scripture grounds, we cannot be surprised at their now entering the kingdom of God's dear Son, before the, as it may be, once bidden Âryans.

Secondly, there is much, no doubt, in human nature alone to account in a very great degree for the difference to which I am drawing attention. The old tale is still acted out—'Have any of the rulers, or of the Pharisees, believed on him?' And the reader may remember, in Dr. Duff's most interesting book, how he describes a Sudra boy, when he was once speaking in Calcutta to a class about the Pharisees, pointing to a Brahmin lad, and saying, 'There is one of *our* Pharisees!' There is a certain amount of simplicity about the lower classes which connects them with the old saying, 'To the poor the gospel is preached.'

But, thirdly, though I spoke above of what may be the working out of the mysterious counsels of the Almighty, as in the case of Israel, even though this might be demonstrably true, which it is not, I do not on any account mean that we are therefore to slacken our efforts for the conversion of the Âryans. God forbid. A man fails miserably when he attempts to *act out* what he conceives to be the secret counsels of the Most High. We must act out *our* duty. We must look to our instrumentality, and see whether there may not be something wrong there. That is *our* duty. We know that God can work by many or by few ; that it is 'not by might, but by my Spirit, saith the Lord.' But none the less are we responsible for our *instrumentalities*. This is the point for us to look at.

The command is plain, ' Go ye into all the world, and *preach* the gospel to *every creature*.' And that does not mean, stand in the bazaars with a stammering tongue and a foreign accent, and an ignorance of the native mode of thought ; but use the best means in your power that the gospel may be preached. And the best and only means in our power is the raising up of a native agency. This is the work for which Europeans are suited. For this work we want men of the calibre of the late Bishop Cotton, Dr. Duff, and others whom I could name, who would do the work in English, and thereby open up to their students the boundless resources of English literature. There is a romance in Europeans preaching in the streets and bazaars of a heathen country : þut in many cases that is nearly all. In a large majority of cases they are very imperfectly understood, in many not at all. Some time since I accompanied a young missionary to an out-station church; the service was about to commence when we reached the place. The native minister politely asked my friend who was in charge of the mission if he would preach. Of course his sermon was extempore. It was not the first time by any means that he had so preached. One European can generally understand another pretty well, and I could follow him throughout: but I learnt afterwards from the native missionary that very few of the sentences were understood either by himself or the people. Indeed, while a European may be very fairly understood by his own congregation, who have become accustomed to his foreign accent and idiom, he may be all but unintelligible to strangers. As I remember a friend, who was an excellent linguist, so far at least as book lore went, being met by a native, to whom he put some question by the roadside as to time or place, with the answer, 'Sir, I do not speak English.' There is a great danger of underrating the difficulty of speaking the native languages really *successfully.* And the natives are too polite to criticise us. I remember, when I had different views myself, being startled by what our ayah, a woman who knew English very fairly, once said after a confirmation address by the Bishop of Madras; she thought the address very beautiful, but added, ' Had I not known English, I should have missed some of it, for I understood the English much better than the interpretation.' The interpreter was a missionary of long standing, and who always preached extempore. For my own part, never do I ascend the pulpit steps to preach in Malayalim but with fear and trembling; and never do I come down without feelings of the deepest humiliation.

Whatever other reasons there may be, there is this one tangible and undoubted reason why we are not greatly influencing the high classes among the Hindus. We have not the necessary gift. To be plain, we cannot speak their language and think their thoughts. I simply state this as a broad—but a very broad—rule. There are, of course, exceptions; notably in the case of some missionaries, who have been born in the country, and have acquired the language, not mechanically, but naturally. Others too, by a natural aptness, have succeeded to a very great degree. And, no doubt, there is a point of proficiency to which all intelligent men may attain. They may, and do, converse with the natives, and that pretty fluently; as, indeed, you must have inferred from much that has gone before. Though even this is what many have not done, even after years of residence. But the instances in which Europeans, who, be it remembered, are generally at least twenty-three years of age when they come out, are able to command such a fluency of expression, and knowledge of native thought, as to secure the sympathies of the educated and fastidious, are not many.

With regard to our theological literature, there aré but few books that have been written by Europeans in the vernaculars. The mass of our vernacular books at present are translations from English books, done under the eye indeed of the missionary, but by some native who has had in his youth a good English education. This alone would go to show how superior as a rule is the English of the native who· is taught when young to the vernacular of the European.

I know that there are those who will deny this altogether; while, on the other hand, there are some who will say that all the world know it, and that we cannot expect it to be otherwise. To the first I would simply say they are deceiving themselves; and to the others, if this be so well known, why are we not looking for a way out of it? All points to the need, as I have before said, but can scarcely repeat too often, of a highly educated native agency. We want either the best men England can give to train the young in India; or else we want the cleverest boys to be selected out of the mission schools, to be sent to our English Universities to receive the most liberal education they are capable of. That such men would be ‘unmanageable’ is a mere bugbear. That will depend upon the way in which they are treated. There are, of course, positions and conditions which are sure to develope a spirit of rebellion, but they may be guarded against.

In the meantime the gospel is chiefly prospering among the simpler aboriginal classes. They come to it with fewer prejudices, and through fewer human obstacles. The doctrine of compensation runs through all nature. If they are further from the refinements and the worldly opportunities of the higher-caste Hindus, they are nearer to the kingdom of heaven. Their more ready enrolment under the banner of Christ is not the first instance of the Almighty having 'raised up the poor out of the dust,' and having 'lifted up the beggar from the dunghill, to set them among princes, and to make them inherit the throne of glory.' And though we lament that the Âryan is so slow to believe, we do not the less bless God that the Drâvidian has been the first to respond to the cry, 'Arise, shine, for thy light is come, and the glory of the Lord is risen upon thee.'

One of our missions is almost exclusively composed of converts from one of these primitive clans. The principal and original work of the Mundakayam mission lies among the Arayans of Travancore, a Drâvidian people, who live on the western slopes of the Southern Ghauts. Some years ago a deputation from several of their villages waited upon the Rev. Henry Baker, jun., who was then the missionary of Pallam, near Cottayam, and asked for Christian instruction. Mr. Baker has himself printed an interesting account of his early connection with them, to which I would refer you. He visited them in their romantic mountain homes, and ere long Christian churches were established in several of the villages. Mr. Baker followed this up by building a small bungalow near to the Ghauts, at some distance, however, from any of the Arayan villages, but pretty centrally between them. Round this bungalow he soon gathered a village, of Syrians and others from the low country, who being Christians, and subscribing to the rules of the village as to attending church, and so forth, had allotted to them by Mr. Baker tracts of forest land in the neighbourhood, which they filled and cultivated, Mr. Baker himself lending them the seed, which is yearly returned in kind with interest. A large paddy chest is built in the mission compound for the reception of this seed paddy; the profits of the hire, of course, going to the mission. Several of the settlers have made a good deal of money by thrift and business habits. The yield of this virgin soil is often enormous. Some of the villagers are also timber merchants, as well as cultivators. The village is called Mundakayam, and gives the name to the whole mission. The name is derived from a pool in the beautiful river which flows close by, Mundakayam meaning the pool of the *Mundi*, or curlew. What was the exact mission problem that Mr. Baker proposed to work out in the agricultural village of Mundakayam, I am unable to say.

It is in no way connected with the Arayans, except so far as it enables the missionary to reside near them during some months in the year. The district is too feverish to allow of a European residing there the year round. It is not impossible that Mr. Baker in the first instance thought that such a village of Syrian and other Christians, in connection with the Church of England, might exert some evangelistic influence on the neighbouring Arayans. I am not aware, however, that this has been the case, at least in any marked manner. Or it is possible that his object was a self-supporting mission.

I undertook a general superintendence of this mission, during Mr. Baker's absence in England a few years since. The Rev. Jacob Chandy, one of the native clergy, was associated with me in the charge; and most ably and conscientiously did he discharge his duties. Owing to the feverishness at certain seasons of the year of the districts near the Ghauts, he was not able to reside in the mission itself: but from his house at Cottayam he used periodically to visit the different stations scattered along a range of nearly thirty miles, performing nearly all the journeys on foot. During this time a deputation from a settlement of Arayans, which was about twenty miles from Mundakayam, came to Cottayam to ask for admission into the Christian Church. The head man of the village was with them, and they gave evidence at once of their sincerity by there and then renouncing their heathen rites and customs, and giving up the insignia of their false worship, the effigies of their ancestors, their devil-dancer's belt, bangles, and other implements. The belt and bangles I retained, and still possess. It was proposed by the people themselves that the remaining implements, chiefly of bronze, should be dedicated to the worship of the true God by being cast into a bell to call them to the house of prayer.

It was grand to see these men as they knelt down in my study, no doubt most of them for the first time in their lives, while the Rev. Jacob Chandy offered up a most suitable and impressive prayer, that the rest of their lives might be in accordance with that beginning. They rose with solemn faces, and I have every reason to believe that they were in earnest. It will, however, no doubt, always happen that, when men come forward in bodies to seek admission to Christian privileges, there will be at least some of them, while well disposed towards Christianity, yet at least equally anxious for the Christian privileges of time, as for those of eternity. This is no reason why we should reject them. But when we reckon the results of missionary work by the numbers of converts, we should always remember that in cases of large bodies applying at once for Christian privileges, we cannot expect that each individual is led by an overpowering sense of the realities of eternity and a personal conviction of the evil of sin, as would presumably be always the case when a single individual seeks baptism in the face of persecution. Accordingly I found these people ready with complaints as to various oppressions they suffered under Sircar and other officials, their being forced to provide a certain amount of wild honey, firewood for a neighbouring pagoda, and other matters, without remuneration. They also had a complaint that some of their cows had lately been killed, and others stolen by the tax-gatherers. But, worse than all, they had been beaten and expelled from lands their forefathers' sweat had bedewed for years untold. Thus a part at least of their ambition was evidently to be under European protection. Not that there is, to my mind, anything whatever unworthy in such a desire : but we should be careful to eliminate all such phases of missionary experience from legitimate missionary results.

These men were put under Christian instruction, and many of them were afterwards baptised by Mr. Baker. Nor have they failed to honour their Christian profession, according to the best of my knowledge.

It is several years since I first visited that part of our mission field. The country has changed greatly since then. There is now a beautiful carriage road from Cottayam to Mundakayam, which is gradually creeping up the Ghaut, and is destined ultimately to connect Travancore with Madura. It is due to the energy and foresight of Mr. Maltby, our late Resident. The mountains to the east of Mundakayam thus opened out are beginning to be studded with coffee plantations, and it is anticipated that this portion of the Southern Ghauts will prove to be a valuable sanitarium for us of the western coast. But when I first went eastwards, there was but a footpath through the nearly forty miles of jungle to Mundakayam. On this we went in Indian file. Starting early in the morning with palanquins, munjils, and poñies, we made the first ten miles of our journey before the sun became too hot for travelling in comfort. We stayed in a native compound under the shade of a cocoanut tope, where with eager appetites we took our breakfast. Resting there till some time after the sun had passed the meridian, we enjoyed the exuberance of tropical scenery about us, passing our time in reading, conversing, or wandering about. The jungle near was beautiful with the scarlet blossoms of the *Gloriosa superba* (the well-known creeping lily), and the nooks and corners with the lovely blue of the Travancore violet (*Torenia Asiatica*). Exquisite little winged lizards were chasing each other, or taking flying leaps from tree to tree, or basking in the sun on the cocoanut stems. Small squirrels, so well known all over India, were chirping like birds on the thatch of the native house. Flying squirrels too, flocks of green parrots with their shrill scream, and lovely little turtle doves now and again invaded our rendezvous. By evening we had reached our half-way house, the family residence of the chief man of the Mundakayam village, a well-to-do Syrian. Here we slept in a small but by no means uncomfortable room.

In the early morning, after a cup of coffee, and while the trees were still dripping heavily with dew, which falls in very great abundance in these leafy solitudes, we resumed our journey. Halting in another native compound till the fiercer heat of the midday sun had again somewhat abated, we completed our journey about seven o'clock in the evening. Some miles before reaching Mundakayam we entered a primeval forest. What a sight was this! Untouched, as we cannot doubt, since the creation of man, these woodland giants, huddled together, and owning no laws but those of nature, had for centuries grown, lived, and died in each other's arms. Standing in the roadway that had been cut through them by Madura merchants, who have long traded with Travancore by this route, the eye could scarcely penetrate the deepening gloom of those mysterious recesses. The dense and unbroken mass of foliage above receives, and all but quenches the light of day: beneath a perpetual sombre twilight reigns. And there what a tangled and inexplicable growth, the giant columns interlaced and bound together with no less gigantic creepers, till the forest is truly one in its compactness! Here and there were huge fragments of dead and rotting trunks that had long since ceased to expand their lofty crests in the glad sunlight, still hanging, as they may have been for how many years, suspended in mid air! And when the road laid open in their full proportions some of these veteran trees still in their prime, we could but exclaim, as we gazed upwards, how grand is creation! On the confines of this forest I obtained a large white thunbergia, and a convolvulus of purest yellow, both of which still flourish in my garden.

On emerging from the forest we came to the Mundakayam river, on the opposite side of which, on rising ground, we got our first glimpse of Mr. Baker's bungalow. It is surrounded by a complete earthwork—not to protect it from rifles, but from elephants, which abound in the neighbourhood, and are very destructive. They sometimes come down in a midnight raid on the village or plantations, and devour or trample down everything before them. I have sometimes heard them when I have been at Mundakayam, among the plantains, of which they are very fond. Grasping the plant with his trunk, the elephant gives it a kick near the ground, when up it comes with a boom like a distant gun. In the paddy grounds too they are very unwelcome visitors. Some protection is obtained by high and strong fences piled up of wood from the trees that have been felled ; but during the time the paddy is growing, there are always watchmen on the ground. Building a small hut up in a tree, they watch with loaded guns, which are generally sufficient to disperse the enemy. When alarmed they throw up their trunks, and scamper off like a herd of cows. The solitary, or rogue elephants are, however, perhaps the most dangerous beasts of the forest ; they are not unfrequently guilty of shedding human blood.

On arriving at Mundakayam we were soon reminded that we were destined to live there a truly woodland life. We were to have a taste for once of how all primitive men have fared. Our table was to be furnished almost entirely from the forest and jungle. The first stirring event that happened after our arrival was the bringing in of a splendid Samber, which had been shot during the afternoon by some Ullâdans, to whom Mr. Baker has given two houses near to his own. These Ullâdans are a true jungle people. They are not very numerous; but are found scattered up and down Travancore. They subsist chiefly on wild yams, arrowroot, and other esculents, which they find in the jungle, and for the grubbing up of which they are generally armed with a long pointed staff. They also further enjoy the fruits of the chase, and are adepts in the use of the bow and arrow. The arrow they use has an iron spear-like head; and so well are many of them versed in the use of this primitive weapon, that I have known of one of them cutting a wriggling cobra in half at the first shot. When armed with guns they make excellent sportsmen; and Mr. Baker encouraged some of them to live near him on this account. One of them also made him a very expert horse-keeper. In physiognomy and habits I fancied they reminded me of the English gipsies.

On the following day, which was Sunday, we found a large congregation in the Mundakayam church in the morning; and in the afternoon we walked about six miles through the jungles, and by the plantations of some of the Mundakayam people, to a small Arayan village, where we also had service. The people, I thought, seemed very attentive and well behaved. The Arayans do not strike one as being very highly intellectual; and they are for the most part short in stature, and not very long-lived. But the feverishness of the climate in the districts they inhabit is enough to account for any physical degeneracy of race. They are undoubtedly a purely Drâvidian people, but are as fair as the high-caste Hindus, proving that the aborigines of India were not black from race peculiarities, but only sometimes black through circumstances, such as I have mentioned in a former chapter.

Many of these men, I rejoice to say, prove themselves

to be worthy members of the Church of Christ. One man, whom I saw first at that time, who had been the head man of a village and a devil-dancer, had once endured a good deal of persecution on account of his adhesion to the Christian faith. It was not from men of his own class, but from men who knew that he would be less under their power as a Christian than he was when a heathen. On one occasion he nearly lost his life. He was bound hand and foot, and fastened down in a river with only his head above the water, exposed to the full blaze of a tropical sun; a species of torture which would probably soon have ended in death, had he not been rescued. But unmoved by these things he still continued steadfast. It is remarkable, however it is to be accounted for, whether as a mere effort of the imagination, or from a more real cause, that this man, having been a devil-dancer, is said to have declared that after his baptism he felt that some peculiar influence, which he was unable to describe, had altogether left him.

On the Monday morning we set out to ascend the mountains, the crest of which was about twelve miles from Mundakayam. We followed the route of the Madura merchants, several gangs of whom we met with their bullocks in single file laden with cotton cloths and chillies. The journey was very charming, the road lying often through exquisite scenery, and for a long way through forest lands which had been partly felled for cultivation. The plan after the forest is felled is to fire it; and terrific is the conflagration. The fire often catches the trees which are still standing: we passed several half burnt through and still smouldering. The most magnificent timbers are often thus sacrificed in great numbers; except when they are near the rivers, where they may be floated during a flood to the low country. There are no means for removing them that would pay expenses. Thus thousands of tons of blackwood, the Indian rosewood (*Dalbergia latifolia*), and other valuable trees, among which are some of the *Cedrelaceæ*, are lost to commerce. I cannot but think it a pity that some means should not be taken by the Government to prevent this waste. The most imposing trees to the eye are those which throw out great buttresses at the base, sometimes twenty or thirty feet high, and ten or twelve feet broad at the bottom, especially a species of cotton tree (*Bombax Malabaricum*), a congener of the famous African giant, the Baobah. One splendid tree I took note of on a hill side, of which we calculated that the stem could not have been less than seventy or eighty feet high to the first bough, and then the tree did not seem to be out of proportion. The whole height must have been considerably above two hundred feet, if not verging on three hundred feet. It is a singular fact that the jungle growth that springs up after these ancient forests have been felled, always consists of plants entirely distinct from the former trees, and equally distinct from anything in the neighbourhood. At an elevation of from 3000 to 5000 feet the result of felling a forest in Travancore is a crop of cardamoms (*Ellettaria cardamomum*).

When we reached the tableland called Peer Merd (more properly *Pír Mêdu*, Mêdu signifying high, or tableland), the cool air was most exhilarating. We were about 3500 feet above the level of the sea; some of the neighbouring peaks being at least 5000 feet. Even at this height there was no longer anything in the scenery distinctively tropical. The trees were all different from those below; and the palms and bamboos had disappeared, except a low kind of date palm. The whole of this tableland, except where it was broken up by rocks or precipices, was divided between tracts of pure grass and forest sholas, the boundaries between the two being as distinctly defined as though they had been marked out by artificial fences. We encamped near to one of the sholas for protection during the night from the land wind, sleeping in a tent that we had brought with us. At sundown we kindled a great fire near to our tent, for protection against the tigers and other wild beasts that abound, and for the comfort of our bearers and servants, for the night was very cold after our experience of the plains. And in the morning we were as fresh as mountain air could make us for our homeward journey.

Scarcely had a European foot up to that time trodden those breezy hills. Occasionally a sportsman had there sought the gaur, or bison, as they are more commonly called here; and no doubt the conservator of forests, who was also in charge of a cardamom district in the neighbourhood, had been there too. But it was a tract of country almost as yet unknown to Europeans. Since then Mr. Maltby's road has been nearly completed, and the sholas are one after another falling to the axe, to be replaced by coffee, the sholas being preferred to the grass lands for that purpose, on account of the greater depth and richness of soil.

On our return to Cottayam we took a new route, which lies through several villages, most of them containing Syrian or Roman Catholic churches. In one part of the jungle we turned aside for a time to examine a partially ruined and desolate pagoda, far from any houses. I have not unfrequently seen similar signs in Travancore of former large villages, or towns, in like ruined pagodas and other signs of a past population. Do these tell of the devastations of past wars? Or are they the results of desertion under an epidemic of the small-pox, or such disease? In this case the pagoda was built entirely of granite, and very elaborately carved. It was in the Tamil style; and may have been built by Madura merchants, not improbably in the midst of a colony from that coast.

In one of the villages we called upon a Roman Catholic priest, whom Mr. Baker had met before on his journeys to and from Mundakayam. He was very civil ; and offered us, I remember, some exceedingly sour and bad sherry. In one of his rooms adjoining the church we found his clerk busily employed in painting an image of the Virgin and Child, which he had himself carved in wood, the copy being a very gaudy affair belonging to a neighbouring church. and which they said had been sent out from Italy. We remonstrated with him, in as kind a way as possible, on the idolatry which they were thus encouraging amongst their people. He said their use of the image was not idolatry, they only used it as a help to devotion. We asked him whether an intelligent heathen would say very much the same thing. But I fear nothing we said made much impression on him. The night, which would have overtaken us long before reaching home, we spent in a Syrian church, the most wretched bedroom I ever honoured—not with a snore, for I did not close my eyes— but with my presence. We had no choice, for we could find no other shelter. Before dawn I was up and outside to breathe the fresh air, for I seemed to be suffocated all night. I found in the morning that I had been lying over a newly made grave.

There is but one other mission, that I have not, I think, touched upon ; I mean Kununkulum. It is the most northerly of all, and is in the Cochin native territory, about 15 miles from Trichoor. It was commenced many years ago, as an out-station, by Mr. Ridsdale, when he was at Cochin. It was subsequently an out-station of the Trichoor mission, and was then formed into a head station by the Rev. J. G. Benttler, who there built a bungalow in 1853, and finally a church, for which I had the honour and privilege of furnishing plans. There are several out-stations connected with it, but none of the congregations have hitherto been very large. The mission house and church are built near to a large and important Syrian bazaar. Fewer, however, of the Syrians have here joined our communion than has been the case in most of the Travancore missions. Most of the converts are from the Chogan and other heathen castes : but the majority of the people in the neighbourhood, as at Trichoor, being high-caste Âryans, the gospel seed appears to have fallen often upon barren ground.

But I must now draw my remarks on the native Church in India to a close. And, unless I am greatly mistaken, my readers will come to the same conclusions, as to general principles, as myself.

1. There is a striking discrepancy between the visible and tangible results of missionary operations, when we regard the un-Âryan classes on the one hand, and the Âryans on the other. The European missionary succeeds

apparently beyond the legitimate results of the gospel message on the one side ; and, on the other, as it appears to me, less than the gospel would warrant us to expect.

2. A European missionary is really at a disadvantage, by reason of his being a member of a dominant race ; for the results of his *protective* influence, which tells greatly on certain classes, should not be reckoned as the legitimate results of evangelism.

3. The fact that he is a foreigner prejudices the higher classes especially against his teaching (and here there is no desired protection to counterbalance the feeling). The early history of our connection with the Syrian Church alone abundantly illustrates this. Indeed, it stands to reason that a foreigner is the last man in the world likely to revolutionise a people. And history tells of no revolution so thorough as that proposed by the gospel.

4. The absence of the gift of tongues is a matter that ought to claim our most anxious consideration.

5. A pressing want in India is an indigenous Christian literature. This is only possible in native hands.

6. Everything points to the necessity for able and learned native evangelists to carry on the work Europeans have begun.

7. The funds of European Protestant Missionary

Societies would be better expended in preparing a powerful native aggressive agency than in sending out a multitudinous European one.

One more topic, and my desultory notes shall close. We are now reaching a most important crisis in the missionary history of South India : a crisis that to my mind points in exactly the same direction as the rest of my missionary experience—the need for a *highly educated native agency.* And here need I say how cordially I endorse the Church Missionary Society's motto, ' Spiritual men for spiritual work ! ' But let us not forget to add to that, *able men for difficult work.* The crisis to which I refer is the growing desire to separate every congregation. where it is possible, from the funds and immediate control of thé home committees. It is a new idea, and we know how men revel in a new idea. Theoretically it is correct, grand. But what does it involve? The necessity more than ever for *leaders* in the native Church.

The system that is fast coming upon us, as I too much fear, of leaving the infant congregations to choose the best men as pastors that they are at present able themselves to afford, will have an undoubted tendency, if it be not counteracted, to lower the tone of education among mission agents. I see strong symptoms of it already. What we shall still want in the native Church will be men of mark and power : and these will not develop themselves among the branches of the wild vine ; they must be cultivated. The State education is fast giving us a number of learned infidels : the Church must rise in emulation, and, using the same weapon, education, give us learned divines. May the great Head of the Church, who alone can give us success in His own work, dispose the hearts of Englishmen to well weigh these most momentous matters.

Finally, there is one idea, that I cannot pass by, that has tended greatly to cripple our mission efforts, but that appears to lurk in almost every European mind as to the Hindus ; and that is, that there are certain things of which they are not *yet* capable. The missionary who is an infidel as to the theory of progressive development, and firmly believes in the unity of the human race, still tells you that the Hindu is not *yet* sufficiently developed (that is, in himself, quite irrespective of education); that he is not yet capable of great responsibilities. What! Does he then believe in physical race development? No; he says. But his acts belie him. Depend upon it Augustine had much the same ideas as to the Saxons, whom he found in England. There is a bias in human nature which tends to encourage the belief in a man, that all who are beneath him by force of circumstances, are beneath him in intelligence and capacity. But it has no foundation in, truth. Least of all people are the Hindus beneath us in intelligence. On this false assumption it is, for instance, that the railway officials have not yet allowed a Hindu to drive an engine on their metals. But let the falsehood die out at least in our missions. Who cannot see that it reacts upon the natives, who in too many cases seem to think that Europeans alone are responsible for spreading the gospel among the nations?

APPENDIX.

RAINFALL AT COTTAYAM AND METEOROLOGICAL NOTES.

The two following Tables represent the rainfall for 1861 and 1865. The average lies between the two; the fall in 1861 having been below, in 1865 above, the average.

December, January, and February are usually without rain. Evening showers commence in March or April from thunder-clouds that gather about the mountains in the East. The S.W. monsoon sets in in the end of May or beginning of June; it closes by the end of August. September gives us occasional showers. In October and November the N.E. monsoon often sends us heavy storms.

Cottayam is, as nearly as possible, in lat. $9\frac{1}{2}$ N., long. $76\frac{1}{2}$ E. It is 17 miles from the coast, and about 150 feet above the level of the sea.

The average of rainfall at Cottayam is very much greater than at Trevandrum.

Rainfall, 1861.

Date	March	April	May	June	July	Aug.	Sept.	Oct.	Nov.
1	(Inches)	2·17	· ·	17·5	22·2	· ·	· ·	1·	· ·
2	· ·	· ·	· ·	· ·	3·3	·15	11·1	4·55	25·
3	· ·	· ·	2·35	14·7	4·7	· ·	5·7	· ·	· ·
4	· ·	· ·	·65	19·8	·17	· ·	7·	· ·	1·75
5	· ·	· ·	· ·	3·	· ·	17·5	4·5	· ·	18·6
6	· ·	2·1	·45	·87	11·75	30·25	1·3	· ·	·9
7	· ·	· ·	· ·	8·9	· ·	9·	2·6	· ·	·75
8	· ·	· ·	· · ·	·57	19·1	9·75	· ·	· ·	· ·
9	· ·	· ·	· ·	2·6	20·45	1·12	19·3	· ·	· ·
10	· ·	· ·	· ·	6·25	15·5	2·	·15	· ·	· ·
11	· ·	15·6	· ·	1·55	16·	· ·	1·5	· ·	· ·
12	· ·	1·2	· ·	2·22	12·8	1·22	2·6	· ·	4·3
13	· ·	· ·	· ·	4·65	7·85	8·32	1·65	· ·	·95
14	· ·	· ·	· ·	2·52	· ·	12·25	1·8	· ·	· ·
15	· ·	10·27	7·25	9·82	18·6	6·8	· ·	· ·	· ·
16	· ·	· ·	· ·	8·47	1·32	3·1	15·2	· ·	1·95
17	· ·	2·67	· ·	2·35	2·75	1·7	2·	· ·	13·5
18	11·	·6	· ·	4·45	4·3	· ·	·35	8·8	4·
19	3·5	3·12	· ·	22·85	4·5	22·3	· ·	3·15	· ·
20	5·4	1·2	9·	1·17	5·25	2·8	·3	· ·	24·15
21	1·37	· ·	· ·	·52	· ·	4·2	3·	·2	· ·
22	11·03	2·45	50·2	20·67	5·1	24·3	· ·	· ·	· ·
23	1·15	10·	3·3	· ·	4·65	·07	·6	· ·	· ·
24	· ·	· ·	2·5	·8	2·2	· ·	3·6	1·9	· ·
25	· ·	· ·	14·35	1·72	1·9	· ·	·3	· ·	5·6
26	· ·	2·52	· ·	10·75	11·	·82	·9	· ·	· ·
27	·27	·45	·1	4·12	·85	· ·	5·5	1·	· ·
28	· ·	· ·	· ·	8·57	· ·	7·7	4·45	3·4	3·2
29	· ·	8·37	10·62	7·7	· ·	13·55	· ·	· ·	· ·
30	· ·	5·6	34·	· ·	· ·	16·8	4·8	· ·	· ·
31	· ·	· ·	36·7	· ·	· ·	13·25	· ·	· ·	· ·
Total	33·72	68·32	171·47	189·09	196·24	198·95	100·2	24·	104·65

GRAND TOTAL .. 1086·64 = 108·664 inches.

In January, February, and December of this year there was
no rain.

Rainfall, 1865.

Date	March	April	May	June	July	Aug.	Sept.	Oct.	Nov.
1	(Inches)	Slight	1·5	6·	·45	5·87	·32	. .	·5
2	. .	rains	1·	1·5	. .	·25	. .	. .	. .
3	. .	on 1st,	. .	1·	4·85	·21	. .	. .	. .
4	. .	2nd &	2·75	·75	2·59	. .	·11	. .	·05
5	. .	3rd	·75	1·	2·21	·80	·16	. .	. .
6	. .	not	. .	1·34	1·43	·07	·2	. .	. .
7	. .	gauged	. .	1·37	1·05	·27	. .	. .	. .
8	. .	. .	·70	·05	1·89	·79	·57	. .	·96
9	. .	. .	1·10	1·25	·38	·55	·79	. .	2·02
10	. .	. .	·5	1·44	. .	1·30	. .	. .	·4
11	. .	. .	. .	1·1	·66	. .	·62	. .	. .
12	. .	. .	. .	2·	1·74	1·30	·15	. .	. .
13	. .	·5	. .	·88	1·65	. .	·13	. .	. .
14	. .	·25	2·	1·3	1·74	1·68	·23	. .	. .
15	. .	. .	. .	·76	4·43	·4	·21	. .	. .
16	. .	. .	. .	·59	5·09	1·03	·41	·95	. .
17	. .	·24	. .	·22	- ·31	. .	. .	. .	. .
18	. .	. .	. .	. .	·75	. .	. .	·45	. .
19	. .	1·	. .	2·65	·35	. .	. .	. .	. .
20	. .	. .	. .	1·2	1·65	. .	·05	·59	. .
21	. .	. .	. .	2·1	3·39	·01	. .	. .	. .
22	. .	·73	. .	. .	1·19	. .	. .	. .	. .
23	. .	. .	. .	·1	. .	. .	. .	·53	. .
24	. .	1·27	2·5	·16	2·8	·25	. .	3·2	. .
25	. .	3·	. .	·69	1·14	1·8	. .	·66	. .
26	. .	. .	. .	. .	·25	3·36	. .	·9	. .
27	. .	. .	. .	·82	1·54	. .	·07	1·98	. .
28	. .	·5	. .	·73	1·70	1·08	. .	·6	. .
29	. .	. .	1·87	·9	·46	. .	. .	. .	. .
30	. .	. .	. .	1·95	. .	. .	. .	1·08	. .
31	. .	. .	1·25	. .	·80	·22	. .	1·63	. .
Total	. .	7·49	15·92	33·85	46·49	21·24	4·02	12·57	3·93

GRAND TOTAL .. 145·51 inches.

In January, February, March, and December of this year there was no rain.

The following notes are selected from the observations of several years, as illustrative of the nature of the climate. They show the general character of the atmospheric pressure, the temperature of the air, and of evaporation, and the state of the wind and clouds for the several months.

Day of Month	Hour	Barometer	Thermometer		Wind — Sea Breeze			Land Breeze
			Dry	Wet	Sets in	Force	Drops	
Jan. 6	7 A.M.	29·94	72	..	10 A.M.	fair breeze	5 P.M.	Land breeze sets in about 6 or 7 P.M. more remarkable for coolness than velocity. Ceases about 7.30, or 8 in the morning.
„ 6	11 A.M.	29·95	80					
„ 6	2 P.M.	29·95	84					
„ 7	7 A.M.	29·95	72	..	12	slight	4 P.M.	
„ 7	9 A.M.	29·95	76					
„ 7	12	29·95	78					
„ 7	2.30 P.M.	29·95	82					
„ 7	10 P.M.	29·95	74					
„ 13	10 A.M.	29·96	84	77	12	slight	3.30	
„ 13	1 P.M.	29·96	86	76				
„ 13	4 P.M.	29·96	85	75				
„ 17	10 A.M.	29·96	81	75	10 A.M.	good breeze	6 P.M.	
„ 17	12	29·96	85	76				
„ 17	2.30 P.M.	29·	88	78				
„ 17	4.30 P.M.	29·87	85	76				
„ 26	8 A.M.	30·02	78	73	10.30	slight	5 P.M.	
„ 26	10.30 A.M.	30·02	82	75				
„ 26	12	30·01	83	73				
„ 26	4 P.M.	29·94	84	73				
Feb. 9	10 A.M.	29·97	84					
„ 9	2 P.M.	29·88	86	76	11 A.M.	slight	4 P.M.	hot land breeze from 10 to 3
„ 18	2 P.M.	29·86	88	77	9 A.M.	strong	4 P.M.	
„ 21	12	29·87	90	79	. . .	nil		
„ 21	3.30 P.M.	29·8	90	78	. . .	slight		
„ 23	10 A.M.	29·8	84					
„ 23	12	29·88	89	78	9 A.M.	strong	6 P.M.	
„ 23	5 P.M.	29·82	88	78				
March 19	8 A.M.	29·9	80					
„ 19	2 P.M.	29·82	86	..	9 A.M.	strong	6.30	
„ 20	9 A.M.	29·83	81	..	9	strong	6.30	slight with rain
„ 20	1 P.M.	29·84	85					
„ 21	2 P.M.	29·88	79	..	. . .	nil		
April 10	8 A.M.	29·89	85	81	7.30	strong	7.30	
„ 10	12	29·87	93	82				

Day of Month	Hour	Barometer	Thermometer Dry	Wet	Wind — Sea Breeze Sets in	Force	Drops	Land Breeze
April 10	9 P.M.	29·95	87					
,, 11	7 A.M.	29·87	84	..	9	gentle	5	
,, 11	8 A.M.	29·89	85	81				
,, 11	9 A.M.	29·91	86	82				
,, 11	11 A.M.	29·91	90	82				
,, 11	12	29·87	92	82				March and April land breeze sets in at 7 P.M., lasts till 7 A.M.
,, 11	1.30 P.M.	29·85	91	82				
,, 11	3 P.M.	29·85	93					
,, 11	9 P.M.	29·9	87					
,, 11	11 P.M.	29·92	85					
May 22	12	29·78	83					
,, 31	8 A.M.	29·76	76		The monsoon S.W. wind takes the place of the sea-breeze from May to Sept., blowing almost constantly, but with varying force.	During this time the heavens are heavily clouded.		
,, 31	12	29·78	82					
,, 31	5 P.M.	29·72	80					
June 1	8 A.M.	29·8	78					
,, 3	8 A.M.	29·77	78					
,, 3	3 P.M.	29·73	84					
,, 14	8 A.M.	29·91	80	78				No land breeze from June to September.
,, 14	12	29·86	84	80				
,, 15	8 A.M.	29·83	79	77				
,, 15	3 P.M.	29·83	80	75				
,, 21	8 A.M.	29·90	80	79				
,, 21	10 A.M.	29·93	82	79				
,, 21	3 P.M.	29·85	85					
July 22	8 A.M.	29·83	77					
,, 22	12	. .	83					
,, 27	8 A.M.	29·87	76					
Aug. 11	8 A.M.	29·84	77					
,, 25	8 A.M.	29·87	77					
,, 25	12	. .	82					
Sept. 15	8 A.M.	29·97	80					slight land breeze at night
,, 15	12	. .	84					
Oct. 12	8 A.M.	29·90	80		During Oct. and Nov. the sea-breeze fitful and un-certain.			
,, 12	12	. .	84					
,, 26	8 A.M.	29·92	79	79				
,, 27	8 A.M.	29·93	79	78				
,, 28	8 A.M.	29·93	79	78				no land breeze
,, 28	12	. .	83	79				
,, 30	8 A.M.	29·88	80					
,, 30	11 A.M.	. .	82	81				
,, 30	12	. .	84	79				
,, 30	3 P.M.	. .	83	78				
Nov. 4	8 A.M.	29·95	79					

Day of Month		Hour	Baro-meter	Thermo-meter		Wind				Land Breeze
							Sea Breeze			
				Dry	Wet	Sets in	Force	Drops		
Nov.	4	12	29·96	83						
Dec.	5	8 A.M.	29·97	78	..	11	slight	3		
,,	5	12	29·96	84						
,,	21	12	30·02	83	78	1	slight	6		
,,	21	9 P.M.	30·02	79	78					
,,	22	8 A.M.	30·02	77	74					
,,	22	12	30·02	84	..	1.30	slight	3		
,,	22	9 P.M.	30·02	80						
,,	23	7 A.M.	30·02	69						
,,	23	8.30 A.M.	30·02	77						
,,	23	12	30·02	83	78	10.30	fitful	5		
,,	23	2.30 P.M.	29·9	84	77					
,,	23	4 P.M.	29·88	84						
,,	23	8.30 P.M.	29·94							
,,	23	9 P.M.	29·96	78	75					
,,	26	11 A.M.	29·97	82	..	10	gentle breeze			
,,	27	9 A.M.	29·97	78						
,,	27	11.30 A.M.	29·96	79	..	11	slight	3		
,,	27	4.30 P.M.	29·89	81						
,,	27	9.30 P.M.	29·95	79						
,,	31	6.30 A.M.	29·91	75						
,,	31	8.30 A.M.	29·94	76						
,,	31	11 A.M.	29·96	81						
,,	31	12.30 P.M.	29·94	82						
,,	31	7 P.M.	29·88	79						
,,	31	10 P.M.	29·92	77						

Land Breeze column: Slight land breeze at night from 7 to 7.

The highest reading for the barometer during ten years was in the months of December and January, 30·02 ; the lowest was on May 31, 1865, at 4 P.M. The S.W. monsoon set in during the night, when the rain-gauge overflowed. The glass stood at 29·67 : thus the greatest range of the barometer in my experience has been only ·35 inch.

The heaviest fall of rain was 12 inches in 12 hours, as registered at Allepie in October, 1863.

The highest temperature was 93° in the month of April ; the lowest 62° at night in January.

The average midday heat is 84°.

OCCASIONAL.

1860. Jan. 1. 6.30 A.M.—Thermometer on grass, 67°.

" " 8.30 A.M.—Heavens spread with fleecy cirri, slowly moving westward. Mountains hazy. Slight uncertain breezes from the north.

" " 11 A.M.—Cumuli in west. Small detached clouds, intensely white, moving from north to south. Below, slight sea-breeze (W. to E.)

" " 12 M.—More sea-breeze.

" " 10 P.M.—Thermometer on grass, 70°. Watery vapour in air seen by moon's halo. Slight land breeze.

" " 6. 11.30 A.M.—Heavens clear, except few cirri. West horizon hazy. Mountains' distinct.

" " 7. 6 A.M.—Thermometer on grass, 62°. Heavens clear, except very faint cirri.

" " 2.30 P.M.—Sky cloudless.

" " 10 P.M. Full moon. Atmosphere clear. Light clouds flying westward, indicating pretty strong current above. Below perfect calm.

" " 8. Heavens clouded; clouds going westward: upper current.

" " 12. Heavens cloudless. Mountains well defined. Sky intense blue. Up to 8 A.M. the barometer has been absolutely stationary since noon of the 6th.

" " 14. Sky cloudless; deep blue.

" " 17. Since noon cumuli arise in East, spread over half the sky, indicating a strong current from E. to W.: below strong sea-breeze (W. to E.)

1860. Jan. 25. Morning cloudless; after 11 A.M. clouds show western current above.

„ „ 28. Sky cloudless.

„ „ 30. Cirri indicate *high* current from S.W. to N.E.

„ „ 31. Clouds indicate upper current from N.E. to S.W.

„ Feb. 13. 7 A.M.—Upper current from W. to E.

„ „ 18. East dark. Thunder in distance.

„ „ 19. In evening minute quantity of rain.

„ „ 22. Slight thunder in distance in evening.

„ „ 27. Heavens clear; mountains distinct.

1861. Mar. 17. Towards evening for several days dark clouds in the East, ending in a thunderstorm at sunset.

„ „ 19. 2 P.M.—East very dark.

„ „ 21. 2 P.M.—Rain; 6.30 P.M., rain; no thunder.

„ „ 22. Early rain from 4 to 7 A.M.

„ „ 29. 1 P.M.—Mountains clear. Cumuli in East.

„ April 9. Light rain evening and night.

„ „ 10. Light rain evening and night.

„ „ 11. 11 A.M.—More rain.

„ „ 12. Rather strong southerly wind. Barometer low (29·72).

„ May 15. Looks almost like S.W. monsoon. Rain in the night from the West, with thunder and lightning.

„ „ 16. Strong West wind this morning

„ „ 22. Monsoon fully set in.

1862. March 5. Thunder lately in the evening or early night.

„ „ 14. Every evening more or less thunder. Slight rains sometimes at night.

1864. June 15. Monsoon set in June 1st, precisely. Rained incessantly for about a fortnight. During that time barometer low. Sea distinctly heard at Cottayam. (Average of barometer from June 1–15, 29·73.)

1864. June 23. Barometer risen 29·97.   Sea not audible.

„   „ 25. Showery weather.   Sea audible this morning.

1865. April 4. No rain this year till April 1st, and again on the 2nd.   On the 3rd, at 4.30 P.M., a strong gale suddenly came from about N.E.; though it lasted only about 15 minutes, many trees were blown down.   An immense Âla (*Ficus religiosa*) near the Mission Church was uprooted; the diameter of the upturned root is about 25 feet. Most of the large Casuarino trees in the church-yard were snapped off or lost large boughs. Such a wind not known here for 20 years, according to the natives.

„   „ 10. Thermometer in verandah window, in the sea-breeze, 94°; in the middle of the house, 93°.

„   „   9 P.M.—Light clouds indicate two currents in the air; the higher from East to West, the lower from West to East.

The barometer, as a rule, falls after 10 A.M., rising again after 6 or 7 P.M.   (See Table for April 10 and 11.)

„   „ 11. 12 M.—Clouds show upper current from East to West, and a lower one from West to East.

„   „   1.30 P.M.—Upper and lower currents seem to be getting mixed, generating whirling clouds.

„   „   3 P.M.—Heavens clouded.   Pretty strong sea-breeze below.

„   May 31. West dark and watery.   Sea occasionally audible. Rain most of the day.

„   June 1. Monsoon set in.

„   „   2. Squall in the night.

„   „ 21. Sea audible until to-day.

„   July 16. The highest flood in the rivers remembered for twelve years.

1865. Oct. 15. N.E. monsoon rain; chiefly in the night.
1866. June 9. First genuine monsoon rain.
  ..   Oct. 18. Thunderstorm in the night.
  „   Nov. 9. Thunderstorm in the North.
  ..   Dec. 13. Severe thunderstorm in the evening.
  „   „   14. 12 M.—Slight shadings of cirrus.
  „   „   9 P.M.—Sky cloudless.
  .,   ., 15. 12 M.—Few cirri.
  „   ..   8.30 P.M.—Sky cloudless. Zodiacal light very
                   striking; though open, not well defined.

  ..   .,   10 P.M.—From appearance of Jupiter through
                   telescope, apparently a good deal of attenuated
                   vapour in the air, causing an undulation, like
                   little globes chasing each other round him. No
                   cloud visible.

  ..   ., 29. 7.30 A.M.—High up cirrus; below dazzling white
                   cloud, drifting eastwards; cirrus slowly moving
                   West.

  .,   .,   10 P.M.—Thermometer on grass, 68°; in the
                   house, 78°.

LONDON: PRINTED BY
SPOTTISWOODE AND CO., NEW-STREET SQUARE
AND PARLIAMENT STREET

A Catalogue

OF

HENRY S. KING & CO.'S

PUBLICATIONS.

LONDON:

65, CORNHILL, AND 12, PATERNOSTER ROW.

1873.

POLITICAL WOMEN.
By SUTHERLAND MENZIES.
2 vols. post 8vo. *[In the press.*

EGYPT AS IT IS.
By HERR HEINRICH STEPHAN,
The German Postmaster-General.
Crown 8vo. With a new Map of the Country. *[Preparing.*

IMPERIAL GERMANY.
By FREDERIC MARTIN,
Author of "The Statesman's Year Book," &c. *[Preparing.*

THE GOVERNMENT OF THE NATIONAL DEFENCE.
By JULES FAVRE.
Demy 8vo. 1 vol. *[Preparing.*

'ILÂM ĔN NÂS. Historical Tales and Anecdotes of the Times of the Early Khalifahs.
TRANSLATED FROM THE ARABIC ORIGINALS
By Mrs. GODFREY CLERK,
Author of "The Antipodes and Round the World."
Crown 8vo. *[In the press.*

IN STRANGE COMPANY;
Or, The NOTE BOOK of a ROVING CORRESPONDENT.
By JAMES GREENWOOD,
"The Amateur Casual."
Crown 8vo. *[Preparing.*

THEOLOGY AND MORALITY.
BEING ESSAYS BY THE REV. J. LLEWELLYN DAVIES.
1 vol., 8vo. *[Preparing.*

65, *Cornhill; & 12, Paternoster Row, London.*

THE RECONCILIATION OF RELIGION AND SCIENCE.

BEING ESSAYS BY THE REV. J. W. FOWLE, M.A.

1 vol., 8vo.　*[In the press.*

A NEW VOLUME OF ACADEMIA ESSAYS.

EDITED BY THE MOST REVEREND ARCHBISHOP MANNING.

[Preparing.

THE FAYOUM; OR, ARTISTS IN EGYPT.

A TOUR WITH M. GÉRÔME AND OTHERS.

BY J. LENOIR.　TRANSLATED BY MRS. CASHEL HOEY.

Crown 8vo, cloth.　Illustrated.　*[In the press.*

TENT LIFE WITH ENGLISH GYPSIES IN NORWAY.　BY HUBERT SMITH.

In 8vo, cloth.　Five full-page Engravings, and 31 smaller Illustrations, with Map of the Country, showing Routes.　Price 21*s.*

THE GATEWAY TO THE POLYNIA; OR, A VOYAGE TO SPITZBERGEN.

BY CAPTAIN JOHN C. WELLS, R.N.

In 8vo, cloth.　Profusely illustrated.　*[In the press.*

A WINTER IN MOROCCO.

BY AMELIA PERRIER.

Large crown 8vo.　Illustrated.　Price 10*s.* 6*d.*　*[In the press.*

AN AUTUMN TOUR IN THE UNITED STATES AND CANADA.

BY LIEUT.-COLONEL JULIUS GEORGE MEDLEY.

Crown 8vo.　Price 5*s.*　*[In the press.*

65, Cornhill; & 12, Paternoster Row, London.

IRELAND IN 1872.

A TOUR OF OBSERVATION, WITH REMARKS ON IRISH PUBLIC QUESTIONS.
By Dr. JAMES MACAULAY.

Crown 8vo. 7s. 6d.

THE GREAT DUTCH ADMIRALS.

By JACOB DE LIEFDE.

Crown 8vo. Illustrated. Price 5s.

NEWMARKET AND ARABIA:

AN EXAMINATION OF THE DESCENT OF RACERS AND COURSERS.

By ROGER D. UPTON.

Crown 8vo. Illustrated. Price 9s.

FIELD AND FOREST RAMBLES OF A NATURALIST IN NEW BRUNSWICK.

WITH NOTES AND OBSERVATIONS ON THE NATURAL
HISTORY OF EASTERN CANADA.

By A. LEITH ADAMS, M.A., &c.,
Author of "Wanderings of a Naturalist in India," &c., &c.

In 8vo, cloth. Illustrated. 14s.

BOKHARA: ITS HISTORY AND CONQUEST.

By Professor ARMINIUS VÀMBÈRY,
Of the University of Pesth, Author of " Travels in Central Asia," &c.

Demy 8vo. 18s.

" We conclude with a cordial recommendation of this valuable book. In former years, Mr. Vambery gave ample proofs of his powers as an observant, easy, and vivid writer. In the present work his moderation, scholarship, insight, and occasionally very impressive style, have raised him to the dignity of an historian."—*Saturday Review.*

" Almost every page abounds with composition of peculiar merit, as well as with an account of some thrilling event more exciting than any to be found in an ordinary work of fiction."—*Morning Post.*

"A work compiled from many rare, private, and unavailable manuscripts and records, which consequently cannot fail to prove a mine of delightful Eastern lore to the Oriental scholar."—*Liverpool Albion.*

OVER VOLCANOES;

Or, THROUGH FRANCE AND SPAIN IN 1871.

By A. KINGSMAN.

Crown 8vo. 10s. 6d.

"The writer's tone is so pleasant, his language is so good, and his spirits are so fresh, buoyant, and exhilarating, that you find yourself inveigled into reading, for the thousand-and-first time, a description of a Spanish bull-fight."—*Illustrated London News.*

"The adventures of our tourists are related with a good deal of pleasantry and humorous dash, which make the narrative agreeable reading."—*Public Opinion.*

"A work which we cordially recommend to such readers as desire to know something of Spain as she is to-day. Indeed, so fresh and original is it, that we could have wished that it had been a bigger book than it is."—*Literary World.*

ALEXIS DE TOCQUEVILLE.

CORRESPONDENCE AND CONVERSATIONS WITH NASSAU W. SENIOR FROM 1833 TO 1859.

EDITED BY MRS. M. C. M. SIMPSON.

2 vols., large post 8vo. 21s.

"Another of those interesting journals in which Mr. Senior has, as it were, crystallized the sayings of some of those many remarkable men with whom he came in contact."—*Morning Post.*

"A book replete with knowledge and thought."—*Quarterly Review.*

"An extremely interesting book, and a singularly good illustration of the value which, even in an age of newspapers and magazines, memoirs have and will always continue to have for the purposes of history."—*Saturday Review.*

JOURNALS KEPT IN FRANCE AND ITALY,

FROM 1848 TO 1852.

WITH A SKETCH OF THE REVOLUTION OF 1848.

BY THE LATE NASSAU WILLIAM SENIOR.

Edited by his Daughter, M. C. M. SIMPSON.

In 2 vols., post 8vo. 24s.

"The present volume gives us conversations with some of the most prominent men in the political history of France and Italy . . . as well as with others whose names are not so familiar or are hidden under initials. Mr. Senior has the art of inspiring all men with frankness, and of persuading them to put themselves unreservedly in his hands without fear of private circulation."—*Athenæum.*

"The book has a genuine historical value."—*Saturday Review.*

"No better, more honest, and more readable view of the state of political society during the existence of the second Republic could well be looked for."—*Examiner.*

A MEMOIR OF NATHANIEL HAWTHORNE,

WITH STORIES NOW FIRST PUBLISHED IN THIS COUNTRY.

BY H. A. PAGE.

Large post 8vo. *7s. 6d.*

"The Memoir is followed by a criticism of Hawthorne as a writer; and the criticism, though we should be inclined to dissent from particular sentiments, is, on the whole, very well written, and exhibits a discriminating enthusiasm for one of the most fascinating of novelists."—*Saturday Review.*

"Seldom has it been our lot to meet with a more appreciative delineation of character than this Memoir of Hawthorne . . . Mr. Page deserves the best thanks of every admirer of Hawthorne for the way in which he has gathered together these relics, and given them to the world, as well as for his admirable portraiture of their author's life and character."—*Morning Post.*

"We sympathise very heartily with an effort of Mr. H. A. Page to make English readers better acquainted with the life and character of Nathaniel Hawthorne . . . He has done full justice to the fine character of the author of 'The Scarlet Letter.'"—*Standard.*

"He has produced a well-written and complete Memoir . . . A model of literary work of art."—*Edinburgh Courant.*

MEMOIRS OF LEONORA CHRISTINA,

DAUGHTER OF CHRISTIAN IV. OF DENMARK:

WRITTEN DURING HER IMPRISONMENT IN THE BLUE TOWER OF THE ROYAL PALACE AT COPENHAGEN, 1663—1685.

TRANSLATED BY F. E. BUNNETT,

Translator of Grimm's "Life of Michael Angelo," &c.

With an Autotype portrait of the Princess. Medium 8vo. *12s. 6d.*

"A valuable addition to history."—*Daily News.*

"This remarkable autobiography, in which we gratefully recognize a valuable addition to the tragic romance of history."—*Spectator.*

LIVES OF ENGLISH POPULAR LEADERS.

No. 1. STEPHEN LANGTON.

BY C. EDMUND MAURICE.

Crown 8vo. *7s. 6d.*

"Mr. Maurice has written a very interesting book, which may be read with equal pleasure and profit."—*Morning Post.*

"The volume contains many interesting details, including some important documents. It will amply repay those who read it, whether as a chapter of the constitutional history of England or as the life of a great Englishman."—*Spectator.*

65, *Cornhill; & 12, Paternoster Row, London.*

ECHOES OF A FAMOUS YEAR.

By HARRIET PARR,

Author of "The Life of Jeanne d'Arc," "In the Silver Age," &c.

Crown 8vo. 8*s.* 6*d.*

"A graceful and touching, as well as truthful account of the Franco-Prussian War. Those who are in the habit of reading books to children will find this at once instructive and delightful."—*Public Opinion.*

"Miss Parr has the great gift of charming simplicity of style; and if children are not interested in her book, many of their seniors will be."—*British Quarterly Review.*

NORMAN MACLEOD, D.D.,

A CONTRIBUTION TOWARDS HIS BIOGRAPHY.

By ALEXANDER STRAHAN.

Crown 8vo, sewed. Price One Shilling.

*** Reprinted, with numerous Additions and many Illustrations from Sketches by Dr. Macleod, from the *Contemporary Review.*

CABINET PORTRAITS.

BIOGRAPHICAL SKETCHES OF LIVING STATESMEN.

By T. WEMYSS REID.

1 vol. crown 8vo. 7*s.* 6*d.*

"We have never met with a work which we can more unreservedly praise. The sketches are absolutely impartial."—*Athenæum.*

"We can heartily commend his work."—*Standard.*

"The 'Sketches of Statesmen' are drawn with a master hand."—*Yorkshire Post.*

THE ENGLISH CONSTITUTION.

By WALTER BAGEHOT.

A New Edition, revised and corrected, with an Introductory Dissertation on recent changes and events. Crown 8vo. 7*s.* 6*d.*

"A pleasing and clever study on the department of higher politics."—*Guardian.*

"No writer before him had set out so

clearly what the efficient part of the English Constitution really is."—*Pall Mall Gazette.*

"Clear and practical."—*Globe.*

REPUBLICAN SUPERSTITIONS.

ILLUSTRATED BY THE POLITICAL HISTORY OF THE UNITED STATES.

INCLUDING A CORRESPONDENCE WITH M. LOUIS BLANC.

By MONCURE D. CONWAY.

Crown 8vo. 5*s.*

"Au moment où j'écris ceci, je reçois d'un écrivain très distingué d'Amérique, M. Conway, une brochure qui est un frappant tableau des maux et des dangers qui résultent aux Etats Unis de l'institu-

tion présidentielle."—*M. Louis Blanc.*

"A very able exposure of the most plausible fallacies of Republicanism, by a writer of remarkable vigour and purity of style."—*Standard.*

THE GENIUS of CHRISTIANITY UNVEILED, BEING ESSAYS BY WILLIAM GODWIN.

AUTHOR OF " POLITICAL JUSTICE," ETC.

Never before published. 1 vol. crown 8vo. 7s. 6d.

" Interesting as the frankly expressed thoughts of a remarkable man, and as a contribution to the history of scepticism."—*Extract from the Editor's Preface.*

" Few have thought more clearly and directly than William Godwin, or expressed their reflections with more simplicity and unreserve."—*Examiner.*

" The deliberate thoughts of Godwin deserve to be put before the world for reading and consideration."—*Athenæum.*

THE PELICAN PAPERS.

REMINISCENCES AND REMAINS OF A DWELLER IN THE WILDERNESS.

By JAMES ASHCROFT NOBLE.

Crown 8vo. 6s.

" Written somewhat after the fashion of Mr. Helps' 'Friends in Council.'"—*Examiner.*

" Will well repay perusal by all thoughtful and intelligent readers."—*Liverpool Leader.*

" The 'Pelican Papers' make a very readable volume."—*Civilian.*

SOLDIERING AND SCRIBBLING.

By ARCHIBALD FORBES,

Of the *Daily News,*

Author of " My Experience of the War between France and Germany."

Crown 8vo. 7s. 6d.

" All who open it will be inclined to read through for the varied entertainment which it affords."—*Daily News.*

" There is a good deal of instruction to outsiders touching military life, in this volume."—*Evening Standard.*

" There is not a paper in the book which is not thoroughly readable and worth reading."—*Scotsman.*

BRIEFS AND PAPERS.

BEING SKETCHES OF THE BAR AND THE PRESS.

By TWO IDLE APPRENTICES.

Crown 8vo. 7s. 6d.

" They are written with spirit and knowledge, and give some curious glimpses into what the majority will regard as strange and unknown territories."—*Daily News.*

" This is one of the best books to while away an hour and cause a generous laugh that we have come across for a long time."—*John Bull.*

THE INTERNATIONAL SCIENTIFIC SERIES.

MESSRS. HENRY S. KING & CO. have the pleasure to announce that under this title they are issuing a SERIES of POPULAR TREATISES, embodying the results of the latest investigations in the various departments of Science at present most prominently before the world.

Although these Works are not specially designed for the instruction of beginners, still, as they are intended to address the *non-scientific public*, they will be, as far as possible, explanatory in character, and free from technicalities. The object of each author will be to bring his subject as near as he can to the general reader.

The volumes will all be crown 8vo size, well printed on good paper, strongly and elegantly bound, and will sell in this country at a price *not exceeding Five Shillings*.

☞ Prospectuses of the Series may be had of the Publishers.

Already published,

THE FORMS OF WATER IN RAIN AND RIVERS, ICE AND GLACIERS.

BY J. TYNDALL, LL.D., F.R.S.

With 26 Illustrations. Crown 8vo. 5s.

"One of Professor Tyndall's best scientific treatises."—*Standard.*

"The most recent findings of science and experiment respecting the nature and properties of water in every possible form, are discussed with remarkable brevity, clearness, and fullness of exposition."—*Graphic.*

"With the clearness and brilliancy of language which have won for him his fame, he considers the subject of ice, snow, and glaciers."—*Morning Post.*

"Before starting for Switzerland next summer every one should study 'The forms of water.'"—*Globe.*

"Eloquent and instructive in an eminent degree."—*British Quarterly.*

PHYSICS AND POLITICS;

Or, Thoughts on the Application of the Principles of "Natural Selection" and "Inheritance" to Political Society.

BY WALTER BAGEHOT.

Crown 8vo. 4s.

"On the whole we can recommend the book as well deserving to be read by thoughtful students of politics."—*Saturday Review.*

"Able and ingenious."—*Spectator.*

"The book has been well thought out, and the writer speaks without fear."—*National Reformer.*

"Contains many points of interest both to the scientific man and to the mere politician."—*Birmingham Daily Gazette.*

The Volumes now preparing are—

PRINCIPLES OF MENTAL PHYSIOLOGY. With their applications to the Training and Discipline of the Mind, and the Study of its Morbid Conditions. By W. B. CARPENTER, LL.D., M.D., F.R.S., &c. Illustrated.

ANIMAL MECHANICS; or, WALKING, SWIMMING, and FLYING. By Dr. J. BELL PETTIGREW, M.D., F.R.S. 125 Illustrations.

MIND AND BODY: THE THEORIES OF THEIR RELATIONS. By ALEXANDER BAIN, LL.D., Professor of Logic at the University of Aberdeen. Illustrated.

ON FOOD. By Dr. EDWARD SMITH, F.R.S. Profusely Illustrated.

THE STUDY OF SOCIOLOGY. By HERBERT SPENCER.

STREAMS FROM HIDDEN SOURCES.
By B. MONTGOMERIE RANKING.

Crown 8vo. 6s.

THE SECRET OF LONG LIFE.
DEDICATED BY SPECIAL PERMISSION TO LORD ST. LEONARDS.

Second Edition. Large crown 8vo. 5s.

"A charming little volume, written with singular felicity of style and illustration."—*Times.*

"A very pleasant little book, which is always, whether it deal in paradox or earnest, cheerful, genial, scholarly."—*Spectator.*

"The bold and striking character of the whole conception is entitled to the warmest admiration."—*Pall Mall Gazette.*

"We should recommend our readers to get this book . . . because they will be amused by the jovial miscellaneous and cultured gossip with which he strews his pages."—*British Quarterly Review.*

CHANGE OF AIR AND SCENE.
A PHYSICIAN'S HINTS ABOUT DOCTORS, PATIENTS, HYGIÈNE, AND SOCIETY ;

WITH NOTES OF EXCURSIONS FOR HEALTH IN THE PYRENEES, AND AMONGST THE WATERING-PLACES OF FRANCE (INLAND AND SEAWARD), SWITZERLAND, CORSICA, AND THE MEDITERRANEAN.

By Dr. ALPHONSE DONNÉ.

Large post 8vo. Price 9s.

"A very readable and serviceable book. . . . The real value of it is to be found in the accurate and minute information given with regard to a large number of places which have gained a reputation on the continent for their mineral waters."—*Pall Mall Gazette.*

"Not only a pleasant book of travel but also a book of considerable value."—*Morning Post.*

"A popular account of some of the most charming health resorts of the Continent ; with suggestive hints about keeping well and getting well, which are characterised by a good deal of robust common sense."—*British Quarterly.*

"A singularly pleasant and chatty as well as instructive book about health."—*Guardian.*

"A useful and pleasantly-written book, containing many valuable hints on the general management of health from a shrewd and experienced medical man."—*Graphic.*

MISS YOUMANS' FIRST BOOK OF BOTANY.
DESIGNED TO CULTIVATE THE OBSERVING POWERS OF CHILDREN.

From the Author's latest Stereotyped Edition.

New and Enlarged Edition, with 300 Engravings. Crown 8vo. 5s.

It is but rarely that a school-book appears which is at once so novel in plan, so successful in execution, and so suited to the general want, as to command universal and unqualified approbation, but such has been the case with Miss Youmans' First Book of Botany. Her work is an outgrowth of the most recent scientific views, and has been practically tested by careful trial with juvenile classes, and it has been everywhere welcomed as a timely and invaluable contribution to the improvement of primary education.

AN ESSAY ON THE CULTURE OF THE OBSERVING POWERS OF CHILDREN,

ESPECIALLY IN CONNECTION WITH THE STUDY OF BOTANY.

By ELIZA A. YOUMANS,

Edited, with Notes and a Supplement

By JOSEPH PAYNE, F.C.P.,

Author of "Lectures on the Science and Art of Education," &c.

Crown 8vo.   2*s.* 6*d.*

"The little book, now under notice, is expressly designed to make the earliest instruction of children a mental discipline. Miss Youmans presents in her work the ripe results of educational experience reduced to a system, wisely conceiving that an education—even the most elementary—should be regarded as a discipline of the mental powers, and that the facts of external nature supply the most suitable materials for this discipline in the case of children. She has applied that principle to the study of botany. This study, according to her just notions on the subject, is to be fundamentally based on the exercise of the pupil's own powers of observation. He is to see and examine the properties of plants and flowers at first hand, not merely to be informed of what others have seen and examined."—*Pall Mall Gazette.*

THE HISTORY OF THE NATURAL CREATION:

BEING A SERIES OF POPULAR SCIENTIFIC LECTURES ON THE GENERAL THEORY OF PROGRESSION OF SPECIES;

WITH A DISSERTATION ON THE THEORIES OF DARWIN, GOETHE, AND LAMARCK: MORE ESPECIALLY APPLYING THEM TO THE ORIGIN OF MAN, AND TO OTHER FUNDAMENTAL QUESTIONS OF NATURAL SCIENCE CONNECTED THEREWITH.

By PROFESSOR ERNST HÆCKEL, of the University of Jena.

8vo.   With Woodcuts and Plates.   *[Preparing.*

AN ARABIC AND ENGLISH DICTIONARY OF THE KORAN.

By MAJOR J. PENRICE, B.A.   4to.

[Just ready.

MODERN GOTHIC ARCHITECTURE.

By T. G. JACKSON.

Crown 8vo.   Price 7*s.* 6*d.*   *[In the press.*

65, Cornhill; & 12, Paternoster Row, London.

A LEGAL HANDBOOK FOR ARCHITECTS.

By EDWARD JENKINS AND JOHN RAYMOND.

Crown 8vo. Price 5s.   [*Nearly ready.*

CONTEMPORARY ENGLISH PSYCHOLOGY.

FROM THE FRENCH OF PROFESSOR TH. RIBOT.

AN ANALYSIS OF THE VIEWS AND OPINIONS OF THE FOLLOWING
METAPHYSICIANS, AS EXPRESSED IN THEIR WRITINGS.

| JAMES MILL. | JOHN STUART MILL. | HERBERT SPENCER. |
| A. BAIN. | GEORGE H. LEWES. | SAMUEL BAILEY. |

Large post 8vo.   [*Preparing.*

PHYSIOLOGY FOR PRACTICAL USE.

BY VARIOUS EMINENT WRITERS.

EDITED BY JAMES HINTON.

With 50 Illustrations.   [*Preparing.*

HEALTH AND DISEASE

AS INFLUENCED BY

THE DAILY, SEASONAL, AND OTHER CYCLICAL CHANGES IN THE HUMAN SYSTEM.

BY DR. EDWARD SMITH, F.R.S.

A New Edition. 7s. 6d.

PRACTICAL DIETARY

FOR FAMILIES, SCHOOLS, & THE LABOURING CLASSES.

By DR. EDWARD SMITH, F.R.S.

A New Edition. Price 3s. 6d.

CONSUMPTION IN ITS EARLY AND REMEDIABLE STAGES.

By DR. EDWARD SMITH, F.R.S.

A New Edition. 7s. 6d.

A TREATISE ON RELAPSING FEVER.

By R. T. LYONS,

Assistant-Surgeon, Bengal Army.

Small post 8vo. *7s. 6d.*

"A practical work thoroughly supported in its views by a series of remarkable cases."—*Standard.*

IN QUEST OF COOLIES.

A SOUTH SEA SKETCH. By JAMES L. A. HOPE.

Second Edition. Crown 8vo, with 15 Illustrations from Sketches by the Author. Price 6s.

"Mr. Hope's description of the natives is graphic and amusing, and the book is altogether well worthy of perusal."—*Standard.*

"Lively and clever sketches."—*Athenæum.*

"This agreeably written and amusingly illustrated volume."—*Public Opinion.*

THE NILE WITHOUT A DRAGOMAN.

By FREDERIC EDEN.

Second Edition. In one vol. Crown 8vo, cloth. *7s. 6d.*

"Should any of our readers care to imitate Mr. Eden's example, and wish to see things with their own eyes, and shift for themselves, next winter in Upper Egypt, they will find this book a very agreeable guide."—*Times.*

"We have in these pages the most minute description of life as it appeared on the banks of the Nile; all that could be seen or was worth seeing in nature or in art is here pleasantly and graphically set down. . . . It is a book to read during an autumn holiday."—*Spectator.*

"Gives, within moderate compass, a suggestive description of the charms, curiosities, dangers, and discomforts of the Nile voyage."—*Saturday Review.*

ROUND THE WORLD IN 1870.

A VOLUME OF TRAVELS, WITH MAPS.

By A. D. CARLISLE, B.A.,

Trin. Coll., Camb.

Demy 8vo. *16s.*

"Makes one understand how going round the world is to be done in the quickest and pleasantest manner, and how the brightest and most cheerful of travellers did it with eyes wide open and keen attention all on the alert, with ready sympathies, with the happiest facility of hitting upon the most interesting features of nature and the most interesting characteristics of man, and all for its own sake."—*Spectator.*

"We can only commend, which we do very heartily, an eminently sensible and readable book."—*British Quarterly Review.*

Military Works.

THE FRONTAL ATTACK OF INFANTRY.

By Capt. LAYMANN, Instructor of Tactics at the Military College, Neisse. Translated by Colonel EDWARD NEWDIGATE. Crown 8vo, limp cloth. Price 2*s.* 6*d.*

"This work has met with special attention in our army."—*Militarin Wochenblatt.*

THE FIRST BAVARIAN ARMY CORPS IN

THE WAR OF 1870–71, UNDER VON DER TANN. Compiled from the Official Records by Capt. HUGO HELVIG. Translated by Capt. G. SALIS SCHWABE. Demy 8vo. With 5 large Maps.

History of the Organisation, Equipment, and War Services of

THE REGIMENT OF BENGAL ARTILLERY.

Compiled from Published Official and other Records, and various private sources, by Major FRANCIS W. STUBBS, Royal (late Bengal) Artillery. Vol. I. will contain WAR SERVICES. The Second Volume will be published separately, and will contain the HISTORY of the ORGANISATION and EQUIPMENT of the REGIMENT. In 2 vols. 8vo. With Maps and Plans. [*Preparing.*

THE ABOLITION OF PURCHASE AND THE

ARMY REGULATION BILL OF 1871. By Lieut.-Col. the Hon. A. ANSON, V.C., M.P. Crown 8vo. Price One Shilling.

THE STORY OF THE SUPERSESSIONS. By

Lieut.-Col. the Hon. A. ANSON, V.C., M.P. Crown. 8vo. Price Sixpence.

ARMY RESERVES AND MILITIA REFORMS.

By Lieut.-Colonel the Hon. C. ANSON. Crown 8vo. Sewed. Price One Shilling.

ELEMENTARY MILITARY GEOGRAPHY,

RECONNOITRING, AND SKETCHING. Compiled for Non-Commissioned Officers and Soldiers of all Arms. By Lieut. C. E. H. VINCENT, Royal Welsh Fusileers. Small crown 8vo. 2*s.* 6*d.*

VICTORIES AND DEFEATS.

An Attempt to explain the Causes which have led to them. An Officer's Manual. By Col. R. P. ANDERSON. Demy 8vo. 14*s*. [*In preparation.*

STUDIES IN THE NEW INFANTRY

TACTICS. Parts I. & II. By Major W. VON SCHEREFF. Translated from the German by Col. LUMLEY GRAHAM. [*Shortly.*

THE OPERATIONS OF THE FIRST ARMY

TO THE CAPITULATION OF METZ. By Major VON SCHELL, with Maps, including one of Metz and of the country around. Translated by Capt. E. O. HOLLIST. In demy 8vo. [*In preparation.*

*** The most important events described in this work are the battles of Spichern, those before Metz on the 14th and 18th August, and (on this point nothing authentic has yet been published) the history of the investment of Metz (battle of Noisseville).

This work, however, possesses a greater importance than that derived from these points, because it represents for the first time from the official documents the generalship of Von Steinmetz. Hitherto we have had no exact reports on the deeds and motives of this celebrated general. This work has the special object of unfolding carefully the relations in which the commander of the First Army acted, the plan of operations which he drew up, and the manner in which he carried it out.

THE OPERATIONS OF THE FIRST ARMY

IN NORTHERN FRANCE AGAINST FAIDHERBE. By Colonel COUNT HERMANN VON WARTENSLEBEN, Chief of the Staff of the First Army. Translated by Colonel C. H. VON WRIGHT. In demy 8vo. Uniform with the above.

[*In preparation.*

THE OPERATIONS OF THE FIRST ARMY,

UNDER GEN. VON GOEBEN. Translated by Col. C. H. VON WRIGHT. With Maps. Demy 8vo.

TACTICAL DEDUCTIONS FROM THE WAR

OF 1870–1. By Captain A. VON BOGUSLAWSKI. Translated by Colonel LUMLEY GRAHAM, late 18th (Royal Irish) Regiment. Demy 8vo. Uniform with the above. Price 7*s*.

"Major Boguslawski's tactical deductions from the war are, that infantry still preserve their superiority over cavalry, that open order must henceforth be the main principles of all drill, and that the chassepot is the best of all small arms for precision. . . . We must, without delay, impress brain and forethought into the British Service; and we cannot commence the good work too soon, or better, than by placing the two books ('The Operations of the German Armies' and 'Tactical Deductions') we have here criticised, in every military library, and introducing them as class-books in every tactical school."—*United Service Gazette.*

Books on Indian Subjects.

THE EUROPEAN IN INDIA.

A HAND-BOOK OF PRACTICAL INFORMATION FOR THOSE PROCEEDING TO, OR RESIDING IN, THE EAST INDIES,

RELATING TO OUTFITS, ROUTES, TIME FOR DEPARTURE, INDIAN CLIMATE, ETC.

BY EDMUND C. P. HULL.

WITH A MEDICAL GUIDE FOR ANGLO-INDIANS.

BEING A COMPENDIUM OF ADVICE TO EUROPEANS IN INDIA, RELATING TO THE PRESERVATION AND REGULATION OF HEALTH.

BY R. S. MAIR, M.D., F.R.C.S.E.,
Late Deputy Coroner of Madras.

In 1 vol. Post 8vo. 6s.

"Full of all sorts of useful information to the English settler or traveller in India."—*Standard.*

"One of the most valuable books ever published in India—valuable for its sound information, its careful array of pertinent facts, and its sterling common sense. It is a publisher's as well as an author's 'hit,' for it supplies a want which few persons may have discovered, but which everybody will at once recognise when once the contents of the book have been mastered. The medical part of the work is invaluable."—*Calcutta Guardian.*

EASTERN EXPERIENCES.

BY L. BOWRING, C.S.I.,
Lord Canning's Private Secretary, and for many years the Chief Commissioner of Mysore and Coorg.

In 1 vol. Demy 8vo. 16s. Illustrated with Maps and Diagrams.

"An admirable and exhaustive geographical, political, and industrial survey."—*Athenæum.*

"The usefulness of this compact and methodical summary of the most authentic information relating to countries whose welfare is intimately connected with our own, should obtain for Mr. Lewin Bowring's work a good place among treatises of its kind."—*Daily News.*

"Interesting even to the general reader, but more especially so to those who may have a special concern in that portion of our Indian Empire."—*Post.*

"An elaborately got up and carefully compiled work."—*Home News.*

A MEMOIR OF THE INDIAN SURVEYS.

BY CLEMENT R. MARKHAM.
Printed by order of Her Majesty's Secretary of State for India in Council.
Imperial 8vo. 10s. 6d.

Juvenile Books.

LOST GIP. By HESBA STRETTON, Author of "Little Meg," "Alone in London." Square crown 8vo. Six Illustrations. Price 1s. 6d.

BRAVE MEN'S FOOTSTEPS. A Book of Example and Anecdote for Young People. By the Editor of "MEN WHO HAVE RISEN." With Four Illustrations. By C. DOYLE. 3s. 6d.

"The little volume is precisely of the stamp to win the favour of those who, in choosing a gift for a boy, would consult his moral development as well as his temporary pleasure."—*Daily Telegraph.*

"A readable and instructive volume."—*Examiner.*

"No more welcome book for the school-boy could be imagined."—*Birmingham Daily Gazette.*

THE LITTLE WONDER-HORN. By JEAN INGELOW. A Second Series of "Stories told to a Child." Fifteen Illustrations. Cloth, gilt. 3s. 6d.

"Full of fresh and vigorous fancy: it is worthy of the author of some of the best of our modern verse."—*Standard.*

"We like all the contents of the 'Little Wonder-Horn' very much."—*Athenæum.*

"We recommend it with confidence."—*Pall-Mall Gazette.*

STORIES IN PRECIOUS STONES. By HELEN ZIMMERN. With Six Illustrations. Crown 8vo. 5s.

"A series of pretty tales which are half fantastic, half natural, and pleasantly quaint, as befits stories intended for the young."—*Daily Telegraph.*

"Certainly the book is well worth a perusal, and will not be soon laid down when once taken up."—*Daily Bristol Times.*

GUTTA-PERCHA WILLIE, THE WORKING GENIUS. By GEORGE MACDONALD. With Illustrations. By ARTHUR HUGHES. Crown 8vo. 3s. 6d.

THE TRAVELLING MENAGERIE. By CHARLES CAMDEN, Author of "Hoity Toity." Illustrated by J. MAHONEY. Crown 8vo. 3s. 6d.

PLUCKY FELLOWS. A Book for Boys. By STEPHEN J. MACKENNA. With Six Illustrations. Crown 8vo. Price 3s. 6d.

Poetry.

POT-POURRI. Collected Verses. By AUSTIN DOBSON. Crown 8vo.

IMITATIONS FROM THE GERMAN OF SPITTA AND TERSTEGEN. By Lady DURAND. Crown 8vo. 5s.   *[In the press.*

EASTERN LEGENDS AND STORIES IN ENGLISH VERSE. By Lieutenant NORTON POWLETT, Royal Artillery. Crown 8vo. 5s.

EDITH; or, LOVE AND LIFE IN CHESHIRE. By T. ASHE, Author of the "Sorrows of Hypsipylé," etc. Sewed. Price 6d.

"A really fine poem, full of tender, subtle touches of feeling."—*Manchester News.*

"Pregnant from beginning to end with the results of careful observation and imaginative power."—*Chester Chronicle.*

THE GALLERY OF PIGEONS, AND OTHER POEMS. By THEO. MARZIALS. Crown 8vo. 4s. 6d.   *[In the press.*

A NEW VOLUME OF SONNETS. By the Rev. C. TENNYSON TURNER. Crown 8vo.   *[In the press.*

ENGLISH SONNETS. Collected and Arranged by JOHN DENNIS. Small crown 8vo.   *[In the press.*

GOETHE'S FAUST. A New Translation in Rime. By the Rev. C. KEGAN PAUL. Crown 8vo. 6s.

WILLIAM CULLEN BRYANT'S POEMS. Handsomely bound, with Illustrations. A Cheaper Edition. A Pocket Edition.   *[Preparing.*

POETRY—*continued.*

CALDERON'S DRAMAS.
THE PURGATORY OF ST. PATRICK.
THE WONDERFUL MAGICIAN.
LIFE IS A DREAM.
Translated from the Spanish. By DENIS FLORENCE MAC-CARTHY.

SONGS FOR SAILORS. By Dr. W. C. BENNETT.
Dedicated by Special Request to H.R.H. the Duke of Edinburgh. Crown 8vo. 3*s.* 6*d.* With Steel Portrait and Illustrations. An Edition in Illustrated paper Covers. Price 1*s.*

DR. W. C. BENNETT'S POEMS will be shortly
Re-issued, with additions to each part, in Five Parts, at 1*s.* each.

WALLED IN, AND OTHER POEMS. By the
Rev. HENRY J. BULKELY. Crown 8vo. 5*s.*

THE POETICAL AND PROSE WORKS OF
ROBERT BUCHANAN. Preparing for publication, a Collected Edition in 5 vols.
CONTENTS OF VOL. I.—
DAUGHTERS OF EVE.
UNDERTONES AND ANTIQUES.
COUNTRY AND PASTORAL POEMS. *[In the Press.*

SONGS OF LIFE AND DEATH. By JOHN
PAYNE, Author of "Intaglios," "Sonnets," "The Masque of Shadows," etc. Crown 8vo. 5*s.* *[Just out.*

SONGS OF TWO WORLDS. By a NEW WRITER.
Fcap. 8vo, cloth, 5*s.* Second Edition.

"The 'New Writer' is certainly no tyro. No one after reading the first two poems, almost perfect in rhythm and all the graceful reserve of true lyrical strength, can doubt that this book is the result of lengthened thought and assiduous training in poetical form. . . . These poems will assuredly take high rank among the class to which they belong."—*British Quarterly Review, April 1st.*

"If these poems are the mere preludes of a mind growing in power and in inclination for verse, we have in them the promise of a fine poet. . . . The verse describing Socrates has the highest note of critical poetry."—*Spectator, February 17th.*

"No extracts could do justice to the exquisite tones, the felicitous phrasing and delicately wrought harmonies of some of these poems." — *Nonconformist, March 27th.*

"Are we in this book making the acquaintance of a fine and original poet, or of a most artistic imitator? And our deliberate opinion is that the former hypothesis is the right one. It has a purity and delicacy of feeling like morning air."—*Graphic, March 16th.*

THE INN OF STRANGE MEETINGS, AND
OTHER POEMS. By MORTIMER COLLINS. Crown 8vo. 5*s.*

"Abounding in quiet humour, in bright fancy, in sweetness and melody of expression, and, at times, in the tenderest touches of pathos."—*Graphic*

"Mr. Collins has an undercurrent of chivalry and romance beneath the trifling vein of good humoured banter which is the special characteristic of his verse. . . . The 'Inn of Strange Meetings' is a sprightly piece."—*Athenæum.*

EROS AGONISTES. By E. B. D. Crown 8vo. 3*s.* 6*d.*

"The author of these verses has written a very touching story of the human heart in the story he tells with such pathos and power, of an affection cherished so long and so secretly. . . . It is not the least merit of these pages that they are everywhere illumined with moral and religious sentiment suggested, not paraded, of the brightest, purest character."—*Standard.*

THE LEGENDS OF ST. PATRICK & OTHER
POEMS. By AUBREY DE VERE. Crown 8vo. 5*s.*

"Mr. De Vere's versification in his earlier poems is characterised by great sweetness and simplicity. He is master of his instrument, and rarely offends the ear with false notes. Poems such as these scarcely admit of quotation, for their charm is not, and ought not to be, found in isolated passages ; but we can promise the patient and thoughtful reader much pleasure in the perusal of this volume." — *Pall-Mall Gazette.*

"We have marked, in almost every page, excellent touches from which we know not how to select. We have but space to commend the varied structure of his verse, the carefulness of his grammar, and his excellent English. All who believe that poetry should raise and not debase the social ideal, all who think that wit should exalt our standard of thought and manners, must welcome this contribution at once to our knowledge of the past and to the science of noble life."—*Saturday Review.*

ASPROMONTE, AND OTHER POEMS. Second
Edition, cloth. 4*s.* 6*d.*

"The volume is anonymous, but there is no reason for the author to be ashamed of it. The 'Poems of Italy' are evidently inspired by genuine enthusiasm in the cause espoused ; and one of them, 'The Execution of Felice Orsini,' has much poetic merit, the event celebrated being told with dramatic force."—*Athenæum.*

"The verse is fluent and free."—*Spectator.*

THE DREAM AND THE DEED, AND OTHER
POEMS. By PATRICK SCOTT, Author of "Footpaths between Two Worlds," etc. Fcap. 8vo, cloth, 5*s.*

"A bitter and able satire on the vice and follies of the day, literary, social, and political."—*Standard.*

"Shows real poetic power coupled with evidences of satirical energy."—*Edinburgh Daily Review.*

𝔉iction.

—♦—

WHAT 'TIS TO LOVE. By the Author of "Flora Adair," "The Value of Fosterstown." 3 vols.

CHESTERLEIGH. By ANSLEY CONYERS. 3 vols. Crown 8vo.

SQUIRE SILCHESTER'S WHIM. By MORTIMER COLLINS, Author of "Marquis and Merchant," "The Princess Clarice," &c. Crown 8vo. 3 vols.

"We think it the best (story) Mr. Collins has yet written."—*Pall Mall Gazette.*

SEETA. By Colonel MEADOWS TAYLOR, Author of "Tara," "Ralph Darnell," &c. Crown 8vo. 3 vols.

"The story is well told, native life is admirably described, and the petty intrigues of native rulers, and their hatred of the English, mingled with fear lest the latter should eventually prove the victors, are cleverly depicted."—*Athenæum.*

"We cannot speak too highly of Colonel Meadows Taylor's book. . . . We would recommend all novel-readers to purchase it at the earliest opportunity."—*John Bull.*

"Thoroughly interesting and enjoyable reading."—*Examiner.*

A New and Cheaper Edition, in 1 vol., each Illustrated, price 6s., of

COL. MEADOWS TAYLOR'S INDIAN TALES is preparing for publication.

The Confessions of a Thug *is in the press.*

JOHANNES OLAF. By E. DE WILLE. Translated by F. E. BUNNETT. Crown 8vo. 3 vols.

The author of this story enjoys a high reputation in Germany; and both English and German critics have spoken in terms of the warmest praise of this and her previous stories. She has been called "The 'George Eliot' of Germany."

"The book gives evidence of consider-able capacity in every branch of a novelist's faculty. The art of description is fully exhibited; perception of character and capacity for delineating it are obvious; while there is great breadth and comprehensiveness in the plan of the story."——*Morning Post.*

OFF THE SKELLIGS. By JEAN INGELOW. (Her First Romance.) Crown 8vo. In 4 vols.

"Clever and sparkling. . . . The descriptive passages are bright with colour."—*Standard.*

"We read each succeeding volume with increasing interest, going almost to the point of wishing there was a fifth."—*Athenæum.*

"The novel as a whole is a remarkable one, because it is uncompromisingly true to life."—*Daily News.*

FICTION—*continued.*

HONOR BLAKE: The Story of a Plain Woman.
By Mrs. KEATINGE, Author of "English Homes in India," &c. 2 vols.   Crown 8vo.

"One of the best novels we have met with for some time."—*Morning Post.*

"A story which must do good to all, young and old, who read it."—*Daily News.*

THE DOCTOR'S DILEMMA.   By HESBA STRETTON, Author of "Little Meg," &c., &c.   Crown 8vo.   3 vols.

THE PRINCESS CLARICE.   A Story of 1871.
By MORTIMER COLLINS.   2 vols.   Crown 8vo.

"Mr. Collins has produced a readable book, amusingly characteristic. There is good description of Devonshire scenery; and lastly there is Clarice, a most successful heroine, who must speak to the reader for herself."—*Athenæum.*

"Very readable and amusing.   We would especially give an honourable men-

tion to Mr. Collins's '*vers de société,*' the writing of which has almost become a lost art."—*Pall Mall Gazette.*

"A bright, fresh, and original book, with which we recommend all genuine novel readers to become acquainted at the earliest opportunity."—*Standard.*

A GOOD MATCH.   By AMELIA PERRIER, Author of "Mea Culpa."   2 vols.

"Racy and lively."—*Athenæum.*
"As pleasant and readable a novel as we have seen this season."—*Examiner.*

"This clever and amusing novel."—*Pall Mall Gazette.*
"Agreeably written."—*Public Opinion.*

THE SPINSTERS OF BLATCHINGTON.   By MAR. TRAVERS.   2 vols.   Crown 8vo.

"A pretty story.   Deserving of a favourable reception."—*Graphic.*

"A book of more than average merits, worth reading."—*Examiner.*

THOMASINA.   By the Author of "DOROTHY," "DE CRESSY," etc.   2 vols.   Crown 8vo.

"A finished and delicate cabinet picture, no line is without its purpose, but all contribute to the unity of the work."—*Athenæum.*

"For the delicacies of character-drawing,

for play of incident, and for finish of style, we must refer our readers to the story itself."—*Daily News.*
"This undeniably pleasing story."—*Pall Mall Gazette.*

FICTION—*continued.*

THE STORY OF SIR EDWARD'S WIFE. By HAMILTON MARSHALL, Author of "For Very Life." 1 vol. Crown 8vo.

"A quiet graceful little story."—*Spectator*.

"There are many clever conceits in it.

. . . Mr. Hamilton Marshall can tell a story closely and pleasantly."—*Pall Mall Gazette*.

LINKED AT LAST. By F. E. BUNNETT. 1 vol. Crown 8vo.

"'Linked at Last' contains so much of pretty description, natural incident, and delicate portraiture, that the reader who once takes it up will not be inclined to re-

linquish it without concluding the volume."—*Morning Post*.

"A very charming story." — *John Bull*.

PERPLEXITY. By SYDNEY MOSTYN. 3 vols. Crown 8vo.

"Written with very considerable power . . . original . . . worked out with great cleverness and sustained interest."—*Standard*.

"Shows much lucidity—much power of portraiture."—*Examiner*.

"Forcibly and graphically told."—*Daily News*.

"Written with very considerable power,

the plot is original and . . . worked out with great cleverness and sustained interest."—*Standard*.

"Shows much lucidity, much power of portraiture, and no inconsiderable sense of humour."—*Examiner*.

"The literary workmanship is good, and the story forcibly and graphically told."—*Daily News*.

HER TITLE OF HONOUR. By HOLME LEE. Second Edition. 1 vol. Crown 8vo.

"With the interest of a pathetic story is united the value of a definite and high purpose."—*Spectator*.

"A most exquisitely written story."—*Literary Churchman*.

CRUEL AS THE GRAVE. By the Countess VON BOTHMER. 3 vols. Crown 8vo.

"Jealousy is cruel as the Grave."

"An interesting, though somewhat tragic story."—*Athenæum*.

"An agreeable, unaffected, and eminently readable novel."—*Daily News*.

MEMOIRS OF MRS. LÆTITIA BOOTHBY. By WILLIAM CLARK RUSSELL, Author of "The Book of Authors." Crown 8vo. 7s. 6d.

"The book is clever and ingenious."—*Saturday Review*.

"One of the most delightful books I have read for a very long while. Very few works of truth or fiction are so thoroughly

entertaining from the first page to the last."—*Judy*.

"This is a very clever book, one of the best imitations of the productions of the last century that we have seen."—*Guardian*.

FICTION—*continued.*

LITTLE HODGE.
A Christmas Country Carol. By EDWARD JENKINS, Author of "Ginx's Baby," &c. Illustrated. Crown 8vo. 5*s.* A Cheap Edition in paper covers price One Shilling.

"We shall be mistaken if it does not obtain a very wide circle of readers."—*United Service Gazette.*

"Wise and humorous, but yet most pathetic."—*Nonconformist.*

"The pathos of some of the passages is extremely touching."—*Manchester Examiner.*

"One of the most seasonable of Christmas stories."—*Literary World.*

GINX'S BABY; HIS BIRTH AND OTHER
MISFORTUNES. By EDWARD JENKINS. Twenty-ninth Edition. Crown 8vo. Price 2*s.*

LORD BANTAM.
By EDWARD JENKINS, Author of "Ginx's Baby." Sixth Edition. Crown 8vo. Price 2*s.*|

HERMANN AGHA: An Eastern Narrative.
By W. GIFFORD PALGRAVE, Author of "Travels in Central Arabia," &c. Second Edition. 2 vols. Crown 8vo, cloth, extra gilt. 18*s.*

"Reads like a tale of life, with all its incidents. The young will take to it for its love portions, the older for its descriptions, some in this day for its Arab philosophy."—*Athenæum.*

"The cardinal merit, however, of the story is, to our thinking, the exquisite simplicity and purity of the love portion. There is a positive fragrance as of newly-mown hay about it, as compared with the artificially perfumed passions which are detailed to us with such gusto by our ordinary novel-writers in their endless volumes."—*Observer.*

SEPTIMIUS.
A Romance. By NATHANIEL HAWTHORNE. Author of "The Scarlet Letter," "Transformation," &c. Second Edition. 1 vol. Crown 8vo, cloth, extra gilt. 9*s.*

A peculiar interest attaches to this work. It was the last thing the author wrote, and he may be said to have died as he finished it.

The *Athenæum* says that "the book is full of Hawthorne's most characteristic writing."

"One of the best examples of Hawthorne's writing; every page is impressed with his peculiar view of thought, conveyed in his own familiar way."—*Post.*

PANDURANG HARI; Or, Memoirs of a Hindoo.
A Tale of Mahratta Life sixty years ago. With a Preface, by Sir H. BARTLE E. FRERE, G.C.S.I., &c. 2 vols. Crown 8vo.

THE TASMANIAN LILY.
By JAMES BONWICK, Author of "Curious Facts of Old Colonial Days," &c. Crown 8vo. Illustrated. [*Preparing.*

The Cornhill Library of Fiction.

3s. 6d. per Volume.

IT is intended in this Series to produce books of such merit that readers will care to preserve them on their shelves.

They are well printed on good paper, handsomely bound, with a Frontispiece, and are sold at the moderate price of 3s. 6d. each.

ROBIN GRAY. By CHARLES GIBBON. With a Frontispiece by HENNESSY.

KITTY. By Miss M. BETHAM-EDWARDS.

READY MONEY MORTI-BOY. A Matter-of-Fact Story.

HIRELL. By JOHN SAUNDERS, Author of "Abel Drake's Wife."

ONE OF TWO. By J. HAIN FRISWELL, Author of "The Gentle Life," etc.

GOD'S PROVIDENCE HOUSE. By Mrs. G. L. BANKS.

OTHER STANDARD NOVELS TO FOLLOW.

Forthcoming Novels.

BRESSANT. A Romance. By JULIAN HAWTHORNE. 2 vols. Crown 8vo. [*Preparing.*

CIVIL SERVICE. By J. T. LISTADO, Author of "Maurice Reynhart." 2 vols.

VANESSA. By the Author of "THOMASINA," etc. 2 vols.

A LITTLE WORLD. By GEO. MANVILLE FENN, Author of "The Sapphire Cross," "Mad," etc.

TOO LATE. By Mrs. NEWMAN. 2 vols. Crown 8vo.

THE QUEEN'S SHILLING. By Capt. ARTHUR GRIFFITHS, Author of "Peccavi; or, Geoffrey Singleton's Mistake." 2 vols.

TWO GIRLS. By FREDK. WEDMORE, Author of "A Snapt Gold Ring." 2 vols. Crown 8vo.

MIRANDA: a Midsummer Madness. By MORTIMER COLLINS.

EFFIE'S GAME; How she Lost and how she Won. By CECIL CLAYTON. 2 vols.

HEATHERGATE. In 2 vols.

Religious.

HYMNS AND VERSES, Original and Translated. By the Rev. HENRY DOWNTON. Small crown 8vo.

THE ETERNAL LIFE. Being Fourteen Sermons. By the Rev. JAS. NOBLE BENNIE, M.A. Crown 8vo. 6*s.*

MISSIONARY ENTERPRISE IN THE EAST. By the Rev. RICHARD COLLINS. Illustrated. Crown 8vo.
[Preparing.

THE REALM OF TRUTH. By Miss E. CARNE. Crown 8vo.
[Preparing.

HYMNS FOR THE CHURCH AND HOME. By the Rev. W. FLEMING STEVENSON, Author of "Praying and Working."
[Preparing.

THE YOUNG LIFE EQUIPPING ITSELF FOR GOD'S SERVICE. Being Four Sermons Preached before the University of Cambridge in November, 1872. By the Rev. J. C. VAUGHAN, D.D., Master of the Temple. Third Edition. Crown 8vo. Price 3*s.* 6d.

WORDS & WORKS IN A LONDON PARISH. Edited by the Rev. CHARLES ANDERSON, M.A. Demy 8vo. 6*s.*

LIFE: Conferences delivered at Toulouse. By the Rev. PÈRE LACORDAIRE. Crown 8vo. 6*s.*

THOUGHTS FOR THE TIMES. By the Rev. H. R. HAWEIS, M.A., "Author of Music and Morals," etc. Third Edition. Crown 8vo. 7*s.* 6*d.*

CATHOLICISM AND THE VATICAN. With a Narrative of the Old Catholic Congress at Munich. By J. LOWRY WHITTLE, A.M., Trin. Coll., Dublin. Second Edition. Crown 8vo. 7*s.* 6*d.*

"A valuable and philosophic contribution to the solution of one of the greatest questions of this stirring age."—*Church Times.*

"We cannot follow the author through his graphic and lucid sketch of the Catholic movement in Germany and of the Munich Congress, at which he was present; but we may cordially recommend his book to all who wish to follow the course of the movement."—*Saturday Review.*

Life & Works of the Rev. Fred. W. Robertson.

NEW AND CHEAPER EDITIONS.

LIFE AND LETTERS. Edited by STOPFORD BROOKE, M.A., Chaplain in Ordinary to the Queen.

In 2 vols., uniform with the Sermons. Price 7s. 6d.

Library Edition, in demy 8vo, with Two Steel Portraits. 12s.

A Popular Edition, in 1 vol. Price 6s.

SERMONS. FOUR SERIES. 4 vols. small crown 8vo, price 3s. 6d. per vol.

EXPOSITORY LECTURES ON ST. PAUL'S EPISTLE TO THE CORINTHIANS. Small crown 8vo. 5s.

AN ANALYSIS OF MR. TENNYSON'S "IN MEMO-RIAM." (Dedicated by permission to the Poet-Laureate.) Fcap. 8vo. 2s.

THE EDUCATION OF THE HUMAN RACE. Translated from the German of GOTTHOLD EPHRAIM LESSING. Fcap. 8vo. 2s. 6d.

LECTURES & ADDRESSES ON LITERARY AND SOCIAL TOPICS. Small crown 8vo. 3s. 6d.
[*Preparing.*

A LECTURE ON FRED. W. ROBERTSON, M.A. By the Rev. F. A. NOBLE, delivered before the Young Men's Christian Association of Pittsburgh, U.S. 1s. 6d.

Sermons by the Rev. Stopford A. Brooke, M.A.,

Chaplain in Ordinary to Her Majesty the Queen.

CHRIST IN MODERN LIFE. Sermons Preached in St. James's Chapel, York Street, London. Third Edition. Crown 8vo. 7s. 6d.

"Nobly fearless and singularly strong. . . . carries our admiration throughout."—*British Quarterly Review.*

FREEDOM IN THE CHURCH OF ENGLAND. Six Sermons suggested by the Voysey Judgment. Second Edition. In 1 vol. Crown 8vo, cloth. 3s. 6d.

"A very fair statement of the views in respect to freedom of thought held by the liberal party in the Church of England."—*Blackwood's Magazine.*

"Interesting and readable, and characterised by great clearness of thought, frankness of statement, and moderation of tone."—*Church Opinion.*

SERMONS Preached in St. James's Chapel, York Street, London. Sixth Edition. Crown 8vo. 6s.

"No one who reads these sermons will wonder that Mr. Brooke is a great power in London, that his chapel is thronged, and his followers large and enthusiastic.

They are fiery, energetic, impetuous sermons, rich with the treasures of a cultivated imagination."—*Guardian.*

THE LIFE AND WORK OF FREDERICK DENISON MAURICE: A Memorial Sermon. Crown 8vo, sewed. 1s.